D0651234

Gregg

I just met the most extraordinary man...

© St. Martin's Paperbacks/ Artwork by Greg Gulbronson

PLACE
STAMP
HERE

NO ORDINARY MAN

in bookstores now

TOREY WOULD PROBABLY never know why she had allowed him to kiss her. It wasn't as if it was unexpected. It wasn't as if she hadn't seen it coming. She'd clearly understood his intent. She'd gone into it with her eyes wide open.

Trouble.

She had known the man was going to be trouble from the first moment she'd laid eyes on him earlier that evening. She just hadn't known what kind of trouble.

The trouble was he was handsome and intelligent and sexy and strong and a hundred other things she had always looked for in a man and had never found until tonight.

The trouble was he kissed better than any man who had ever kissed her.

The trouble was she wanted him.

She was wise enough, however, to accept the fact that she didn't always get what she wanted, and sometimes— many times—it was for the best.

But could it matter so very much if she were to indulge herself for another minute or two?

Torey answered her own question.

No.

Liar!

St. Martin's Paperbacks Titles
by Suzanne Simmons

THE PARADISE MAN
NO ORDINARY MAN

NO ORDINARY MAN

SUZANNE SIMMONS

St. Martin's Paperbacks

NOTE: If you purchased this book without a cover you should be aware that this book is stolen property. It was reported as "unsold and destroyed" to the publisher, and neither the author nor the publisher has received any payment for this "stripped book."

NO ORDINARY MAN

Copyright © 1998 by Suzanne Simmons Guntrum.

All rights reserved. No part of this book may be used or reproduced in any manner whatsoever without written permission except in the case of brief quotations embodied in critical articles or reviews. For information address St. Martin's Press, 175 Fifth Avenue, New York, NY 10010.

ISBN: 0-312-96495-1

Printed in the United States of America

St. Martin's Paperbacks edition/April 1998

St. Martin's Paperbacks are published by St. Martin's Press, 175 Fifth Avenue, New York, NY 10010.

10 9 8 7 6 5 4 3 2 1

This one is for our dear friends, Stella and Jerry Cameron.
You promised we'd love Scotland,
and we did.

"Breathes there the man, with soul so dead,
Who never to himself hath said,
This is my own, my native land?"
—Sir Walter Scott

"But to see her was to love her,
love but her, and love forever . . ."
—Robert Burns

Chapter 1

He'd made a mistake.

A big mistake.

Mitchell Storm stood at the bottom of the marble staircase and, like the four hundred guests crowded into the Great Hall below, gazed up at the young woman in the shimmering evening gown.

Even from this distance he could see that she was tall and slender and fine-boned in that way French women had of being fine-boned, although he knew she wasn't French.

Her neck was long and swanlike. Her shoulders were narrow, but not too narrow, and straight. Her posture was perfect. Her figure was exquisite: that was clearly evident despite the fact that she was dressed in the fashion of the Victorian era.

Her features were delicate, yet defined: high cheekbones, a small, aristocratic nose, a chin that was neither too pointed nor too rounded, and an altogether lovely mouth.

Her skin was flawless—it was the color and texture of fine porcelain. Her hair was upswept in the style of the period with a few tasteful wisps left free to frame her face.

She held her gloved hands in front of her: a silk fan clasped in the right, a small jeweled evening bag dangling from the left. The gemstones glittering at her ears and throat were huge, blood red, and, from all accounts, priceless.

Mitchell had been circulating among the guests for the past quarter hour, eavesdropping on their conversations. In the process he had learned that Storm Point had been built for Andrew Storm more than a century ago by Richard Morris Hunt, *the* architect of the famed Newport, Rhode Island "cottages."

That the cost of the mansion had been an astronomical twelve million dollars: four million dollars for its construction and the balance going toward interior decoration.

That so much marble had been used in building the estate—yellow Siena and black-veined Brescia from Italy, pink-veined Numidian from western Algeria, and white stone for the facade from rural New York—that a private wharf and warehouse had been needed to unload and store the materials.

That the ceiling of the Great Hall—the very hall in which they now stood—Rubenesque cherubs, gilded cornices, magnificent rococo relief work and all, soared fifty feet overhead.

That Dickens, the butler, was left over from the "previous administration."

And that Victoria Storm—Torey, as her closest friends called her—was one of the richest women in the United States.

But he had known that before he'd left Scotland.

Mitchell swore softly under his breath. He'd made a mistake all right. A huge mistake. He had pinned his hopes for the future—and the hopes of three villages, several dozen sheep farms, and some eight hundred people—on a young woman of rare privilege and even rarer wealth who had obviously never had to worry about where her next designer ball gown was coming from, let alone her next meal.

"Doesn't Victoria look sensational?" came a sibilant whisper from nearby.

The imposing matron in front of Mitchell, elaborate hairdo and ample bosom dramatically draped with a king's ransom in diamonds, leaned slightly to one side, waggled her head and mouthed to her acquaintance, "Yes, she does."

Her response was apparently seen by the second female as a signal to continue the conversation. "I understand the inspiration for her costume was a nineteenth-century ball gown designed by Charles Worth, the founding father of *haute couture*."

"Indeed." The richly attired matron managed to look down her nose even as she gazed up at the subject under their collective scrutiny. "I must confess that I've always been puzzled by the proclivity of redheads to wear pink." There was a particular emphasis on the word pink, as if it were something contagious.

The other woman studied the engraved card clasped in her hand. "The description in the program states that Victoria's gown is magnolia satin embroidered with thousands of tiny multicolored beads that give the material a rosy, iridescent tint. Her evening slippers are covered with magnolia satin as well, and her shoe buckles are fashioned of rubies and diamonds."

Leaning closer still, bosom and diamonds quivering in the wake of her sudden movement, the bejeweled doyenne announced in a stage whisper that carried halfway across the Great Hall, "I see Victoria is also wearing the Storm rubies tonight."

Her companion appeared to be momentarily taken aback. "They aren't being auctioned off as well, are they?"

"Of course they aren't, Lola." The glare Lola received said she had clearly taken leave of her senses if she thought that was true. "Victoria Storm sell her great-great-grandmother's jewels?" There was an incredulous sniff. "Not in a thousand years. Not in a million years. Not even for charity." She adjusted the corsage on her costume before adding, "Why, I'll wager those rubies haven't been out of the bank vault since Marilyn Storm died."

The second woman took in a deep breath and released it on a sigh. "Poor Victoria." She gave her head a shake and heaved another sigh. "And poor Marilyn."

"Poor?" Another perfectly executed ladylike sniff that managed to convey a wealth of implication. "I scarcely think so."

The more timid of the two women became flustered. "I only meant because Victoria lost both of her parents . . . because Marilyn died so young . . ." She became even more flustered and began to fan herself with the evening's program. After a brief period, in which she apparently managed to collect her wits, she spoke up in a hopeful voice. "Perhaps we'll get a good look at the rubies."

"Of course we will." There seemed to be no doubt about it in the matron's mind. "Victoria understands her responsibilities as the charity ball's hostess. She'll make

4

sure everyone has a look-see. After all, we each made a sizeable donation to her pet projects for the privilege of being in attendance tonight.''

"It's for a good cause," her companion volunteered. "Several good causes."

"I suppose so," the woman allowed, somewhat belatedly, before she finally fell silent.

The young woman at the center of their attention reached the bottom of the Grand Staircase, accepted the arm of the handsome, middle-aged man waiting there for her, turned, and then glided into the adjoining crystal-chandeliered ballroom, passing within several feet of Mitchell.

He blew out his breath expressively.

Victoria Storm was beautiful.

He'd give her that.

And she was Scottish through and through. The red hair, the blue-green eyes, and the fair skin with the slightest smattering of freckles fairly shouted her heritage.

Unfortunately, he just knew in his gut that she was going to be one of those supercilious young women with an annoying laugh, a well-bred nose perpetually raised in the air, and feet perpetually several inches off the ground; an essentially brainless creature who knew a great deal about art and literature and a wide variety of esoteric subjects, and absolutely nothing about real life.

Beautiful but brainless.

"This is bloody ridiculous," came an indignant whisper from somewhere behind his right shoulder.

Mitchell swung around. It was Iain MacClumpha, a serving platter of large, pink, plump shrimp grasped in his beefy hands and a furious expression on his forty-five-year-old face.

Without moving his lips, Mitchell said, "Keep your voice down and follow me."

He wended his way through the stragglers at the back of the crowd, checking every now and then to make sure the red-faced and red-haired giant was behind him.

There was a table beside a row of French doors. Mitchell took the platter of seafood from his companion and right-hand man, plunked it down on the table, and stepped out into the night.

"This is sheer madness, laddie," Iain MacClumpha gritted through his front teeth, his soft Scottish burr all the more pronounced for his indignation.

"Yes. It is," he agreed.

But no more so than a number of things he'd done in the past year, Mitchell reminded himself.

For a minute or two, the only sound was the scuff of their ghillie brogues on the crushed seashell path as they put a discreet distance between themselves and the house.

The man beside him asked in a sharp tone, "Did you see she was wearing the plaid and the *suaicheantas*?"

Mitchell had.

Although he'd caught only a brief glimpse of the silk evening sash and the silver clan badge pinned at her shoulder as Victoria had made her way down the Grand Staircase.

"Crist," his companion swore, thumping his muscular thigh with the palm of his broad hand, "I canna believe the local constables thought we were a couple of gussied-up waiters hired for the fancy party the lass is throwing."

Mitchell almost laughed.

Earlier that evening *not* local constables, but uniformed security guards had mistaken the two of them for members of the catering staff. He and Iain had been summarily dispatched to the service entrance of the mansion and put to work.

Frankly they hadn't argued the point. After all, he and The MacClumpha weren't exactly guests, either. Mitchell had decided on the spot not to try to explain the situation to a hired guard or anyone besides the woman it concerned.

Hell, it was going to be tough enough explaining it to Victoria Storm when the time came.

"And that bloody Englishman in charge."

He knew Iain meant the butler, Dickens.

"It's the kilts," Mitchell explained.

It had seemed like a good idea: both of them dressing in traditional Scottish kilts to make a lasting first impression on their American relation. The MacClumpha rarely wore trousers, of course, but it was a fairly new experience for Mitchell.

They'd had no way of knowing the staff was going to be dressed in kilts. Or, for that matter, that they were arriving on the eve of Victoria Storm's annual costume ball.

The other man failed to see the humor in the situation. That much was apparent.

"Obviously I need to take a different approach to confronting—" Mitchell immediately corrected himself "—to meeting with my cousin." He made another quick correction. "With *our* cousin."

Iain MacClumpha's branch of the family had descended through an illegitimate son of the third earl. Even though generations had passed, everyone knew who were legitimate septs of Clan Storm—and who were not.

The big man's voice had the timbre of a bass drum. "I lay no claim to the lass."

Mitchell would like to be able to say the same, but he

couldn't. Victoria Storm was his fourth cousin, and he had traveled to the United States specifically to meet her.

Actually he was here on a mission; a mission that he was a far cry from accomplishing. He would just have to put up with a snub or two, or a case of mistaken identity, if that's what it took.

Beggars couldn't be choosers.

"Maybe this wasn't my best idea," Mitchell conceded, rubbing a hand across his tired eyes as he finished the thought out loud.

Iain MacClumpha shook his head. "Hell of a time to start second-guessing yourself, if you don't mind my saying so. Not that your side of the family ever did lay claim to having the *Da-Shealladh*."

The Gaelic word rolled awkwardly off Mitchell's tongue. "The *Da-Shealladh*?"

"The Second Sight."

He made an interested sound. "You mean the ability to predict events?"

"I do. The vision may come in any place, and at any time of the day or night, and it comes unbidden. Too bad there was none on your side of the blanket with the gift. It'd come in handy about now." An additional bit of philosophy was tacked on. " 'Course, some say the Sight isn't a gift at all, but a terrible burden."

His burden was of another kind altogether, Mitchell acknowledged, picturing the crumbling castle, the great, brooding mountains, and the wild, windswept island an ocean away.

In the past few months he'd come to rely on Iain MacClumpha's brusque opinion. The man was outspoken and too big for anyone—except, perhaps, Mitchell—to argue with.

Uneasiness and weariness—he hadn't slept since leaving Glasgow yesterday—made Mitchell shift his stance. "So far it hasn't exactly gone according to our plans, has it, my friend?"

His traveling companion seemed to recover a portion of his sense of humor. He raised his arm and slapped Mitchell between the shoulder blades. "Burns had somethin' to say on the subject."

"Did he?"

Iain MacClumpha was fond of quoting Scotland's favorite son and poet, Robert Burns, who had had something to say on just about every subject.

The MacClumpha bobbed his shaggy head up and down. "Rabbie Burns wrote that they tend to 'gang aft a-gley.' "

"Who does?"

"Not who, laddie. What."

Mitchell was willing to play along for a minute. "What tends to go 'aft a-gley?' "

The Scotsman smiled and his face was transformed. "Why, 'the best laid schemes o' mice and men.' "

Both men laughed.

"Now, do you mind telling me again what we're doin' here?" Iain inquired in better humor.

Mitchell answered the question, without really answering it. "We're here to see the lady."

The Scotsman tugged on the sleeve of his evening jacket—a Prince Charlie Coatee with matching vest—and made a sound halfway between a chuckle and a snort. "This is MacClumpha you're talkin' to, *my lord*, lest you've forgotten." Iain only referred to Mitchell formally when he was trying to make a very particular point.

Mitchell reconsidered his answer. " 'Know thy enemy,' " he finally said tersely.

Thick, reddish-blond eyebrows drew into a frown.

9

"Did you learn that lesson at your grandfather's knee?"

Mitchell indicated otherwise as he walked on some small distance. "The London School of Economics by way of Jakarta and the University of Texas."

The seashell path curved around a large flagstone terrace that extended past the stately home and onto an expanse of rolling, green lawn. The impressive row of French doors—glass panes sparkling like faceted diamonds, brass knobs and fittings gleaming like burnished gold—had been thrown open to the summer night. Light poured from every window and door of the house, and the melodious strains of an orchestra playing a waltz could be heard somewhere in the background.

Mitchell Storm raised his face to the night air. He could make out the distinctive tang of salt and sea. The ocean must be very close by. Then he heard the solitary screech of a gull and the sound of waves pounding rhythmically against the shoreline.

He closed his eyes for a moment. He could almost imagine himself back on the Isle of Storm. Scotland seemed so near . . . and yet so far away.

"Is she the enemy?"

He came out of his reverie. "Is who the enemy?"

"The lass."

"Everyone is an enemy until they prove themselves to be a friend," he stated pragmatically.

Iain MacClumpha appeared to be biting his tongue. "Sounds like somethin' a clansman might have said two hundred and fifty years ago during the Rising."

"I suppose we picked the wrong side back then, too."

"We tried not to pick sides. We tried to stay neutral. The story goes that your great-great-great-great-great-grandfather entertained, in turn, both Bonnie Prince Charlie and the 'Butcher' Cumberland just before the Battle of Culloden.''

He needed to bone up on his Scottish history. "The 'Butcher' Cumberland?''

"The Duke of Cumberland. He led the English forces—recorded to be nine thousand strong—against half that number of Highlanders. The battle lasted an hour, but the slaughter continued through that bleak day and into the next, and for weeks to come. The moor at Culloden was stained with the best blood of Scotland.''

"How fortunate that we remained neutral then,'' Mitchell said sardonically.

"A man does what a man has to do.''

He arched an eyebrow in The MacClumpha's direction. "Burns again?''

The burly man shook his head. "My dad.'' The Scotsman wasn't above giving a small history lesson every chance he got. "We're neither Highlanders nor Lowlanders when it comes to that, laddie. The Storms have always been a law unto themselves.''

"It's a pity all that neutrality and diplomacy hasn't paid the bills and shored up the crumbling walls.''

"These are hard times for the people of the Western Isles,'' he was informed.

And it was his responsibility to find a way to restore the family's fortunes, and, in the process, bring prosperity—or at least guarantee survival—to the people who depended on him, Mitchell had discovered with his grandfather's death.

But he was having second and third thoughts about approaching Victoria Storm for help. She didn't seem like the type, somehow, who would give a damn about the fate of the inhabitants of a small island an ocean away. Maybe this whole thing, including the long trip from Scotland, had been a mistake from beginning to end.

"Why not wait and call on your cousin tomorrow?" his friend suggested.

"The morning after a formal ball?" Mitchell shook his head. "I wouldn't call that an opportune moment. And I have no intentions of waiting around until it's convenient for my dear cousin to grant me an audience."

Iain MacClumpha stepped back, folded his arms across his massive chest, planted his feet and gazed up at the imposing four-story stone edifice. "It's a bloody big house."

"It is."

He took another step backward and replanted his feet. "I suppose they refer to it as a mansion in this country."

"I suppose they do."

"It must take a great walloping lot of money to keep up a place like this."

"I'm sure it does." Mitchell decided he might as well tell Iain what he knew. "Our cousin inherited not only this house, but a luxury penthouse apartment in New York City, a villa on the Mediterranean, and a ski chalet in the Swiss Alps."

Breath whistled out between Iain MacClumpha's teeth. "By the blessed bones of St. Columba!"

He couldn't have said it better himself. "Victoria Storm has a great deal of money."

"Andrew did all right for himself."

"He certainly did." Mitchell could tell that the man beside him was duly impressed. "Do you know what men like Andrew Storm were called in this country during the last century?"

The MacClumpha gave a grimace. "Naw."

"Robber barons."

The MacClumpha grunted. "Seems appropriate."

"Yes, it does."

They turned and made their way back to the great house. Mitchell followed a kilted waiter through the service entrance and into the kitchen: it was all stainless steel and polished brass, what seemed like miles of marble countertops and walls of cupboards, huge ovens and rows of cooking stoves, a bank of subzero refrigerators, and a walk-in freezer. There were chefs in their distinctive white hats, maids in neat, black, aproned uniforms, and waiters in plaid.

Out of the corner of his mouth, Mitchell instructed: "Grab another tray of canapés and circulate."

He could tell Iain wasn't thrilled by the prospect of playing waiter again.

"Then what?" the man inquired with a scowl.

"Keep your eyes and ears open."

Iain MacClumpha picked up the first tray he came to. "What am I looking for?"

"Any of the Victorias. And keep in mind they could come in any form or shape or size, especially the marble one. The list I have only makes it clear there were at least a half dozen different Victorias disposed of at the 1879 auction."

"And if I find one?"

"Then I'll approach my dear cousin and offer her a deal she can't refuse."

"Do you think she'll go for it?"

"I'll make certain that she does," Mitchell said confidently as he hoisted an oversized serving tray ladened with mounds of black Beluga caviar and wafer-thin slices of pink Scottish salmon.

"Not above using your charms on the lass, are you?"

"You said it yourself: 'A man does what a man has

to do.' " A short silence followed. "On second thought, why don't you start with the terrace and the gardens, then move inside to the Billiard Room and the Great Hall?" His suggestion would give the headstrong Scot additional time to cool off.

Iain gladly set his tray back down. "Where are you headed?"

"I'm going to follow our dear cousin around her own party for a while."

"Mind your p's and q's, laddie."

"Believe me," Mitchell Storm assured him, putting his shoulder to the swinging door between kitchen and service hallway—a cacophony of music, laughter and voices from the formal reception rooms beyond washed over him—"I intend to."

He had to.

There was too damned much at stake not to.

Chapter 2

Someone was following her.

She hadn't actually seen him, but she knew it all the same. Well, she *sensed* it.

It had started as a slight niggling sensation at the back of her mind, like a mental itch that couldn't be scratched.

Then the small, nearly infinitesimal hairs at her nape had stood straight up on end, and a rash of goose bumps had been raised on her arms despite the warmth of the July night.

Finally there were the butterflies that had inexplicably begun to flutter about in her stomach.

Torey didn't believe for a minute that she was imagining the whole thing. Or that her sudden attack of "nerves" had anything to do with the four hundred people—society's elite—who had watched her descend the Grand Staircase. Or the fact that she, and she alone, was responsible for tonight's fund-raiser. Since the death of her mother, Marilyn, some ten years ago, she had been responsible for performing these duties and more... much more.

No, it wasn't her imagination, and there was certainly nothing wrong with her nerves.

She was being followed.

She'd almost caught a glimpse of him once or twice in her peripheral vision—some sixth sense told Torey it was a man—but by the time she was able to disengage herself from the conversation and turn to look, he had vanished.

Into thin air.

Torey accepted a glass of champagne from one of the kilted waiters and circulated among her guests. She took a sip; no more, no less. The crystal flute of vintage Cristal was more of a prop than anything else. For tonight of all nights she knew that she needed to keep a clear head and have her wits about her.

"Good evening, Victoria. Lovely party," mewed a breathless blonde, clinging to the arm of her escort as they promenaded from one room to the next.

For some, it wasn't enough apparently to see; they also had to be seen.

Torey nodded in acknowledgment and smiled: it was her duty smile. Then she spotted Beatrice Van Allen and Lola Albright sitting across the room, fans *and* tongues wagging, and extended her smile to include the gossiping duo.

Mrs. Van Allen had outdone herself tonight. Her mass of silver hair was artistically arranged on top of an already impressive head, and she was dressed in a black silk gown truly worthy of a Victorian "grande dame." In addition, she was decked out from bow to stern in the fabled Van Allen diamonds, including the tiara once rumored to have been among the Russian crown jewels.

Lola Albright, half her companion's size and consequence, was wearing a soft shade of yellow brocaded satin that did little for her sallow complexion. Beatrice

Van Allen had, no doubt, already lectured her friend on the error of her sartorial ways.

The two women had been the first to arrive for the evening's festivities. They had appeared at the front entrance at nine o'clock sharp. The dowagers of Newport, Rhode Island society did not believe in being fashionably late.

As she gazed out over the ballroom and its gaily costumed dancers, Torey could almost picture Storm Point as it must have been in the day of her great-great-grandparents.

Indeed, the theme for this year's *bal rose* had been inspired by photographs of Andrew and Annelise Storm, and the legendary parties they had given during the Gilded Age—a time as much about spending fortunes as making them.

Money had been no object when it came to Annelise's little "fêtes," as her great-great-grandmother had referred to her gala dinners and dances; they had often included elaborate decorations and costumes, exotic animals and entertainments imported specifically for the occasion, and titled guests from every royal house in Europe.

The Prince of Wales, affectionately dubbed Bertie by his family and friends, had attended one such gala at Storm Point in 1871 costumed as Lord of the Isles: kilt, sporran, and all.

Torey had seen the proof for herself: a vintage, and slightly out-of-focus, daguerreotype of the man who would one day become Edward VII of England.

Permitting herself a small sigh, she resisted the temptation to tug at the revealing bodice of her dress.

It was no small feat, Torey had discovered, dealing with the intricacies of a Victorian evening gown. Learning to manage the petticoat and the bustle, the flounces and the corset, the elaborate train and the bouffant puffs, not to mention the décolletage, had given her a newfound respect for the women of that era.

She glanced down at the silk evening sash draped diagonally across the front of her ball gown. The sash was affixed to her shoulder with a silver brooch, representing a sprig of cranberry, and then looped across her right breast to the opposite hip. Hand-tied five-knot fringe hung down past her waist in both the front and the back.

The sash was more than a fashion statement, however. It was her family tartan.

Indeed, that very afternoon, during a last-minute fitting, the couturier had complained about the sash, pointing out the obvious and lamenting, "It's plaid, Miss Storm."

"Yes, well, a plaid would be, wouldn't it?"

The elegant woman had crossed her arms, raised her nose a fraction in the air, cleared her throat and waited, as if expecting some kind of explanation.

"I'm a direct descendent of Clan Storm," Torey had stated.

That had brought no discernible reaction from the dressmaker beyond the slightest arch of a finely penciled eyebrow.

Torey had tried again. "The theme of this year's ball is Victorian Scotland."

"I am aware of that, Miss Storm."

"Ms. Fraser and I came up with the theme ourselves. We're both of Scottish descent."

A terribly genteel nose had been raised even higher in the air. "Indeed."

"The sash must be included in my costume." Torey had decided she would brook no argument on that point.

The sash had stayed.

She was a Scot, after all, and proud of it. Not that she had ever been back to the family seat—an island off the western coast of Scotland—but she wasn't above using the Scottish theme for her own purposes. The charity ball was for a worthy cause.

Actually several worthy causes would benefit from tonight's fund-raiser.

The entrance of the ball's hostess down the Grand Staircase, wearing an elegant designer creation, was considered by many of the guests to be the high point of the evening.

As a matter of fact, a silent auction was held with the gown going by the end of the night to the highest bidder and the money to the designated charities. The tradition had begun between the World Wars and had been passed down ever since from generation to generation. For the past decade, the privileges and duties—and the burdens—had fallen on Torey's shoulders.

She took another sip of champagne and went through the motions of speaking to several of her eminent guests before finding herself alone for a moment.

Truth to tell, there were times when she would like nothing better than to forget the whole blasted business of holding a charity ball, of sitting on the board of directors of a dozen philanthropic organizations from child-care facilities to health clinics to art museums, however necessary and worthwhile they might be—and, of course, they were all necessary and worthwhile—of maintaining her family's position in society and the myriad responsibilities that went with being a Storm.

But she was not only a Storm, Torey reminded herself. She was the last of the Storms.

She gave a heavy sigh. Being a Storm had never been

easy. It seemed like she had spent her entire life either being sheltered by her dear parents, mourning her dear parents, or following in her dear parents' footsteps.

It was a preordained path that she trod.

Even Peter Nicholson—dear, dependable, and thoroughly safe Peter—was part of what her parents had intended for her, practically from birth. After all, she and Peter made the perfect couple. Everyone said so. They were from the same social circle, the same moneyed background, the same elite schooling. They were like two peas in a pod . . . an utterly predictable pod.

The only unpredictable thing Peter had done in recent memory was plead an unavoidable out-of-town business trip to Dallas this weekend. It was the first time in over a decade that he had missed the annual ball.

Torey sighed again, more heavily, and then abruptly halted in the middle of the exhalation: the sharp point of a straight pin was pressed against the underside of her right breast. Apparently the seamstress had missed one. She paused and discreetly adjusted the bodice of her evening gown before returning to her daydreaming.

Monte Carlo.

She would like to chuck it all and escape to Monte Carlo for the summer.

No, not Monte Carlo. She'd had quite enough of bright lights and elegant society and smart, chic people.

Provence, then.

Or Portofino.

Or a Caribbean island . . . like her best friend, Jane Bennett. Now Jane Hollister.

Torey had to admit that she envied her former college roommate, not only for her handsome husband, Jake Hollister, but because the newlyweds had a remote Caribbean island that they disappeared to whenever the world got to be too much for them.

She wished she had a place to run away to and someone to run away with.

Strange, but it never occurred to her for a moment that that someone should be Peter.

Torey snapped out of her reverie and straightened her back; not that she had ever been one to slouch. A young woman of good breeding never slouched, according to the dictates of the headmistress at Miss Porter's School for Young Ladies where Torey—always referred to as Victoria or Miss Storm by the establishment's staff—had been enrolled as a student from the age of nine until a pubescent fourteen.

She suddenly froze.

There it was.

That sensation of being watched.

She looked up and found herself staring into the huge gilt-framed mirror hanging on the wall in front of her. Then she saw the reflection of a man standing in the doorway between the ballroom and the Great Hall beyond.

It was him.

Somehow she knew it was.

And he'd been watching her. She had seen him quickly avert his eyes and pretend to be contemplating one of the paintings on the wall opposite: a turn-of-the-century masterpiece by the renowned portraitist, John Singer Sargent. The portrait had been painted of her great-grandmother and her great-aunt when they were girls: two redheaded young beauties on the verge of womanhood, dressed in white muslin dresses with blue satin ribbons in their hair.

Of all the priceless artworks in the house, it was her personal favorite.

So, while the stranger made a pretext of studying the painting, Torey studied him.

He was dressed in a traditional kilt, and it briefly registered somewhere in her memory that the plaid was a familiar one.

Nevertheless, it wasn't the man's kilt that caught and held her attention. It was something far less tangible. It was something in the way he stood there, surveying the room around him: as if he were to the manor born.

Out of the blue, the words to an old Scottish folk song flitted through her mind:

> *Speed, bonnie boat, like a bird on the wing;*
> *Onward, the sailors cry:*
> *Carry the lad that's born to be king*
> *Over the sea to Skye.*

The man was noble, even regal.

And intimidating.

But he was far more than that, Torey acknowledged.

He was gorgeous.

His age was somewhere between thirty and forty, probably slightly closer to forty. Broad shoulders. Muscular arms and chest. Lean waistline. Long legs. Very long legs. Thick, dark hair that brushed his collar at the sides and in the back. High forehead. Arching eyebrows. Dark, intelligent, piercing eyes.

Were his eyes black or brown in color, or something in between? Or something else altogether?

The man's nose bordered on the patrician, but had obviously been broken at some point in his life. The flaw saved him from ever being described as picture-perfect.

His mouth was expressive; the lower lip was slightly fuller than the upper. His chin was well-formed and jutted with determination. His ears were nicely shaped and tucked close to his head. His hands were long-fingered, masculine yet graceful.

Torey had met many men in her life: giants of industry, leaders of political parties, and even of countries—those of royal birth and of royal circumstances. She had seen that implacable air of self-confidence, that mantle of power, that core of inner strength that some men, a very few men, that *this* man seemed to possess.

She imagined that no matter where he was, it would always be the right time and the right place, and he would always know exactly the right thing to say and do.

She had a flash of insight. It happened sometimes at the oddest moments.

This was no ordinary man.

There was something mysterious and more than a little dangerous about him.

"Excuse me, Victoria."

Alice Fraser appeared at her side.

She turned. "Yes, Alice."

The woman lowered her voice and quietly informed Torey of the latest developments: "Dickens has given the caterers permission to open another case of champagne. And I've seen to it that each lady has a corsage, as you requested."

Torey's attention was momentarily diverted. "Thank you, Alice. I don't know what I'd do without you."

It was true.

Alice was the perfect personal secretary. She was formidable and forty-five, unmarried and unattached, intelligent, well-organized, and fiercely loyal to Torey. In the ten years they had been together, including the painful period in Victoria's life when she had lost both her parents within a tragically short span of time, Alice Fraser had also become her friend and confidante.

The always-capable Ms. Fraser knew where to obtain, on a moment's notice, coveted tickets to a sold-out performance of a Broadway play; which was the best florist for orchids in Seattle, Phoenix, or Rome; and the size, style, and color—a shade of rose somewhere between pale pink and ivory—of the Parisian-made silk undergarments that Torey preferred.

In short, Alice Fraser was indispensable.

Especially when they had all been working eighteen-hour days in preparation for what the society columns had dubbed *the* event of the Newport season: the charity ball at Storm Point.

Torey moistened her lips. "Who is that man?" she asked nonchalantly, her hand going to her throat.

Alice turned and, without making a production of it, peered out over the ballroom. "Which man?"

"The tall, dark, and handsome one standing in the doorway," she said without once looking directly at him.

"Waiter."

That took Torey by surprise. She dropped the strand of rubies that she had been nervously fingering with her free hand. "Are you certain?"

"Yes."

Torey again raised the glass of champagne to her mouth and pretended to take a drink. "He doesn't look like a waiter to me," she murmured from behind the crystal rim.

Alice inquired in her usual no-nonsense tone: "What does he look like?"

Victoria Storm took a deep, fortifying breath and slowly released it. "Trouble."

Chapter 3

"I've found one," Iain MacClumpha declared when the two men met up with each other again more than an hour later in a seldom-used corner of a back hallway.

Mitchell was relieved. Their initial search seemed to be paying off. "Where is yours?" he asked.

The brawny Scot gestured toward a vague point somewhere behind him. "The formal gardens."

He made a mental note of the fact. "What is it?"

"A piece of statuary."

"How large is the statue?"

Iain raised and lowered his arm several notches, finally indicating a height that was more or less level with his own shoulder. "Life-size." He rubbed his hand back and forth along his jawline and confessed, " 'Course, it's a mite difficult to tell since the statue is sitting up on some kind of pedestal."

Mitchell cast a meaningful glance at his coconspirator. "It sounds like it could be a logistics problem."

There was no argument from The MacClumpha. "The bloody thing must weigh at least a dozen hundredweights . . . that's over a half ton to you."

Mitchell bit off a short, succinct expletive. "Make that a logistics nightmare."

"What'll we do?"

There was only one thing they could do. "I guess we'll figure out a way to cross that bridge when we get to it," Mitchell told him through stiff lips.

Iain MacClumpha paused and considered, and eventually nodded his head slowly. "Only thing we can do," he said, echoing the sentiment. Then he inquired, "Did you find anything?"

That was right. He hadn't told the other man about his own discoveries.

"I've located two. One is a portrait of the young Queen Victoria hanging above the fireplace in the study."

"And the other?"

"The second is a small, standing bronze mirror, about twelve or fourteen inches in height, with a figure of a mythical winged woman at its base. The bronze is done in the Greek style, and probably dates from the fifth or sixth century B.C. It's not only a valuable antiquity, but I would be willing to guarantee that it's the 'Winged Victory' mentioned in the accounts of the auction."

"What the family affectionately dubbed 'Vicky.' "

"The very one."

The lines defining Iain MacClumpha's craggy features deepened. "Andrew has much to answer for."

"Andrew may have done us a favor."

The Scot's face shot up. "A favor?"

"At least they're all in the same place," Mitchell pointed out to him. "It would be virtually impossible for us to locate the missing Victorias if they had been purchased by a number of bidders and scattered more than a century ago to the four corners of the earth."

Iain wasn't an unreasonable man. Not once he'd had sufficient time to reflect on the matter. "You've got a point."

Yes. He did.

But it didn't make Mitchell's task any easier when it came to approaching his cousin.

"By the by, have you introduced yourself to the young lady?" the big man came right out and asked him.

Sometimes he wondered if Iain MacClumpha could read his mind. "Not yet."

"What are you waiting for?" The MacClumpha's reddish-blond eyebrows, the same color and texture as his shaggy head of hair, drew together into an impertinent arch. "You're a *buirdly* lad. No doubt she'll take to you like a duck to water."

Mitchell brought his teeth together. "I was hoping to find her alone for a few minutes."

The Scot bit off the edges of a smile and, with an undertone of amusement in his voice, suggested, "Are you tellin' me you're too *blate* to speak to her?"

Mitchell Storm did not require the English translation from the Gaelic. He got the gist of what was being said—and certainly implied—well enough on his own. Lord knows, either way, he wasn't about to try to repeat the Gaelic.

An elderly man, appropriately called Old Ned by the locals back home on the Isle of Storm, had cautioned Mitchell—only partly in jest, he'd come to realize over the past few months—that to utter the guttural sounds correctly in the old tongue, "without strangling yerself, my lord, ye need generations of Scots blood in yer veins, and it wouldn't hurt to be born with the peat-reek in yer nostrils and the sight of the hills as the first thing ever ye clapped your eyes on."

27

At least he qualified on one count: there were innumerable generations of Scots blood flowing through his veins.

The MacClumpha made a disbelieving sound. "You're waiting until you find the lass alone? In case you hadn't noticed, laddie, the bloody house is filled with hundreds of bloody guests and there's a fancy dress ball going on."

It sounded ludicrous when put like that.

But Mitchell told himself that he'd know instinctively when and how to approach Victoria Storm.

He firmly told The MacClumpha, "In my own time and in my own way."

"Now you sound like your grandfather."

Mitchell knew that was meant as a compliment. Indeed, the highest compliment. Iain MacClumpha had been devoted to William Storm, direct descendant of the ancient kings of Dalriada, thirty-fourth chief of the clan, laird of the Isles, and a peer of the Realm.

The two men had been bound by blood, tradition, friendship, and kinship. A MacClumpha had served as the trusted right-hand man of the chief of Clan Storm for longer than recorded history. There was never one without the other.

With more than a hint of frustration, Iain asked, "Are you certain the old earl said Victoria was the key?"

"I'm positive." Mitchell would have dismissed that last conversation with his grandfather as the ramblings of a dying man, but something had clicked in his memory, something from his own past, from the single childhood trip he had made to the Western Isles at the age of twelve or thirteen. "My grandfather pulled my head down close to his mouth"—the skin on the old man's hands had appeared rice-paper thin—"and managed to say in a raspy but perfectly clear voice: 'You must find the treasure. The key is in America. Go to America and bring back Victoria."

Iain scratched his head. "Which Victoria?"

That was the question.

It was, unfortunately, the question to which he didn't have the answer.

Mitchell raised and then lowered his shoulders. "I don't know which Victoria."

Iain brightened. "Look at it this way. So far we've found three of them."

Mitchell held up the fingers of one hand. "Four."

"Four?"

"Don't forget our cousin."

"You mean the lass?"

He did.

"You believe the lass herself may hold the key to finding the treasure?"

"She might." Admittedly it was a long shot. But he wasn't taking any chances. There was too much at stake to overlook even the remotest possibility.

Iain shook his head in bemusement. "What are you going to do once we've found them all?"

"Take them back to Scotland with us."

"Every last one?"

"Every last one." Mitchell set his jaw, along with his resolve. "I'm not sure how a Victoria is the key to finding the missing treasure, but taking them all back is the only way to be certain we have the right one."

Iain turned his head and glanced down the hallway. "I suppose you want me to return to the party now and circulate with another tray of fancy food."

"I do."

"And keep my eyes and ears open."

"And keep your eyes and ears open."

Iain scowled. "I don't mind so much fetching and carrying for the old biddies, even though one of them ordered me to the kitchen to get her a dish of fresh strawberries and cream, and another demanded that I bring her a cup of tea laced with exactly two ounces of the 'water of life.' "

"The 'water of life?' "

"Uisge beatha." He translated. "Scotch whisky."

Mitchell started to sympathize.

Iain wasn't finished. "But the next time a young gentleman—and I employ the term gentleman loosely— sneers at me and demands a peek under my Scotsman's 'skirt,' I may just have to show the buggering fool what a real *dowp* looks like."

Mitchell didn't want to know what a *dowp* was.

"Remember what we're trying to accomplish here, Iain," he admonished his companion.

The big man grumbled under his breath.

Mitchell placed a hand on his friend's shoulder. "Stay calm, and don't do anything rash."

Those were to be famous last words.

Something was wrong.

Only this time it wasn't some sixth sense that told Torey there was trouble, it was an astonished female shriek and a loud, raucous burst of male laughter from the next room.

She only hoped and prayed it wasn't Ronnie Flynn-Frye again. At last year's Louis Quatorze ball he had downed one too many snifters of her fine French brandy and had propositioned most of the female guests under the age of fifty. Torey had been adamant about not inviting Ronnie this year, but his mother had begged and pleaded and cajoled and had even promised her son would behave himself.

Mrs. Flynn-Frye had also pledged one quarter of a million dollars to Torey's favorite charity.

Under the circumstances, how could she refuse?

Quickly darting into the formal dining room—huge buffet tables, ladened with everything from iced lobster to pickled ortolan, lined both lengthwise mirrored walls— Torey spotted several dozen people gathered in the far corner.

Before she could work her way closer, Beatrice Van Allen, with the ever-faithful Lola Albright in tow, planted herself squarely in Torey's path. There was no avoiding her.

"What is it, Mrs. Allen?" she inquired, unhappy with the delay, however well intentioned. And there was no telling about the woman's intentions.

"Tell her, Beatrice," urged Lola, fan fluttering, cheeks pink, eyes bright. "Do tell her."

Mrs. Van Allen had obviously decided the job of informing their hostess what was what was hers whether or not she wished it to be. "Well, my dear, it's about one of your waiters."

She would prefer not to be having this conversation, but it seemed inescapable. Just as Beatrice Van Allen herself was inescapable. "What about one of my waiters?"

Lola Albright interjected her two-cent's worth. "It wasn't entirely his fault, you must understand, Victoria. One of the young men had had too much to drink, as young men so frequently do at these affairs."

"That is no excuse for improper behavior on the part of the hired help," declared the dowager in black silk, snapping her fan shut with a flick of a diamond-encrusted wrist. "As I'm sure you agree, Victoria."

"I do."

"Decorum must be maintained."

"Of course."

"Good manners are good manners."

Lola nodded her head in parroted agreement. Torey didn't think she'd ever seen the usually pale creature quite so animated or quite so flush with color.

Apparently a little scandal agreed with Lola Albright.

Mrs. Van Allen had not completed her diatribe. "Behavior is either proper or it isn't. There is never any middle ground when it comes to that sort of thing."

"There were extentuating circumstances," piped up her faithful shadow.

A half turn of a regal head, priceless gemstones glittering under chandelier light. "Breeding always exposes itself, Lola."

Lola Albright appeared to choke on her own saliva.

Doggedly, Beatrice Van Allen continued. "Lack of breeding, I presume, must do the same."

Torey's voice was silky. "Expose itself?"

"Precisely."

"He is a foreigner," was volunteered plucklessly.

Torey admitted to a certain confusion. "Who is a foreigner?" she asked. There were no less than thirty nationalities represented among her guests.

"The man in question."

"Is there a man in question?"

"There is a man of questionable behavior."

"I see." But, of course, Torey didn't see. These two had intervened and prevented her from seeing. "If you two ladies will excuse me, I really must see to the matter myself." She swept the train of her skirt out behind her and left in the wake of a well-meaning "but" or two.

Making her way toward the commotion, Torey wondered where in the dickens Dickens was.

She was finally close enough to make out a head of unruly red hair among the crowd of onlookers. Through a small opening she managed to catch a glimpse of a tartan—undoubtedly a kilt—and something rather white and fleshly.

Ohmigod.

Torey felt as if the air had been sucked from her lungs. For a moment she couldn't seem to breathe. One kid-gloved hand flew to cover her mouth. She squeezed her eyes shut and then reluctantly opened them again.

Unbelievably.

Unmistakably.

Bare buttocks.

Dear God, someone was mooning her guests.

As she tried to force her way through the throng, she ran straight into a hard, male body.

Well, a hard, male chest.

A deep masculine voice said in a quietly commanding tone, "Don't worry. It's under control."

Torey looked up. It was him. The man in the mirror. The man who had been following her.

"I beg your pardon?"

He grasped her lightly by the elbows. "The incident is over. The situation is under control."

Torey wasn't convinced. "Who is he?" she demanded to know at once, motioning toward the giant.

"A hotheaded Scot."

She expected to be told more than that.

As if he'd read her thoughts, the stranger elaborated on his answer. "My piper."

Torey knitted her eyebrows. "Your what?"

"My piper." The man puffed up his cheeks, blew out the air, and freed one hand momentarily in order to wiggle his fingers as if he were playing a musical instrument. "Bagpipes."

Torey's mouth formed a perfectly round O.

"By now, Dickens and several of your staff will be escorting Iain to the kitchen."

They'd better be.

She gazed up into the stranger's handsome face. "I don't know you, do I?"

"No."

Suspicion was an immediate and appropriate response on Torey's part. Not that she knew every single guest who had been invited to tonight's charity ball on sight, of course.

Her eyes narrowed. "Were you sent an invitation?"

"No."

Her suspicions grew. "Did you crash my party?"

"Not exactly."

She was becoming exasperated. "Then exactly how did you get in?"

"The MacClumpha—"

She interrupted him. "The MacClumpha?"

A gesture was made over a broad shoulder toward the man being ushered through the dispersing group of oglers. "His name is Iain MacClumpha."

"He plays the bagpipes for you."

"Yes. Among other things."

She didn't inquire what those other things might be.

The man gazed down at her and smiled with his entire face: crinkling eyes, straight, white teeth, and beautiful mouth. Torey found herself more than a little fascinated by him. He was even more handsome—and even more enchanting, if that were possible—when he smiled.

She finally cleared her throat and prompted him with, "As you were saying . . ."

He appeared perfectly willing to expound on the subject. "When Iain and I arrived on your doorstep earlier this evening, the security guard assumed we were waiters."

She glanced down at the expanse of bare, muscular leg between plaid hose and kilt, and felt a flood of unexpected warmth spread across her cheeks. "It's the kilt."

He nodded. "I realize that now."

She stated the obvious aloud. "You're no waiter."

"I'm no waiter."

Was there the merest hint of sarcasm in his otherwise velvety baritone voice?

She went on. "You're probably not with the catering company, either."

"I'm not with the catering company."

Torey's curiosity got the best of her. "Then what are you doing here?"

"It's a long story."

She inclined her head slightly to one side and informed her uninvited guest, "I like long stories."

"Look, Miss Storm—"

Torey interrupted. "You know who I am."

"You're Victoria Storm."

She'd had enough. Moistening her lips, she demanded to know: "Who are you?"

The man facing her only hesitated briefly before answering, "I'm Mitchell Storm."

He'd made another mistake.

Mitchell stood in front of Victoria Storm and looked down into a sea of color: the blue of the straits as the setting sun reflected off the water's surface; the green of the hills after a misting rain; the particular shade of heather—blue and gray and lavender all at once—that grew only on the island.

There was also self-awareness and a keen intelligence and even anger in those unusual blue-green eyes of hers.

More remarkably, his cousin appeared to be completely lacking in feminine wiles, or girlish flirtations, artifice, or a sense of self-importance, or any of the usual character flaws he had come to expect when initially meeting a beautiful young woman.

Maybe she was beautiful but *not* brainless, after all.

Victoria Storm said to him, "Would you mind explaining what that was all about?"

"I think one too many of your guests insulted The MacClumpha," he replied.

She appeared to be biting the corners of her mouth. "I suppose the lesson to be learned here is—"

He arched an eyebrow in anticipation.

"—Don't insult The MacClumpha," she finished.

She had a sense of humor. He hadn't expected that, either. A beautiful and intelligent woman with a sense of how funny—and sometimes how downright ridiculous— life could be.

The best-laid schemes were definitely going "aft a-gley."

Her intent gaze pinned him to the spot where he stood. They were nearly chest to chest. She put her head back, lifted her determined chin—this woman was no shrinking violet, that was for damned sure—and stared up at him. "Is it purely coincidence that both of us have the last name of Storm?"

"No."

"Are we related in some way?"

"We are."

"Would you care to tell me how we're related?"

Mitchell took his eyes off her for the first time in five minutes, and glanced around at the roomful of people. "I'm not sure this is the time or the place."

"I'll be the judge of that."

She had a definite mind of her own.

He gave it to her short and sweet. "We're distant cousins."

"How distant?"

"Fourth cousins."

"Go on."

"My great-great-grandfather, Angus Storm, and your great-great-grandfather, Andrew Storm, were twin brothers."

Fine nostrils flared.

He continued. "Angus was the older by fifteen minutes and, consequently, he inherited the lands, the titles,"— the debts—"and became the chief of Clan Storm."

"And Andrew?"

"I'm sure you know your history of Scotland and its economic woes during the middle of the nineteenth century."

"The potato famine."

"It hit not only Ireland, but the Highlands and the Hebrides, reducing whole towns to scavenging for cockles and seaweed. Anyway, like many a young Scot in his position—a younger son with no land of his own and no money to speak of—Andrew decided to emigrate to America and make his own way in the world." Mitchell looked around the incredibly and richly furnished mansion. "He apparently did very well for himself."

Her eyes became unblinking. She nailed him with that stare. "No thanks to his identical twin from the family tales I've heard. I don't know all the details, but I was given the impression that Andrew was kicked out of Scotland by his 'beloved' brother.''

Mitchell felt the sudden heat in his face. ''There's a little more to the story than that.''

There was a lot more to the story.

''As I told you before, Mr. Storm, I like long stories.''

''And I'll be happy to tell you this one, Miss Storm, but not now and not here.''

''Another time, then,'' she suggested smoothly.

''Another time.''

''Tomorrow?''

Why not? Wasn't that why he had come all the way from Scotland?

''Tomorrow,'' Mitchell agreed, then added, ''People are beginning to stare at us.''

He noticed that she didn't even bother to verify whether it was true or not. Either Victoria Storm didn't care, or the occurrence was so commonplace as to be utterly unremarkable to her.

The orchestra began to play one of those long, slow, moody love songs. The words were out of his mouth before Mitchell Storm could consider the wisdom of his actions. ''Would you like to dance?''

That caught her by surprise. ''Dance?''

He motioned toward the ballroom floor. ''I'm asking you to dance with me, dear cousin.''

Chapter 4

Torey went into his arms.

The orchestra was playing a vintage Rodgers and Hammerstein tune and a fragment of the lyrics floated though her mind; something about an enchanted evening and seeing a stranger across a crowded room.

They danced for a minute or two without speaking. Torey hadn't realized how tall Mitchell Storm was until his shoulders blocked her view of the other couples on the floor.

She put her head back slightly, looked up at him, and, picking the safest topic she could think of, initiated the conversation. "I believe I recognize your tartan."

"I'm not surprised."

"It's one of the tartans of Clan Storm, isn't it?" she said, seeking confirmation.

"It is."

She glanced down at the green and red plaid silk sash draped across the front of her evening gown. "Mine is, too."

Her dance partner stared at her décolletage, then nodded his head. "Modern dress tartan."

She would not allow the man to intimidate her. She stepped back, placed him at arm's length and looked down at his sporran and kilt. The pouch was soft, gray fur—probably rabbit—with a silver cantle and chain strap; the plaid was muted green and blue with a distinctive lavender-gray stripe. "Which is yours?"

"The ancient hunting tartan."

"Are you a hunter, Mr. Storm?"

"Under the circumstances, don't you think you should call me Mitchell?"

"Are you a hunter, Mitchell?"

His smile was predatory. "In a manner of speaking."

Torey was beginning to have misgivings. "In exactly which manner of speaking?"

Her recently self-introduced cousin took the lead and smoothly guided her around the ballroom floor. He held her close, but not too close. He had a firm grasp on her waist and her hand, but he wasn't squeezing or crushing her. In fact, he was a surprisingly good dancer for a large, athletic man with large feet. She would almost call him graceful.

"It's all part of the long story I'll relate to you tomorrow," he finally promised.

Torey wondered if she was going to like the story Mitchell Storm intended to tell her.

She chose another topic of conversation off the top of her head. "Your piper is a most unusual man."

"Yes. He is."

"He's very large." It was an obvious observation; nevertheless it was true.

"Very large."

"A gentle giant?" she speculated.

Mitchell seemed to need a second or two to think about it, then he shook his head. "I wouldn't go that far."

She moistened her lips. "Is he violent?"

A semblance of a smile flitted across the handsome features. "Not normally."

Torey's beaded satin skirt and train, with its pleatings and double-shirred ruche, brushed the hardwood floor with a distinctive *swish-swish* as it swept around her ankles—and his—as they danced.

She suggested, "Of course, tonight wasn't a normal situation . . ."

"Let's just say an insulted Scotsman can be dangerous," he said noncommittally.

"Aren't you Scottish?"

She felt him hesitate. "Yes. I am," he said.

Torey wasn't sure why she was so interested in pursuing the subject, but she was. "How do you retaliate when you're insulted?"

Her distant cousin didn't appear to understand her question. "I beg your pardon?"

"We've seen how The MacClumpha reacts: He gets mad and goes off . . ."

"Half-cocked?" was proposed, deadpan.

Torey bit her bottom lip and nodded. "Yes." She kept pressing. "What do you do in retaliation when someone insults you?" Assuming anyone ever had the nerve—or imprudence—to insult this man. "Do you get angry?"

"I like to think I'm slow to anger," Mitchell answered without answering her question.

"Why is that?" Without waiting for a response, she put forth, "Temperament?"

"Training."

That wasn't what Torey had expected him to say. Now she was more than a little curious; she was fascinated. "What kind of training?"

"Physical. Mental. Spiritual," came the cryptic response.

Didn't that just about cover them all? "So you've mastered self-control through training?"

"Yes."

She straightened her back ever so slightly. "And where did you learn such enviable self-control?"

A shrug of broad, masculine shoulders and another vague answer. "A number of places."

She could be persistent. It was required in a successful society hostess and even more in a successful fund-raiser: she was both. "Your lessons in self-mastery, where did they begin?"

"Jakarta."

"Jakarta?"

"Actually at a special school my parents sent me to one summer outside Jakarta. The school was run by a monk who practiced, among other things, *agama Jawa*: a peculiar brand of religion that encompasses Hinduism, Buddhism, and Islam."

It took several moments for Torey to realize that Mitchell was perfectly serious.

"I also played football."

"In this country we would call it soccer," she corrected.

"I played quarterback for the University of Texas Longhorns for four years," he countered, successfully maneuvering her through a potential bottleneck of swaying couples.

Torey realized that she had just been nicely put in her place. The man had said football and he'd meant football.

She kept her attention focused on his mouth. "I suppose that explains the accent."

His brow furrowed into a frown. "Most people in the U.S. don't think I have an accent."

That was the most surprising part of all. He didn't. No Texas drawl. No Scottish burr. No upper-crust English accent. Nothing. "You don't," she agreed.

Why?

Almost as if he'd heard the unspoken question in her mind, he explained, "My parents moved around a great deal while I was growing up."

"Then you didn't live in Scotland?"

"My father considered Scotland, especially the Isle of Storm and all that it represented, a virtual prison. At the age of twenty-five he left with my mother and never returned."

"Not to this day?"

Something altered in Mitchell's eyes and in the way he held her in his arms as they danced. It was a subtle, nearly imperceptible change. Yet Torey sensed it immediately.

"My parents were killed in an airplane crash on their way back to Hong Kong while I was still in college."

"I'm sorry."

"So was I." He seemed to loosen his grip on her waist fractionally. "I understand you've lost both of your parents as well."

"Yes, I have."

"You're the last of the American Storms."

"I am."

"I'm the last of the Scottish Storms," he stated.

Neither spoke for a minute or two. The Rodgers and Hammerstein song ended, but the orchestra immediately began to play another classic tune. Without a word, they kept on dancing.

Torey passed her tongue over her lips. "What did you do, then?"

Mitchell's eyes met hers. "When?"

Her voice went a shade softer. "After your parents died?"

"I finished college."

Mitchell Storm wasn't exactly forthcoming about himself. But it had been his decision to enter her life, and not the other way around, and Torey was curious about him. She would have that curiosity satisfied. "And after college?"

He seemed intent on giving vague replies. "I kicked around for a while."

She wasn't sure what he meant. "Kicked around?"

"Traveled."

Ah.

When he didn't volunteer more information, she asked, "Where did you go on your travels?"

He threw out the names of a few exotic locales. "Marrakech. Timbuktu. Tabora. Komodo."

Torey herself was widely traveled, of course. England. France. She loved the Riviera. Monaco. Italy. Spain. The Moorish influence intrigued her. Greece. The Netherlands. Switzerland. She had a lovely place in the Swiss Alps, and her friend, Jane Bennett Hollister had an apartment in Paris that she occasionally used.

Still, when she traveled, it was all very neat and tidy, Torey realized. All very civilized. She wasn't certain she'd ever been anywhere that wasn't civilized.

She nudged him again. "And where did you go once your travels were over?"

"Eventually I wound up in London and spent a year there studying before I returned to Hong Kong and took over my father's share in an import-export business."

"Until—?"

"Until last year when my grandfather became ill."

The pieces of the puzzle were beginning to fit into place. Well, the very large pieces, perhaps.

"Then you went home to Scotland," she concluded.

"Then I went home to Scotland," he said.

Mitchell snapped his mouth shut.

He'd been talking too much. Hell, he'd practically spilled his guts to the woman.

It didn't make sense.

Admittedly, Victoria Storm was beautiful. She was intelligent and witty, contrary to his initial impression of her. She was an accomplished conversationalist and a damned good listener. And he liked the sound of her voice.

But that was no excuse.

She also stood between him and what he wanted; what he needed most in the world. That made her the enemy, even if only on a temporary basis. Besides, strictly on principle, it was never wise to give out any more personal information than was absolutely necessary. He should know that by now.

He was a fool.

His American relation now knew a great deal about him, and he knew very little of her outside of a few hard, cold facts: mostly financial and statistical information that almost anyone clever enough to know where to look and what questions to ask could obtain.

Silently Mitchell swore at himself. He was worse than a fool; he was an idiot.

He'd lost the element of surprise.

He'd forfeited his advantage.

He had given her the upper hand.

As the second song came to an end, he quickly dropped his arms, took half a step in retreat from his dance partner, and said to her, "I've taken up too much of your time, dear cousin. You can't neglect your other guests on my account."

"Indeed, I can't, *dear cousin*," Victoria Storm countered with a regal nod of her head. She turned her lovely back to him and started to walk away. Then she paused and glanced over her shoulder. "By the way, there will be fireworks a little later. I'm sure you wouldn't want to miss all the excitement."

He'd already had more than enough excitement for one evening, Mitchell grumbled under his breath as he went in search of the errant Iain MacClumpha.

She had danced all of her duty dances. She'd had her dress, and her toes, repeatedly stepped on. Her décolletage stared at. Her ear bent. And her patience tried.

It was always a relief when the fireworks began. It was an even greater relief tonight.

The waiting crowd was noisy: laughing and talking and toasting each other with champagne. Then came the first loud boom and a burst of brilliant color showered down from a midnight-blue sky overhead, followed by the usual appreciative *oohs* and *ahs* from the guests assembled on the patio to watch.

Traditionally this was Torey's favorite part of the evening. To her it always signalled that another grand ball at Storm Point had come off without a hitch.

Well, nearly without a hitch.

She sighed deeply. It was strange, but there was only one man she could actually remember having danced with tonight. She knew exactly how he had held her in his arms, and how he had swept her around the ballroom floor.

She seemed to have memorized the jut of his chin, the arch of his dark eyebrows, the aristocratic line of his nose, the enticing shape of his mouth. In fact, she could close her eyes and see every minute detail of his features.

She could measure the width of his shoulders and the tensile strength in his arms. She could hear the resonance in his voice, especially when he laughed.

She loved his laugh.

One would almost think she was infatuated with him.

Ridiculous.

Mitchell Storm was a stranger to her. And, yet, he wasn't really a stranger.

Perhaps she needed a change of scenery even more than she'd realized, Torey conceded to herself. Although there was no denying her newfound Scottish relation was an attractive man with more—far more—than his fair share of male sex appeal.

She slipped away from the crowd and sought a secluded corner of the flagstone terrace where, as a child, she used to hide, perched atop a low, stone urn, to watch the fireworks. Her hiding place had the perfect vantage point.

There was a sudden burst of gold dust in the sky over their heads, and then a glittering shower of silver. And then yet another of red, white, and blue. Man-made stars of every color and hue that lasted for only a few magical moments.

A wistful sigh escaped Torey's lips. She could picture her parents gathering with their guests on this very terrace to watch the annual fireworks display. Sometimes she would spy her mother and father stealing away into the night to dance alone, arms wrapped around each other, on the dew-damp lawn.

" 'We danced till the stars went out, my darling Torey,' " she murmured, repeating what her doting mother used to tell her the next morning.

Torey took another step into the shadows.

She stopped dead in her tracks. She knew that he was there. She could *sense* that he was there.

"What is it you've really come for?" she whispered, without turning to look at him.

"I've come for you," the man behind her admitted as if that wasn't at all what he had intended to say, as if he'd consumed too much champagne and it had unwisely loosened his tongue, and yet she was certain he'd had nothing to drink at all.

"Me?"

"It wasn't part of the plan," he confessed in a tone that conveyed his own bewilderment.

"*I* wasn't part of the plan?"

"You were part of the plan." He hesitated. "I just didn't expect you to be as you are."

"Is that good or bad?"

She knew there was a sardonic smile on those lips of his. "That depends on your point of view," he said.

"In your point of view?"

She felt his chest move as he breathed in and out. "It's good *and* bad."

She had to ask. "Why?"

A masculine hand—she could hear the telltale sound—was driven in frustration through soft, dark, thick hair. "It makes the whole damnable business easier and yet infinitely more difficult."

Torey didn't even pretend to understand. "I'm not sure that makes sense."

"It will."

Her heart beat hard. "When?"

"Eventually."

She was suddenly chilled. She wrapped her arms around herself. "How soon is eventually?"

His tone of voice changed, became softer, less harsh. "When you've heard the whole story."

"The one you're going to tell me tomorrow? That story?"

She didn't turn around, but she could imagine Mitchell's mouth—that beautiful mouth of his—turning up slightly at the corners, not exactly in a smile, but not in a frown, either. "Yes, that story."

She shivered.

"Are you cold?"

"A little."

There was a distinctive rustling behind her. Then she felt his dress jacket—still warm from his own body heat—being placed around her bare shoulders. "Better?"

Her throat tightened. "Yes. Thank you."

"You're welcome."

Mitchell didn't remove his hands. They stayed on her shoulders, however lightly, however nonchalantly at first. And Torey found that she didn't mind. Not in the least.

"Victoria—?" he said in a scarcely audible whisper that she clearly heard.

"Yes, Mitchell."

"Turn around and look at me."

She slowly turned and faced him. For a moment—that split second between bright bursts of fireworks—there wasn't enough light to make out anything but a vague form in the shadows.

"I'm looking at you, but I can't see you," she told him.

The night sky behind her suddenly became illuminated. And there he was, cast in a golden glow, his features sharp and intense and dangerously handsome.

"Now you see me."

"Now I see you."

Why was it so important that she see him? The reason soon became clear. Mitchell Storm raised his hand and caressed her cheek, then brushed his thumb across her lips.

And she knew.

He was going to kiss her.

Chapter 5

He would probably never know why he'd decided to kiss her. It certainly wasn't the smartest thing he had ever done. In fact, it was downright stupid. It could jeopardize his entire mission.

The mission be damned.

Blame it on jet lag: how many hours—or had it been several days now—since he'd slept? Call it temporary insanity. Or label it plain old lust. Or simple curiosity. All Mitchell knew was that he wanted to kiss Victoria Storm and he was going to kiss her.

And she knew it, too.

He'd seen the awareness in her eyes in one of those fleeting moments when the fireworks had lit up the night sky.

Where's your famous self-control now, Storm?

That was Mitchell's last thought before he lowered his head and touched his lips to hers. He didn't deepen the kiss, or grind his teeth against hers, or thrust his tongue into her mouth.

Although the temptation was there.

He didn't press his face to the enticing and inordinate

amount of inviting flesh exposed by the low-cut neckline of her evening gown, or fill his hands with her, or do any of a dozen things that had entered his mind at the sight of her.

Although the temptation was definitely there.

He still retained some measure of self-control, some modicum of decency and common sense, not to mention a few good basic instincts, Mitchell reminded himself. And all of his instincts were cautioning him to take it slow and easy.

But he didn't take his mouth away. He left it touching hers, even as he stood there, even as he continued to breathe, even as he said to Torey, with just a trace of self-deprecating humor in his voice, "I suppose this makes us kissing cousins."

"I suppose it does," she murmured, her breath wafting against his face like the gentlest of breezes. "I don't think this is wise," she added after a minute, maybe longer. But he noticed that she made no attempt to pull away, and she'd had every opportunity to do so.

With his lips still lightly brushing back and forth along hers, he asked, "Do you always do what is wise?"

"I try to," came on the wave of a small, wistful sigh.

There was another burst of bright, revealing light. Then a shower of shooting stars—brilliant blues and glittering greens—that matched her eyes, Mitchell mused as he opened his own eyes and found himself staring straight into Torey's.

Suddenly he had the sensation of falling. He couldn't seem to save himself, and there was only one way he could think of—although, heaven knows, he wasn't thinking rationally—to stop the feeling of vertigo. He closed his eyes again and deepened the kiss.

His right hand cupped her face; his left hand went

around her waist and urged her even farther back into the shadows. There wasn't a sound of protest. Nor a moment's hesitation. Victoria went with him, willingly, eagerly. Some small part of his brain alerted Mitchell to the fact; he'd have to figure out why later.

But not now.

Now all he wanted to think about was kissing Torey.

His senses were bombarded. He had never touched anything softer than the smooth, satiny skin on her lips, her cheek, her lovely neck, her bare shoulder.

He inhaled. He could detect the scents of the night: salt on the wind and the briny sea; dusky roses heady with fragrance and evening dew, climbing a trellis somewhere nearby; and something he couldn't quite put his finger on, something subtle, possibly perfume, but unlike any perfume he'd ever smelled before.

He inhaled again. It was Victoria. It was her scent that he couldn't quite identify. It was feminine, elusive, sensual, surprising—like the woman herself.

She sighed and murmured something unintelligible against his mouth. Mitchell realized that he liked—like was such an insipid word for the way he felt—the sound of her voice and the sound of her laughter. It hadn't occurred to him until now how important that could be between a man and a woman.

He withdrew his lips a fraction of an inch. "Do you like the way I laugh?"

She blinked several times in rapid succession and stared up at him. "I beg your pardon?"

"Do you like the sound of my voice?"

"Yes. Very much," she said at last.

"What about the way I laugh?"

"I love your laugh," she confessed, laughing lightly. It was as if, in that instant, she had remembered the sound

53

of his laughter and she had to laugh herself.

Mitchell was pleased.

He found himself kissing her again. One moment the taste of her was like a clear, cool mountain stream. The next it was slightly sweet, similar to an exotic fruit, yet with subtle undertones of something richer, something darker, something infinitely more intriguing. Her taste was compelling, complex, ever-changing.

It aroused him.

Hell, he'd been so preoccupied with the woman in his arms that he had failed to notice the reaction of his own body.

Thank God for his sporran. Hanging at the front of his kilt, the traditional fur pouch, with its silver targe and cantle, provided at least some coverage.

And thank God for the layers of petticoats and the heavily beaded fabric of Torey's costume: it provided even more of a barrier between the two of them. A barrier he might have cursed at some other time; but one which he was thankful for, under the circumstances.

Mitchell discovered that he had only one regret. Torey's mass of ringlets were aflame with the same deep, burning, inner fire as the priceless rubies at her ears and throat. Yet her hair was arranged in a formal, upswept style that prevented him from running his fingers through it.

He imagined what it would feel like. "Silk." He hadn't realized he had spoken aloud.

"Silk?" she puzzled in a dreamy, preoccupied tone. "My sash is silk." She glanced down at her evening gown. "I'm sure there must be silk somewhere on my dress."

"Your hair," he said.

She reached for one of the tendrils that had been left

free to frame her face, but Mitchell beat her to it. He wrapped the strand of fire around his index finger and brought it to his lips. It was cool to the touch, soft and fine, and smelled faintly of roses.

"Silk," he pronounced.

She reached up and tentatively stroked the hair at his temple, threading her fingers through it, brushing it back into place when she mussed it.

"Silk," she echoed.

Torey would probably never know why she had allowed him to kiss her. It wasn't as if it was unexpected. It wasn't as if she hadn't seen it coming. She'd clearly understood his intent. She'd gone into it with her eyes wide open.

Trouble.

She had known the man was going to be trouble from the first moment she'd laid eyes on him earlier that evening. She just hadn't known what kind of trouble.

The trouble was he was handsome and intelligent and sexy and strong and a hundred other things she had always looked for in a man and had never found until tonight.

The trouble was he kissed better than any man who had ever kissed her.

The trouble was she wanted him.

She was wise enough, however, to accept the fact that she didn't always get what she wanted, and sometimes—many times—it was for the best.

But could it matter so very much if she were to indulge herself for another minute or two?

Torey answered her own question.

No.

Liar!

Yes.

She shoved the argument to the back of her mind, reached up to stroke the thick, dark hair at Mitchell's temple and anticipated, then savored, the sensation of him kissing her again.

What made him taste delicious? What made his kiss, his touch, the way he looked into her eyes thrilling? Why was he intriguing, while the next man left her feeling only cold and indifferent? What made one man so much to her liking, while the others, all the others, were of absolutely no interest to her?

She didn't know the answers.

Suddenly Torey was aware of silence. The fireworks were finished. The night sky was pitch black again. Then, out of the darkness, came a distinctive sound.

"I have a surprise for you," she said, slipping from his arms and turning to face the water.

"I believe I've had quite enough surprises for one evening," Mitchell confessed to her.

"You'll like this one."

"I liked nearly all of the others, but one most of all," he murmured meaningfully, resting his hand on her shoulder.

"Look."

"Where?"

She pointed. "There."

On a rocky cliff, with the ocean at his back, a lone Highlander in full regalia was profiled by torchlight. He began to play his bagpipes. The song was the traditional tune, "Scotland the Brave."

Torey knew the words by heart. She had since she was a little girl. She opened her mouth to sing along, but discovered that her emotions and the threat of tears had closed her throat.

She managed to whisper only the final refrain: " 'Scotland the home, Scotland the brave.' "

"Have my eyes deceived me, or did I see Victoria dancing with a waiter earlier this evening?" Beatrice Van Allen demanded of her companion, her voice heavy with reproach.

"He was no waiter," Lola Albright said smugly as the two women made their way back inside the house after the conclusion of the fireworks and the piper's playing of "Scotland the Brave."

Beatrice Van Allen halted for a moment and turned a skeptical eye on her friend. "How do you know he wasn't a waiter?"

Lola Albright took great pleasure in claiming, "I have it on the best authority."

Alice Fraser nodded her head with satisfaction and followed the pair at a discreet distance. She listened to every word. To make certain, in part, that Miss Albright had gotten it right.

Mrs. Van Allen was all ears. "*What* do you have on the best authority?"

Lola lowered her voice to a conspiratorial whisper and stated, "He's her cousin."

The aging dowager raised a hand to cup her ear and repeated in a slightly louder voice, "He's her what?"

"Cousin," was practically shouted.

Beatrice Van Allen brought her nose up a fraction of an inch and sniffed as only she could: an act that conveyed both her disdain and her disapproval. "He may still be a waiter."

"He's not a waiter, I tell you." Lola Albright was losing her patience. She snapped her fan shut and stuffed it into her evening bag. "He's a peer."

"A pear, you say?"

"Not a pear, Beatrice." She sighed long-sufferingly. "The man is a peer. A peer of the realm."

"Whose realm?"

Miss Albright was out of patience. "The Queen's, I presume."

"What queen? This isn't getting us anywhere," declared the dowager. "It's so terribly noisy in here. I can scarcely hear a word you're saying, Lola."

The diminutive woman took her more substantial friend aside and clarified: "The man Victoria was dancing with is her cousin. His name is Mitchell Storm. But if one were to address him formally he would be Lord Storm."

"*Lord* Storm?"

"He is a baron and a viscount and an earl and heaven knows what else." Lola instilled a certain reverence into her usually shrill voice. "He has more titles than you can shake a stick at, Beatrice."

Beatrice was speechless.

"And they are some of the oldest and most respected and prestigious titles in all of Great Britain." Lola nodded her head once, twice, then thrice. "And he has inherited a great castle on an island off the coast of Scotland. Actually, I believe he owns the entire island and everything and everyone on it."

"Well, I'll be."

Very likely, Mrs. Van Allen, Alice Fraser thought to herself with a certain amount of enjoyment.

It had certainly paid off to put a bug in Miss Albright's ear. The woman couldn't keep a secret if her life depended on it.

Lola Albright was still chomping at the bit to share every choice tidbit of information she had been made privy to. ''And the gentleman involved earlier in that most unfortunate incident in the dining room, the very large one with the bright red hair, is Lord Storm's most valued adviser and right-hand man.''

Beatrice Van Allen was beside herself. She raised her fan and vigorously waved it back and forth in front of her color-stained cheeks. ''You don't say.''

''I do say.''

''Then he isn't a waiter, either.''

Lola shook her head.

The society matron appeared nonplussed for a moment. ''Oh, dear. And I instructed him to fetch me a cup of my medicinal tea.''

''Oh, dear,'' echoed Lola Albright.

Always a woman quick to recover from a nasty shock, as she was fond of boasting to her friends and acquaintances alike, Beatrice Van Allen gave a heave of her rather generous bosom, cleared her throat, and announced in surprisingly good humor, ''I must remember to tell our dear Victoria that she has the most unforgettable balls . . .''

Alice Fraser heaved a sigh of relief.

By morning everyone in Newport would know exactly who and what Mitchell Storm and Iain MacClumpha were. Her mission had been accomplished.

For she wasn't about to allow anyone—and that included Beatrice Van Allen or Lola Albright or any of their kind—to speak a word against Victoria, or even hint at a breath of scandal.

At the age forty-five, Alice told herself she wasn't really old enough to be the mother of a thirty-year-old, yet she considered Victoria Storm the daughter she would never have.

And no one would be allowed to harm Torey.

To that end, she would also need to keep a sharp eye on those two Scotsmen. Especially that handsome devil of a younger one she had seen with Torey during the fireworks.

For that matter, the older Scot was still in his prime, as well. And he had a temper. His behavior, in a moment of anger, had been unpardonable. But not, perhaps, entirely unexpected.

A real man, a man like Iain MacClumpha, was a warrior at heart. He wasn't some soft, sensitive, namby-pamby modern male, and certainly not one to take an insult lying down.

These men were basically uncivilized under the veneer of twentieth-century manners and customs. They could be ruthless. They would do whatever it took to get what they wanted, what they needed.

Torey might not understand that.

She did.

But she was, after all, a Fraser.

An old and honored name, and a powerful clan in their own right, the "bold" Frasers, as they were called, had played an important part in Scottish history since the twelfth century. They had fought alongside The Bruce, they had fallen at Culloden and they had raised their own regiment, the Fraser Highlanders, to do battle for king and country in one war after another.

Loyal and fiercely protective of their own, it was best not to cross swords with a Fraser.

Alice stepped around from behind a decorative archway and came upon the pair of Newport dowagers seemingly by accident.

"Mrs. Van Allen. Miss Albright." She greeted the pair with deference and issued them a special invitation. "Victoria and her other guests are about to gather in the

Great Hall for the traditional farewell. Won't you ladies please join her?''

"We would be delighted to, Ms. Fraser."

A short time later, the sound of several hundred voices raised in song echoed through the marble corridors of Storm Point. It was the same poignant tune that had been sung at the conclusion of every grand ball for more than a century.

The words were those of Robert Burns:

> *Should auld acquaintance be forgot.*
> *And never brought to min'?*
> *Should auld acquaintance be forgot,*
> *And days o' auld lang syne?*

Chapter 6

"Where is everybody?" Mitchell asked, his curiosity getting the better of him. In sharp contrast to the night before, the house and grounds of Storm Point appeared deserted.

"They're still asleep," Torey replied.

Which explained, no doubt, why she had answered the door herself. It'd caught Mitchell off guard. Frankly he had expected to be facing the butler, Dickens. Instead, he found himself staring down into the lovely face of Victoria Storm.

The woman kept doing the unexpected. It intrigued him.

It irritated him.

She looked like she had been up for hours. On the other hand, he'd rolled out of bed exactly thirty minutes ago and had yet to ingest his first cup of coffee. He needed one badly, too.

"You're not," he pointed out.

"I'm not what?" she inquired amicably enough, stepping back and indicating he should come inside. Then she closed the huge front door behind him.

"Still asleep."

"I'm an early riser," was given as her reason.

This morning she was dressed in a pair of black silk trousers, a pink cashmere tunic and a pair of strappy little black European sandals that laced around her ankles.

Very chic, very simple, very stylish.

She had nice ankles, too.

He also noticed that her toenails had a coat of pale pink polish on them, and she was wearing a long gold chain around her neck with an antique locket dangling from the end.

In the bright sunlight, her hair was an absolute blaze of red. It was casually tied back into a ponytail with a length of pink silk ribbon. She didn't appear to be wearing any makeup, only a touch of pink lipstick. She looked even younger and more beautiful—and more pink—than she had the evening before.

Mrs. Van Allen's comment last night, while they had all been standing in the Great Hall watching Torey as she descended the main staircase, popped into Mitchell's mind. The old battle-ax had said something about not understanding or, at least, not approving of the propensity for redheads to wear pink.

He preferred Torey in pink.

Mitchell found himself voicing an inane question. "Aren't your staff early risers?"

"Normally." There was a short pause. "But I always give them the morning after off."

"The morning after?" His brain was refusing to function properly without a heavy dose of caffeine.

Must be jet lag.

Or the lack of sleep.

Whatever the cause, he'd give anything right now for a cup of strong, black coffee.

"The morning after the annual ball," she said. "The staff work harder than anyone to make the event a success, and it's usually close to dawn before they get to bed."

"What time did you go to bed this morning?" He hadn't meant the question to sound impertinent. Impertinence wasn't his style. But he was curious.

"Six-thirty," she finally replied.

He glanced down at his watch. It was now eleven o'clock. "You had a short night."

"I had a short night."

Mitchell had almost forgotten. "These are for you." He thrust the white florist's box, fastened with pink cord and embellished with a matching pink bow, into her hands.

Her face lit up with pleasure. "For me?"

"For you."

Torey placed the box on a gilded Louis-something-or-other table just inside the front door and, without regard for the table's value or apparent antiquity, quickly tore off the lid, sending pink cord, pink bow, and pink tissue paper flying in every direction.

"Long-stemmed pink roses," she exclaimed. "They're my very favorite."

"I'm glad."

"How did you know?"

"I didn't," he confessed.

It had been purely a lucky guess on his part.

Torey bent over and inhaled the delicate fragrance of the dewy roses. "Why?"

Mitchell cleared his throat. "I wanted to bring you what the French would call a *douceur*."

"A conciliatory gift," she quickly translated and glanced up at him. "Have we quarreled?"

"No."

Not yet.

She laughed and the sound was like the melodious tinkling of wind chimes stirred by the slightest breeze. "Are you trying to tell me that we're about to quarrel?"

He certainly hoped not.

"Ahhhh," Torey murmured knowledgeably, stretching the small interjection out to three times its normal length. "The roses are in anticipation of needing a *douceur*."

She'd seen right through him.

"You might say so," was all Mitchell was willing to admit to at the moment.

"I suppose it has something to do with the story—" She paused for a brief time and reconsidered. "—The *long* story that you came here today to tell me. You're afraid that I'm not going to like your story." She gathered up the florist's box and the discarded debris and turned around. "Let's go put these in water."

"Where are we headed?"

"To the kitchen."

"I know the way well."

Torey laughed again. Her laugh made his spine tingle. "I suppose you do, after last night," she tossed back over her shoulder. "How is The MacClumpha feeling this morning?"

"Better."

"I'm glad to hear that."

He caught up with her in three easy strides. "I believe it's primarily due to your Miss Fraser."

Torey gave him a sidelong glance. "Alice?"

He nodded his head. "Apparently she was able to convince Iain last night that no real harm was done, and that the whole incident will be forgotten within the week."

"Alice Fraser is a remarkable woman," Torey stated

as they turned the next corner and found themselves in the corridor outside the kitchen. "She is definitely a treasure."

"You're fond of her."

"I'm very fond of her."

"How long have you known her?"

"Alice and I have been together for ten years." Mitchell saw the muscles in her neck and shoulders tense. "A little more than ten years, actually." It was another minute or two before she quietly added, "Since just before my parents died."

He didn't know what to say.

Torey was suddenly busy. She searched for and found a large, crystal vase in a cupboard, filled the vase with water from the faucet, removed the roses from the box and skillfully arranged them with the greenery supplied by the florist shop.

She worked diligently for a few minutes, then stepped back to admire her handiwork and exclaimed, "There."

"They look great," he said in genuine praise. He wondered if all young women of her social class and privileged upbringing learned flower arranging at some juncture in their lives, or if it was a particular talent of hers.

"Thank you for the roses, Mitchell."

"You're welcome."

She went on to the next item presumably on their agenda. "Have you eaten?"

"No." His stomach picked that instant to growl loudly as if to emphasize the point.

That definitely got her attention. "Have you even had a cup of coffee this morning?"

He shook his head.

"Would you like some coffee?"

He'd be willing to sell his soul for a cup of coffee. He settled for, "Yes, please."

That's all it took. Torey quickly and efficiently went about the business of preparing fresh coffee in some kind of fancy contraption sitting on the kitchen counter. Once the "pot" of coffee was going, she opened one of the huge stainless-fronted refrigerators and peered inside. Then she glanced back over her shoulder at him. "Hungry?"

"Famished."

"Let's eat."

"Good idea." Great idea.

"One should never tell—or, for that matter, listen—to a long story on an empty stomach, don't you agree?"

"Heartily."

"Are you in the mood for breakfast or lunch?"

Before he could express an opinion—truthfully, he didn't have a preference either way; he was in the mood for food, period—she volunteered, "I'm better at lunch."

Eating it or making it?

"Lunch it is, then," he stated.

She stopped long enough to pour a mug of steaming, black coffee and press it into his hands. "You look like you could use this."

"I could. Thanks."

"You're welcome." She returned to her perusal of the fully stocked refrigerator. "Lunch—hmm." Her head came up, ponytail swinging from side to side. "Do you like cold chicken breasts?"

"Yes."

"Lobster salad?"

"Yes."

"An assortment of cheeses?"

Mitchell inhaled the aroma of fresh coffee wafting under his nose, took a drink—more of a sip, since it was strong and very hot—and gave a contented sigh before answering, "Yes."

Torey paused, removed a container from the second shelf, snapped off the lid, studied its contents, and speculated, "Some kind of relish. Possibly cucumber, possibly pickle?"

"Yes."

She turned on the heel of one skimpy sandal, stared at him for a full thirty seconds and then came out and asked, "How long has it been since you've had anything to eat?"

Mitchell gave some thought to his answer. "I guess prior to the flight from Glasgow."

"Before you left Glasgow?"

He nodded. "That would make it the night before last."

Her eyes widened. "Why?"

He wrinkled up his nose and made a face. "You know what airline food is like."

She shot him a frown. "Why in the world haven't you eaten since then? That's nearly two days ago."

Hell, he guessed it was for the same reason he hadn't slept until last night. Or he should say until this morning?

Mitchell shrugged. "No opportunity. No time."

"You should have helped yourself to something last night at the party." Torey appeared visibly distressed at the thought that he had actually gone without food.

"Most of the evening The MacClumpha and I were expected to serve the refreshments, not consume them," he informed her.

Her face became flush with color. "I'll fix you something to eat immediately. You sit down right there," she ordered, pointing to a small, pleasant table in front of a sunny window, "and I'll serve you a plate of food."

And she did.

This morning he looked like a Texan.

He was dressed in well-laundered blue jeans, a denim shirt with the sleeves rolled up to the elbows, and a pair of slightly worn brown leather cowboy boots. All that was missing was the accent.

And the Stetson.

"Aren't you going to join me?" Mitchell stopped eating long enough to glance up and realize that she was watching him eat; she herself wasn't eating.

"Yes. Of course, I'm going to join you," Torey assured him, helping herself to a small serving of lobster salad and one of Antoine's delectable home-baked *pomme de terre* rolls. Bread and rolls were the assistant chef's specialty.

Torey took a bite of lobster salad, and told herself for the tenth time in as many minutes that she couldn't get over the difference in Mitchell Storm.

He wasn't the same man.

Yet he was obviously the same man who had been dressed in a traditional Scottish kilt at last night's gala. The same man who had surreptitiously followed her around her own party. The same man she had finally met and talked to and danced with. The same man who had held her in his arms and kissed her.

Good Lord, she hoped he wasn't going to turn out to be a Jekyll and Hyde.

"Why *did* you kiss me last night?" She hadn't meant to blurt it out like that in between bites of lobster salad and flaky *pomme de terres*, but there it was, and it was too late now to take it back.

His hand and fork became suspended in midair.

"I shouldn't have asked that question," Torey stammered, quickly attempting to backtrack.

"There's nothing wrong with asking the question," he said, putting his fork down, planting his elbows on the kitchen table in front of him, bringing his hands together, intertwining his fingers, and then leaning forward slightly to rest his chin on them.

"But—?"

"But I'm not sure I know the answer." Mitchell turned his head and gazed out the window, staring at the expanse of green lawn that stretched down to the rocky shoreline at the water's edge. After some time he looked back at her. Torey realized that his eyes weren't brown or black or even something in between. In this light, they were a silvery gunmetal gray. "Why did you kiss me?"

It occurred to her to protest that she hadn't kissed him. But it wasn't true. She may have started out kissing him back, but before it was all said and done, yes, she had been kissing him eagerly, willingly, wholeheartedly.

"I suppose," she said after several moments of honest self-appraisal, "it seemed like a good idea at the time."

He picked up his fork and pushed the food around his plate. "I suppose it did."

Muscles in her stomach clenched. "Are you sorry it happened?"

He shook his head vigorously. "Not in the least."

Her stomach relaxed.

His expression was unreadable to her as he added, "In fact, I'd do it again in a minute."

So would she.

Mitchell stared at her across the table. "Are you sorry about last night?"

She couldn't lie to him, and there was no purpose served by being coy. "I'm not sorry." Her voice came out low and husky; it didn't even sound like her.

"I meant what I said."

"About what?" She didn't understand.

He narrowed his eyes. "It wasn't part of the plan."

"Kissing me?"

He nodded.

"But *I* was part of the plan." She distinctly remembered Mitchell telling her that.

"You had to be," he said, regarding her with a frown. "Not that much has gone according to our plans."

"Yours and The MacClumpha's?"

He nodded again and drove his fingers through his hair in agitation. "It makes the whole business so bloody complicated."

Torey took a sip of the coffee that she had poured for herself. "You told me it would all make sense once I'd heard the entire story."

"It will." He shoved another bite of chicken into his mouth, chewed, swallowed, and muttered, "I hope."

"Maybe you should start while we finish our lunch since you said it was going to be a long story."

"Okay." Mitchell Storm drew a breath. "Once—"

Torey immediately interrupted him. "This isn't going to be one of those stories that begins with 'Once upon a time,' is it?"

Chapter 7

"Once there were two brothers, fraternal twins, born on the Isle of Storm, a wild, windswept jut of rock off the western coast of the Scottish mainland. The Isle of Storm lies beyond Holy Island and the Isle of Arran. It is north of Islay, capital to the legendary Lords of the Isles, but not quite as northerly as Mull, and not far distant from sacred Iona."

Mitchell recited the beginning of the story using the identical words as when it had been told to him, over and over again, in those months after he had returned home to Scotland, and before his grandfather, William Storm, thirty-fourth chief of Clan Storm, had finally succumbed to advancing age and ill health.

"Romulus and Remus," Torey murmured over the rim of her coffee cup.

Mitchell frowned.

"The legendary founders of Rome. They were also twin brothers," she remarked.

Mitchell liked to think that he knew his ancient history as well as the next man . . . or woman. "Fathered by Mars, the Roman god of war, Romulus and Remus were thrown into the river Tiber, somehow survived against incredible odds, were raised and suckled by a she-wolf and eventually restored their family to power.''

"But in the end they quarreled bitterly. Romulus won and Remus was killed," Torey said, tilting her head to one side.

"How fortunate, then, that the twins in our own ancestral background simply had a falling-out. Or it's possible, I suppose, that one of us might not be here today," he theorized.

Torey took another drink of coffee and inquired, with what seemed to him to be genuine interest, "What year were the twins born on the Isle of Storm?"

"1837. The same year the young Victoria came to the throne," he stated.

"Alexandrina Victoria. Born 1819. Officially crowned queen of Great Britain and Ireland, and empress of India in 1838. Married her beloved Prince Albert in 1840. Mothered nine children. Was widowed in 1861 and left inconsolable. She died on the Isle of Wight in the dead of winter, 1901.''

Torey sounded like a turn-of-the-century schoolgirl, standing in front of the class, reciting her lessons by rote.

Mitchell was tempted to laugh, but somehow restrained himself. "How in the world?"

Torey put her cup down and smiled at him knowingly. "Don't you mean *why* in the world?"

"All right. Why?"

"Miss Porter, of Miss Porter's School for Young Ladies, assumed I was named for the late and great Victoria and, therefore, I was required to commit to memory the facts of the queen's life."

"How old were you at the time?"

"Nine."

Mitchell found himself staring into her eyes and saying, "I wonder what you were like at nine."

Torey rattled off, "I had awful, bright red hair, freckles galore, and I was short for my age."

"What happened?"

In his opinion, she wasn't particularly short now. She wasn't exactly tall, either, of course.

"I started growing the following year."

"Did you like Miss Porter's School for Young Ladies?"

"I loathed it," she confessed, with fervor in her voice. "At least at that time. Several years later, when I had *auburn* hair and my freckles seemed to have magically disappeared and I had grown nearly a foot in height and I was one of the upperclassmen"—she gave him a devilish grin—"then it wasn't quite so loathsome." A moment later she asked, "What were you like at the age of nine?"

"Nine?" He rubbed his jaw. "That was a long time ago."

"It wasn't *that* long ago."

"Longer than you might think," he told her.

That brought a raised auburn eyebrow. "How old are you?"

"Thirty-seven." He didn't particularly care if it was socially correct or not; he posed the same question to her. "How old are you?"

She didn't hesitate to tell him. "Thirty."

"Single?"

"Yes. And you?"

"Definitely."

"So what were you like as a boy?"

"I don't think that has anything to do with the story I'm trying to tell you."

"I want to know, anyway." She sounded absolutely adamant.

Mitchell decided he might as well not fight her on this one. There would be plenty of opportunities for disagreement between them soon enough, he feared.

"I was tall," he began.

"And—?" she prompted.

"And I had dark hair and was slightly on the thin side in those days," he recalled.

"But what were you like?" she insisted.

He wasn't starving any longer; that made it a whole lot easier to be sociable. He finished off the last bite of chicken, put his fork down on the plate, raised the coffee mug to his mouth, and took another swallow before he answered. "I was different."

"Different than what?"

Not *what*, my dear, sweet, lovely, sexy cousin, Mitchell thought to himself as he watched Torey across the kitchen table, *who*.

"Different than the other children," he finally said to her. "My family had moved so often and I'd lived in so many exotic places and, don't forget, like you I was an only child."

Surely she would see.

"I see," she said slowly, at last. "You were more self-reliant than most kids."

So she did understand. He'd thought she might.

Mitchell nodded his head and felt the hair at his nape brush along his shirt collar. He should have gotten a haircut before leaving Scotland, but there hadn't been time.

"I felt older, too." He had always felt older than the other boys and girls his age. "I was older in a lot of ways."

"I was, too," she stated simply.

He believed her.

"Sometimes it was lonely," she added without any intimation of feeling sorry for herself.

"Sometimes it was lonely," he agreed.

It seemed to Mitchell that she suddenly brightened. "Why don't we take our coffee and stroll down to the shore while you tell me the entire story of our great-greats?"

He found himself volunteering to rinse their dishes before they left, and she took him up on the offer.

Then she had to change into a pair of sturdier shoes. After all, flimsy little designer sandals wouldn't be practical for hiking along the rocky coastline.

Finally they refilled their coffee mugs and took off at a casual pace across the expanse of perfectly manicured green lawn toward the blue, blue water.

"Once there were two brothers, fraternal twins, born on the Isle of Storm, a wild, windswept jut of rock off the western coast of the Scottish mainland. The Isle of Storm lies beyond Holy Island and the Isle of Arran. It is north of Islay, capital to the legendary Lords of the Isles, but not quite as northerly as Mull, and not far distant from sacred Iona." Mitchell had started over at her request.

It wasn't that she couldn't remember the story so far, but there was such an enchanting rhythm to the words when he recited the opening lines, almost as if they were part of some great epic poem, that Torey had asked him to begin again, and he had.

Mitchell went on. "The laird and his lady—the parents of the twin sons—rejoiced and all the people of Clan Storm with them. The firstborn was called Angus, and he was my great-great-grandfather."

"And his slightly, and we do mean slightly, younger

brother was christened Andrew, and he was my great-great-grandfather," Torey chipped in.

The storyteller nodded and took a sip or two of his coffee. Then he paused for a few quiet moments to enjoy—no, Torey decided, watching him, *savor* was the better word—the sight of a seagull gliding along overhead on a gentle sea breeze.

"All was well between the brothers for many years, or at least so it appeared," he continued. "They were very much alike, and, maybe, in the end, that was part of the problem."

Torey was inquisitive. "How were they alike?"

Mitchell squinted into the bright noonday sun. "When I was a boy of twelve or thirteen I was sent back to Scotland to spend a summer on the Isle of Storm."

She distinctly remembered being told last night that his father and mother had never returned to Scotland once they'd gone into self-imposed exile. "Your parents didn't accompany you?"

"No. They didn't. We were living in Singapore at the time. They claimed there was only enough money for one of us to make the flight. We all knew it wasn't true."

"There was plenty of money."

"Enough," came the cryptic reply.

"So you made the trip by yourself."

"Yes." Mitchell passed his tongue along the edges of his teeth. "Anyway, I was given free rein of the castle and grounds that summer. One day, on my explorations, I discovered a portrait of the twins hanging in a wing of Castle Storm that was no longer in use. In the painting the two brothers were dressed in traditional kilts and full Highland regalia—in defiance of British law at the time, according to my grandfather."

"It was against the law?"

He nodded. "Wearing the tartan had been strictly forbidden for nearly a century before the artist had daringly painted the picture of Angus and Andrew."

"And—?"

"And they looked like twin brothers. They had the same reddish-blond hair, the same distinctive square cut to their jaws, the same blue-green eyes, the same straightforward look in those eyes, the same broad shoulders, the same everything."

Torey's hand went to her throat. She wound the gold chain around and around her index finger as she often did when she was thinking.

They walked on for some time, putting the house behind them and heading for the rocky cliffs, the beach some distance below and the open sea on the horizon.

"I wonder what could have gone wrong between them," she speculated aloud.

Mitchell flexed his shoulders. "We may never know for certain how it started. They may have quarreled over money, or power, or a prize mare, or who received what rents from what crofts."

Torey held up one hand to partially shield her eyes from the sun's glare and watched, transfixed, as a white sailboat came floating like a huge, majestic swan, around the point. "Maybe they quarreled over a woman."

"Maybe."

"Whatever the cause of their argument, I take it there was a falling-out between Angus and Andrew."

"You might call it a falling-out."

Actually, if memory served her correctly, he had been the first to use the term.

Torey slowly lowered her hand and turned to him. "What would you call it?"

"War."

"War?" she repeated in a sharper tone than she had intended to use with him.

There was no compromise in the hard eyes that stared back at her. "They declared war on each other."

"Why?" she asked.

Handsome features momentarily darkened. "It's something in the Scottish blood."

He wasn't serious. He couldn't be serious.

He started to explain, "A true son of Scotland lived and died by the sword."

He was serious, Torey realized.

"In his heart and soul every Scotsman's a warrior," Mitchell declared unequivocally.

"Was or is?"

The absurdly simple question was given about thirty seconds of thought. "Is."

He meant it.

"Even you?"

"Yes, even me."

"Then forewarned is forearmed."

"There won't be any warning," Mitchell cautioned her.

He'd frightened her.

Good.

She should be afraid of him.

Yet there didn't seem to be any trepidation in her voice or in her manner when she suggested to him several minutes later, "This is the best path to take down to the beach."

"Why don't we sit here for a few minutes?" he said, indicating a grassy knoll.

"All right." Torey proceeded to plunk herself down on a soft mound of earth.

Mitchell finished off the lukewarm coffee in the bottom of his mug and set it beside him in the sandy soil. "I'll try to keep to the high points for the sake of brevity."

She gazed straight ahead toward the horizon where blue water met blue sky. "By all means, do."

This wasn't getting any easier. "Whatever caused the rift between the brothers, they both paid a price. As the oldest, and according to the legal practice of primogeniture, when their father died, Angus inherited the Isle of Storm and Castle Storm, the long list of titles that had passed down through the centuries from eldest son to eldest son, and, most important, he became chief of Clan Storm."

Mitchell wondered if Torey had any real idea of what it meant to be the head of a clan.

"That meant Angus became responsible for the well-being of nearly eight hundred people—men, women, and children—mostly clansmen, who lived on the island," he said. "Times were hard. The potato famine stretched on year after year. Food was scarce. Luxuries were unknown. Money was hard to come by. Debts piled up."

"It must have been a very difficult time for everyone," Torey conceded.

"It was."

"And Andrew?"

"Contrary to what you may have heard, Andrew wasn't kicked out of Scotland. Driven by a younger son's bitterness and a young man's ambition and perhaps a desire to show the clan that he, too, was worthy to be their leader, he emigrated to America."

"To make his fortune."

"Which he obviously did."

"Well," Torey said, getting to her feet and brushing

the sand from her silk trousers. "That, as they say, is that."

Mitchell stood. "I wish it were true."

She turned. "Isn't it?"

He shook his head. "The story doesn't end with Angus staying in Scotland and doing his duty, or with Andrew coming to America to make his fortune."

Another swipe was taken at the sand stubbornly clinging to her derriere. "Where does it end?"

"It doesn't."

That brought his cousin's head up sharply. "Perhaps you'd better explain."

First he offered her the steady support of his hand as they climbed down the embankment. It was a beautiful day for a walk on the beach. It was a shame to ruin the peace and tranquility, but Mitchell was pretty sure his story would do both.

"As the years went by, Angus sank deeper and deeper into debt. The truth was, Andrew had always been the financial wizard of the two, but he wasn't there to help his brother."

"Don't blame Andrew. It wasn't his fault."

"Not then, perhaps."

Her eyes narrowed. "Which implies that at some time it was his fault. At least in your opinion."

"Not just in my opinion, Torey."

"This must be the part you knew I wouldn't like; the reason you brought me a *douceur* in the form of my favorite roses." She stooped to pick up a pretty pink shell that had washed ashore at her feet, apparently discovered it was broken in several places, and tossed it back into the ocean. "What happened?"

"The Civil War. A time in American history when fortunes were made and fortunes were lost. Andrew

Storm made a fortune. In fact, during the decade follow-ing the war he became one of the most successful men in the United States. In the world, for that matter. He prospered in every conceivable way a man can prosper. He had money to burn. And he took some of that money and bought himself a wife: a beautiful, intelligent, and socially prominent young woman.''

''Annelise Morgan.''

''He and Annelise built several mansions, including Storm Point. They entertained on a lavish scale. They traveled in style. They indulged their every whim. And then they had a son, a son to carry on the Storm name and to perpetuate the Storm dynasty in the New World.''

''My great-great-grandparents were no different than the Wetmores or the Vanderbilts or the Astors or a dozen other prominent families in this country who lived like royalty during the Gilded Age.''

''I'm sure Andrew and Annelise were very much like the rest of their social set.''

''Then what is your point?''

''The point is this. While Andrew prospered, Angus was facing financial ruin, and the people of the Isle of Storm were virtually facing starvation. Angus put his per-sonal pride aside, went to his younger brother and begged for help.''

She waited.

He delivered the punch line. ''Andrew turned him down flat.''

He saw the way Torey suddenly wrapped her arms around herself as they walked along the beach.

It was a minute or two before she said in a soft voice, ''Payback time?''

''Something like that.''

''Andrew must have hated his brother.'' Her shoulders

were hunched. "Or perhaps he simply no longer cared for anyone or anything that reminded him of Scotland."

"That, I'm sorry to say, wasn't the case."

"How do you know?"

"Because when Andrew refused to help him, Angus was forced to take drastic measures. He had to put up for sale at auction a large number of prized possessions—paintings, furniture, jewelry, silverplate, even items of national historical significance—that had been in the Storm family for generations."

"He wouldn't be the first impoverished aristocrat to have to sell off the family heirlooms," she pointed out.

"True."

"It happened all the time."

"True again."

"What haven't you told me?" she said as they watched the waves wash away their footprints.

"Angus desperately needed every pound sterling he could obtain from the auction. The date was set. Discreet invitations were sent to everyone who was anyone with money in Great Britain, Canada, the United States, even France."

"And?"

"No one came."

"No one?"

"Andrew made certain they didn't."

"Oh, no."

"Oh, yes. But it gets worse. Andrew did dispatch several men to the auction to bid on his behalf, unbeknownst to Angus or anyone else involved in the sad business. The undercover agents bought up everything in sight at pathetically low prices and then had the entire collection of family heirlooms packed up and shipped off to Andrew in America."

"He cheated his own brother."

"That's about the size of it."

Torey turned and looked back in the direction of the great white stone house. "Then it's likely that those family heirlooms are right here at Storm Point."

"It's likely."

After some minutes, she remarked, "They were called robber barons, you know."

He chose not to respond beyond, "Who was?"

"A number of the so-called gentlemen who made huge fortunes during the last century. There was no personal income tax. Their methods of making money didn't bear much scrutiny and didn't get much scrutiny. They lived like kings."

"So I've heard," he said noncommittally.

"My great-great-grandmother, Annelise, routinely spent three or four hundred thousand dollars entertaining here at Newport, and that was just for several months in the summer when she and Andrew were in residence. It didn't include a penny of what she spent on her own gowns or her jewelry. Or what they lavished on their primary home, a mansion on New York's Fifth Avenue. Why, one entire room of that house was imported from Florence at a cost of sixty thousand dollars. I've seen the records myself, in the family archives. Sixty thousand dollars was a great deal of money in those days, Mitchell." Her voice grew softer. "That one room cost thirty times the price of the average family home at that time." She was very quiet for a number of minutes. Then she opened her mouth and asked, "Are you here to demand restitution?"

"No." At least not in the way she would assume.

"You must want something."

"I do want something," he admitted.

Her back was ramrod straight. "Money?"

He was too angry to speak. He was almost shaking with the force of his anger. He realized in the space of less than twenty-four hours this young woman had made him lose his self-control on two separate occasions.

"I'm sorry, Mitchell." She reached out and placed a hand on his arm. Her touch was ice cold on his sun-warmed flesh. "That was a horrible thing for me to say. Please accept my apology."

It was another minute or two before he trusted himself to speak. "Apology accepted."

"What is it you need?"

He spoke without anger, but with a kind of cold finality. "I need to borrow several items."

She made an attempt at humor. "I assume you don't mean a neighborly bowl of sugar."

"I would like, strictly on temporary loan, several objects from the auction."

"That was at least one hundred years ago."

"Yes, it was."

"Do you really believe they'll still be here?"

"I do." He didn't believe it to be true; he knew it to be true.

She shot a quick sideways glance at him. "Do you mind if I ask what you intend to do with the items?"

"I intend to take them back to Scotland with us."

"Us?"

"The MacClumpha and myself."

"The MacClumpha. Of course. I'd almost forgotten. And what will you do with these borrowed items once you have them back on the Isle of Storm?"

She was asking a lot questions. Not that he blamed her. After all, she had only his word for what had transpired between Angus and Andrew a century earlier.

"I plan to use them to solve a mystery that could finally bring prosperity back to the Isle of Storm."

"Then what?"

"Then I'll arrange to have the items returned here to Storm Point," he vowed.

"Do you know what items you need?"

"In a manner of speaking."

"Is that a yes or a no?"

"It's a maybe."

She regarded him dubiously. "You need certain objects but you don't know exactly what they are."

"Well, I do and I don't."

She sighed and shook her head. "I think you need another cup of coffee."

"I'd love one," he admitted.

They started back toward the house.

"Now, tell me again what it is you're looking for."

"I'm looking for a Victoria."

"Who or what is a Victoria?"

"Well, it could be a painting of Queen Victoria, or a garden statue, or a small bronze," he told her.

"We have all of those."

"I know," he confessed.

"You've been snooping."

"Guilty as charged."

"That's what you and The MacClumpha were doing at the party last night."

"Only when we weren't serving caviar and Scottish salmon, or waiting on demanding society dowagers."

"Oh, dear, *not* Mrs. Van Allen."

"Oh, dear, *yes* Mrs. Van Allen."

"I'm sorry."

"Not as sorry as The MacClumpha."

"Is that what led to the—" Torey stopped and cleared her throat. "—unfortunate incident?"

"Let's just say it was a contributing factor."

She returned to the subject she apparently found of greater interest. "Then you believe you've already located several of the Victorias from the original auction."

He nodded.

"Have you located the one you need?"

"Not exactly."

"Not exactly?"

"The problem is I won't know which Victoria is the right Victoria until I get them all back to Scotland."

"You, my dear cousin, have a logistics problem."

"More like a logistics nightmare."

"I'll try to help in any way I can."

"Thank you."

"I suppose the first order of business is to search the house from top to bottom trying to locate any Victoria that may have come from the auction. Do you have a list, by any chance?"

"Only an incomplete one. And I'd like to keep this quiet. There's more at stake than you can imagine."

"That can be done. But don't you think two pairs of eyes are better than one?"

"Two?"

"Yours and mine. Besides, we can always make up some reasonable explanation like I'm showing my cousin, visiting from Scotland, around Storm Point."

It wasn't a bad idea. "All right."

They were halfway back to the house when her hand flew out and she grasped his arm again. Thank goodness the coffee mug in his hand was empty.

"I have an even better idea."

He waited to hear what it was.

"Four pairs of eyes are twice as good as two pairs of eyes, aren't they?"

He did the math. "Four pairs?"

"Yours. Mine. The MacClumpha's and Alice Fraser's." She added, "You can trust Alice with your life. She's a Scot right down to her bones. And she's discreet."

"Discretion is vital, in this case."

"We'll split up into two teams. You and I on one. Iain and Alice on the other."

"Boy-girl, boy-girl."

"I was thinking more of making sure each team had someone on it who was knowledgeable about the house and its contents."

He felt a little foolish.

"Then it's settled?"

"Then it's settled," he agreed.

"When would you like to start?"

"Tomorrow?"

"Bright and early."

Not too early, he hoped.

"Of course," she rattled on, leapfrogging from one idea to the next, "you and The MacClumpha must come and stay with us at the house."

"Thanks, but—"

"No buts."

"In that case, thank you."

"You're welcome."

They walked on.

"How do you know that a Victoria is the key to your solving the mystery and bringing prosperity back to the Isle of Storm?" she finally inquired.

Mitchell wondered when she'd think of that.

"It's a long story," he told her.

"Another long story?"

And it was one long story that he didn't intend to tell her. Not now, and maybe never.

"Perhaps I'll tell you the whole story one day," he teased, reaching out and tugging on her ponytail. "If you really want me to."

"What do you really want?" she suddenly asked him in a thoughtful tone as they neared the back entrance to Storm Point.

"What do I really want?" Mitchell wasn't sure he understood the question.

"What do you want most in the world?"

That was easy. "To find all of the Victorias and take them back to Scotland with me."

A shadow of a smile crossed Torey's face. "Other than that, what do you want most?"

The answer was not on the tip of his tongue, but very nearly. "A new roof."

"A new roof?"

"There is an African proverb that goes, 'The beginning of wisdom is to get you a roof.' "

"What do you want a roof for?"

"Castle Storm. The one I have now leaks like a sieve." He turned the tables on her. "What do you want most right now?"

She looked up at the great stone house as they approached it from the seaward side. "I've spent my summers at Storm Point for as long as I can remember. I love this house."

"But—?"

"But what I want most is to run away from home."

Sometime later that night, as he lay in bed trying unsuccessfully to put Victoria Storm out of his mind and fall asleep, it occurred to Mitchell that there might be a way.

He tried to think clearly, sorting through the various possibilities and their probable variations. He tried to exercise the self-control that he was supposedly so famous for.

It wasn't working.

Images of Torey kept intruding: the sunlight on her hair as they strolled along the beach that afternoon, the sweetness of her smile, the sexy—and unintentional—way she dropped her voice half an octave when she laughed, the shape of her lovely backside as she reached behind her to brush the sand from her silk slacks.

Oh, he had been sorely tempted to offer his assistance at that moment.

Those exquisite minutes in the shadows the night before, the smell of her, the feel of her, the intimate and intoxicating taste of her as he'd kissed her for the first time.

Mitchell shot straight up in bed, threw off the covers and perched on the edge of the mattress. His body was covered with a sheen of sweat, despite the coolness of the night, and he was aroused.

In fact, he was hard and tight and he felt like he was about to explode.

Restless, impatient, angry with himself—hell, he was downright pissed off at himself—he quickly got up and walked across to the window. He drew back the heavy, brocade draperies, and stood there staring out at the night.

Surely there was a way.

There must be a way.

There had to be a way.

Mitchell Storm, 'The Chief of the Name, Clan, and Family of Storm,' or simply 'The Storm,' made a vow to himself. By God, before it was all said and done, he would find a way for everyone to get what they wanted and what they needed.

As he finally drifted off to sleep—the first gray light of dawn was already a pale shadow on the morning water—the words of another Scotsman, Sir Walter Scott, came to mind:

> *Oh, what a tangled web we weave,*
> *When first we practice to deceive!*

Chapter 8

"It's not fair, of course," Torey pointed out to Mitchell
as the four of them took a break the following afternoon
in time for tea. "You and Mr. MacClumpha have already
found all the obvious ones."

They were in the study, sitting or standing as each
chose to do, around a low, round table that was covered
with a finely embroidered linen tablecloth and a sterling
silver tea service—one of a dozen such sterling silver tea
services utilized at Storm Point—a large, tiered, porcelain platter of freshly baked cookies, a variety of small
iced cakes, traditional English biscuits, crumpets soaked
in melted butter and covered with jam, and a selection
of tea sandwiches that ran the gamut from thinly sliced
cucumber to fish paste.

Alice was pouring. "Milk, Mr. MacClumpha?"

"Yes, please."

"Sugar, Mr. MacClumpha?"

"Please."

"One or two, Mr. MacClumpha?"

"Two, please."

Alice handed the dainty china cup to the red-haired

giant who was trying to look inconspicuous in a leather wingback chair that was approximately half his size.

"Thank you, Miss Fraser."

"You're welcome, Mr. MacClumpha."

"Just MacClumpha," he said, his face a sudden flush of color as he accepted the cup of tea. "Or Iain."

"How do you prefer to be addressed?" Alice Fraser came right out and asked him. She had never been one to beat around the bush.

The big man stared at his hands, then raised his solid chin and looked straight into Alice Fraser's eyes. "Iain, if that wouldn't seem too presumptuous."

"It isn't in the least bit presumptuous," she assured him. "You may call me Alice."

That brought a smile to his face.

"What do you think, Alice?" Torey put her teacup down and reached for another biscuit.

"I think you're right, of course. Mr. MacClumpha—Iain and I have searched the formal gardens twice: once this morning and again after lunch. There is just the one statue that fits the description on the list Lord Storm gave us."

Mitchell swallowed the final bite of a chocolate chip cookie; he had already devoured at least half a dozen of them. Torey had heard him casually mention last evening that chocolate chip cookies were his favorite, and she had immediately requested that the assistant to the assistant chef bake a batch for their honored guest.

He took a gulp of tea to wash down the last crumb and suggested, "I don't think we should stand on formalities, either, Miss Fraser. At the very least I expect you to call me—"

"Call him laddie," Iain MacClumpha butted in with a manly guffaw. "That's what I call him half the time."

"What do you call him the other half?" Torey inquired, then laughed when she saw the expression on the Scotsman's features.

"If it's acceptable to you," Mitchell proposed to the stalwart woman, "I'll refer to you as Alice in private. I'd like you to call me Mitchell. In public we may all choose to be more formal, depending on the circumstances and the company."

"Well put, my lord," Iain offered with a mischievous grin that stretched from ear to ear.

Mitchell rested one elbow on the fireplace mantel, took another drink of his tea, and then gave an exaggerated and somewhat theatrical heave of his chest. "The trouble with being a titled lord in these modern times is that a man receives so little of the respect due him," he announced to the room in general and no one in particular. "Not like in the good old days, I'm told, when the chief of his clan—like the early pagan kings of Scotia—was believed to be semidivine. A chief could do no wrong, then, and loyalty to him was absolute."

"You're right," Torey said, speaking directly to The MacClumpha. "I think we should call him 'laddie.' "

"Why is that, lass?"

Torey was thoroughly enjoying herself. "I do believe he's getting too big for his breeches."

The MacClumpha laughed out loud gustily and slapped his knee, sending a small wave of milky tea spilling over the rim of his cup and into the saucer.

Alice tittered discreetly.

A dark, masculine eyebrow was raised in a suggestive arch, and a sexy, masculine mouth—oh, that mouth!—smiled provocatively at Torey, putting an entirely different, and far more intimate, interpretation on what she'd said.

It was her turn to blush.

Ah, well, Torey reminded herself, everyone claimed that pink was her color.

"Back to the business at hand," she said, calling the informal meeting to order. "Mitchell has discovered the painting of Victoria hanging over the fireplace here in the study."

Not exactly a piece of brilliant detective work, in Torey's opinion. After all, the picture was right out in the open for anyone and everyone to see.

"The portrait of the young queen is on the inventory of auctioned items," Alice confirmed.

Mitchell spoke up, volunteering more information. "I've also located a small bronze figurine, undoubtedly of Greek origin, probably dating from the fifth or sixth century B.C., and affectionately known within the family as 'Vicky.' "

Absentmindedly Torey reached for another biscuit, nibbled on the edge without really taking a bite, and mulled over the facts and figures in their possession. "Including the piece of garden statuary, that brings our current total to three."

"Yes, three," Mitchell corroborated.

"There must be more Victorias somewhere," she said mumbling, and not very subtly masking her frustration. She tossed the uneaten biscuit down on her plate. "But where?"

Alice Fraser got to her feet, straightened the jacket of her serviceable gray suit, rocked back slightly, as was her habit, on the heels of her sensible Oxfords, and suggested in her usual no-nonsense manner, "May I recommend that Iain and I tackle the Prince of Wales wing next, while you and Mitchell concentrate your search on the trophy room and perhaps the library?"

It was a good, sensible plan.

Just like Alice herself.

"We'll meet up again in two hours to see what progress, if any, we've made," Torey added.

"Two hours it is," Alice verified, glancing down at her wristwatch to mark the time. "We'll reconnoiter in the library at six-thirty sharp."

Teatime was officially over.

Nevertheless, Torey noticed that Mitchell grabbed another chocolate chip cookie from the plate and popped it into his mouth on their way out of the study.

Torey pushed open the huge, carved teakwood doors at the end of the long corridor, reached around the corner, and flipped a switch. One spotlight after another blinked on in sequential order: first up one row and then down the next.

She shivered.

Mitchell wasn't certain if he'd actually seen her shiver, or if he had only sensed it.

Or imagined it.

He decided to try the subtle approach. "Did you feel a sudden chill in the air?"

"No." His question must have surprised her. She turned her head. "Why do you ask?"

He shrugged as if it were nothing, really. "I thought I saw you tremble, that's all."

"I did," she granted.

Should he ask her why?

"This was my least favorite room in the entire house— in the entire world—when I was a child," Torey confessed to him as they entered the trophy room.

He looked around, making out the familiar and yet, somehow, grotesque shapes of once living, breathing creatures. "I can certainly see why," he said after a moment.

"This place used to frighten me."

He stuffed his hands into the pockets of his jeans. "I'm surprised it didn't give you nightmares."

"It did."

They paused in front of a stuffed and mounted Bengal tiger: majestic head raised, razor-sharp teeth bared—and now yellowed with age and fading shellac—once-deadly claws extended, eyes glazed and expressionless.

The brass plaque at the tiger's feet proclaimed that it had been bagged by Andrew Storm II, apparently Torey's great-grandfather, in 1910 while he was on safari in eastern India.

There was also an enlarged black-and-white photograph on the wall behind the display. It showed a handsome young man in jodhpurs and a hunting jacket, a rifle tucked under one arm, a hat under the other, posing with a booted foot positioned on his "trophy," and with a smile of self-satisfaction on his face.

"I find this room and its contents pathetic and more than a little sad," she told him.

Mitchell strolled down the aisle of exotic creatures, preserved by a taxidermist's talents. In some instances the whole animal was exhibited; in others it was the head, or the horns, or, in the case, of one unfortunate elephant, only its feet.

"I hate everything about this room," Torey said in a whisper as she walked beside him.

"I'm surprised you haven't gotten rid of them," he said with an all-encompassing gesture.

"Believe me, I've tried," she said without any marked enthusiasm. "It's easier said than done. Nobody will take them off my hands. No one wants them. No one will even agree to dispose of them." She gave a sigh. "Frankly I don't know what to do with the poor things."

"I have a friend who's a curator at the Field Museum in Chicago. I'll give him a call if you like."

"Would you?"

"I can't promise anything."

"I realize that, but it would be such a relief to find them a good home."

They went from one specimen to the next until they had reached the end of the row. Then they started up the opposite side.

"You don't suppose any of them were named Victoria, do you?" Mitchell speculated.

That made Torey laugh.

It was good to hear her laugh.

"There's nothing in here," she finally acknowledged, reaching the same conclusion he already had.

Mitchell flipped the light switch off and closed the carved teak doors behind them. "I believe the library is our next assignment from Miss Fraser."

"Not Miss Fraser," she corrected him. "Alice."

He snapped his fingers together. "That's right. I must remember to call her Alice."

"Now *this* has always been one of my favorite places," Torey told him cheerfully as they strolled into a room of sunlit windows.

The library at Storm Point was a soaring hall with a ceiling frescoed by Pellegrini and imported from a *palazzo* in Venice. There were richly carved larger-than-life wooden figures on either side of a massive fireplace; so massive that a man could stand upright within its bricked interior without ducking his head.

The walls were lined with more than twenty thousand books on every subject from art to gardening to architecture. There was a circular staircase with a wrought-iron and brass railing that led to a second level of bookshelves. Overstuffed chairs and sofas were everywhere, and tables and lamps of every size and description. This was obviously a room created for the comfort of the reader.

There was also a huge globe on a wooden pedestal in one corner, and a mammoth desk beside it.

"That's the Vanderbilt desk," Torey said informatively.

"All right, I'll bite. Why is it called the Vanderbilt desk?" he asked her.

"Because at a gala summer ball at Marble House, a ball very similar to the one we held here earlier this week, my great-grandmother paused for a moment and admired the gilded Sphinxlike heads gracing the four corners of this ornate desk. In a gesture of generosity and to surprise her—and to no doubt impress her; she was a most beautiful woman—her host and neighbor, William K. Vanderbilt, had the massive piece of furniture delivered that very same evening to Storm Point. It was here in the library when she arose the following morning."

"The man had style."

"He certainly did."

"Where are you going?" he inquired as she climbed the circular stairway to the second level of bookshelves.

"I want to check under V in reference books and biographies."

"For Victoria."

She nodded, and with a casual wave of her hand, said, "I'm sure you can find some way to make yourself useful downstairs."

"Make myself useful," Mitchell muttered under his breath. "That's what I thought I'd been doing all along."

It was several minutes before Torey turned and apparently noticed that he was still standing in the middle of the room exactly where she had left him.

"What are you doing?" she asked.

Mitchell thought about *not* telling her. But in the end he did, sticking as close to the truth as he dared. "I'm watching you."

"Watching me?"

"Yup."

She went perfectly still. "Why?"

"I like watching you."

She laughed dismissively, but he thought he heard a trace of feminine pleasure in her laughter as well. "That's no excuse for lollygagging about. Now get to work."

Mitchell noticed that she surreptitiously checked on him when she thought he wasn't looking.

He stood there, without moving, for another minute or two.

"What *are* you doing?" she demanded again.

He walked to the bottom of the circular staircase. "You have very nice . . ." His eyes came to rest on her breasts. He dropped his gaze lower. He was still in dangerous territory. Then even lower still. He finally decided it was safe to say, "You have very nice ankles."

"Nice ankles?"

"Yes. Well-shaped. Fine-boned. Slender without being thin. First-rate ankles, that's what yours are."

"Thank you. I think."

"Nice calves, too."

"Calves?"

"And knees."

"Knees?"

Why was she repeating everything he said?

"Great legs, in general."

Mitchell glimpsed her smile behind the book she was

holding up in front of her. He decided it might be best if he skipped any more specifics. "In fact, you have a lovely figure."

She looked down at him. "So do you."

"Thank you, I think."

"For a man, I mean."

"I know what you mean," he said, slowly climbing the stairs to the second level. He observed that she took a step or two back from him as he approached.

"Perhaps we should talk about something else," she quickly suggested.

Coward.

"What would you like to talk about?"

Torey's expression—and apparently her mind—appeared momentarily blank.

Mitchell made a small production of racking his brains. Then he snapped his fingers as if a remarkable idea had just occurred to him. "I have it."

"You do?"

He crossed his arms. "Let's talk about kissing."

"Kissing?" She was taken aback.

He went through a pantomime, pretending to take a book down from the shelf beside him, leafing through its pages, running the tip of his finger down the printed page and supposedly reading: "Ah, yes, here it is. Kissing. A demonstration of friendship or love or a form of greeting between two people."

"Kissing?" she repeated.

He continued the act. "While certain sexual implications are often recognized by the act of kissing in the West, it is often ceremonial and performed in public in other parts of the world." He rapidly searched his memory. "In some parts of India, for example, the custom is for one person to apply the mouth and nose to the cheek of another, and then inhale. Then there's the custom of the Lapps, which also includes making a nasal-sounding noise and smacking the lips.''

Torey was laughing out loud by the time he concluded his lecture on the subject. Mitchell could see that the tension had left her neck and shoulders.

He took another step toward her. ''Do you know something else interesting about kissing?''

She swallowed. ''No.''

''You've never kissed me in broad daylight.''

Her hand went to her throat. She toyed with the gold chain and locket hanging around her neck. ''I've only kissed you once before.''

He made a small clicking noise with his teeth and tongue. ''That isn't altogether true.''

''It isn't?''

''You may have kissed me on only one occasion, but we kissed a number of individual times.'' He raised and lowered his shoulders. ''Seven or eight . . . but who was counting?''

''Apparently you were.''

He ignored her attempt at wry humor. ''Tell me, my dear cousin, what do you think is the major difference between daytime kissing and nighttime kissing?''

''The amount of light?''

''I mean emotionally.''

Torey licked her lips. ''I suppose one feels less inhibited in the darkness.''

''Good point.'' He came nearer. ''What else?''

She brought the book to her chest and held it tightly against her as if it would somehow provide her with a degree of protection. ''There is a sense of not being seen at night, so one feels a greater freedom to express oneself.''

''Another valid observation.''

"There's something about the night that is sensual, seductive . . . almost erotic."

"Really?"

She breathed in and out. "I suppose so."

"What we need, of course," he pointed out, nearly closing the space between them, "is a method of comparison."

She blinked.

"How can we tell exactly what the difference is if we've never kissed each other in the light of day?"

Torey drew herself up. "That was sneaky."

He tried to appear wounded.

"All right, maybe not sneaky, but definitely devious and cunning and sly like a fox."

He smiled. "Satisfy my curiosity, then."

"Your curiosity, is that all it is?"

"No, but I thought that was safer than saying 'Put me out of my misery.' "

"Are you in misery?"

He might as well confess. "Yes."

"Why?"

A man does what a man has to do.

"Because I haven't kissed you in almost forty-eight hours, and it's all I've been able to think about."

She relaxed her grip on the book in her hands. "I suppose I should be flattered."

"Be honest with me and with yourself. You are flattered," he stated boldly.

It was a calculated risk.

She might turn tail and run. She might laugh in his face. Or she might decide to slap his impertinent mouth and stomp off, angry as hell at him.

She did none of those things.

Instead, Torey took the last step toward him and murmured, "Well, perhaps, for the sake of comparison. . . ."

Chapter 9

She was taken by storm.

It started out as curiosity, of course, not just on Mitchell's part, but on Torey's as well. After all, she had her fair share of questions—okay, doubts—about him, about herself, about the night of the charity ball, and about the way she'd reacted when he had kissed her.

She had asked herself more than once in the intervening two days if it had merely been a fluke.

Had it been the balmy summer night or the shooting stars overhead or the smell of the dew on the grass and the salty sea air or the scent of the roses?

There was a difference in the fragrance of roses at night.

Why wouldn't there be a difference in the way it felt to be kissed by a man at night?

Not *a* man.

Not just *any* man.

This man.

On the one hand, it made absolutely no sense to Torey that she should reach the age of thirty and suddenly discover passion in the arms of a stranger.

On the other hand, she knew there was precious little common sense or logic involved when it came to an emotion like passion.

One minute she was standing by the comfortably familiar bookshelves in the library, a leatherbound volume on Queen Victoria clutched to her breast, watching Mitchell come closer and closer, and wondering what the enigmatic expression on his face meant.

The next minute he was kissing her.

And she was kissing him.

Dear God, but she loved the taste of him, the feel of his mouth on her mouth, the way his lips moved against her lips, lightly brushing back and forth, and then more.

So much more.

She loved the way he held her in his arms. She loved the strength she could feel in him and the stroke of his hand as he held her with fingers splayed at her nape.

She loved the way her body felt pressed to his, her breasts flattened by his chest, her thighs against his muscular legs.

She loved the indisputable fact that she aroused him. That he wanted her. That she wanted him. That whatever was happening between the two of them, it was wild and wonderful and mutual.

She wanted more.

He gave her more.

She wanted even more.

He took more.

He tasted her with the tip of his tongue, then delved deeper and deeper into her mouth until she was no longer certain who was giving and who was taking.

He was devouring her with his lips and teeth and tongue. Let him swallow her whole! Let him take her into himself and she would become a part of his flesh and bone, his very blood. She went willingly, eagerly, mindlessly.

He filled his hands with her hair and she wondered if he said "silk" aloud, or if she had only heard it in her mind.

He filled his hands with her shoulders, her arms, her waist, her hips, her derriere, wanting her nearer, urging her nearer, demanding she come nearer to him as he lifted her, parting her thighs and thrusting his pelvis forward.

There were only his blue jeans, and whatever he wore under them, and the thin layer of her linen shorts and the even thinner layer of her silk panties separating them. Torey could sense his heat, taste his desire, feel his need.

And her own.

She was nearly weeping with her need of him: salty tears, musky tears, erotic tears.

Then she heard her name spoken as she had never heard it spoken before: softly, deeply, intensely, passionately, as if the sound were echoing down through the ages, as though both the question and the answer were contained in a single word and the word was her name: "Victoria."

Day or night, Mitchell discovered, it made no difference. When he kissed her it was like putting a match to kindling: he went up in flames. And Torey went with him.

Caution, common sense, taking it nice and slow and easy, his enviable self-control, the training of his mind and body—it all vanished in an instant, the instant he covered her mouth with his.

It was ironic.

No, it was more than ironic. It was some kind of absurd joke he'd unintentionally ended up playing on himself: he had no self-control when it came to this woman.

He heard her name spoken in a voice he didn't recognize as his own: "Victoria."

"Michell," came the whispered response.

Not Mitchell, the modern translation of his name, but Michell, the old Scottish version.

Hell, he must have heard her wrong. It shouldn't come as any surprise. His attention wasn't focused on what Torey was saying to him, but on what Torey was doing to him.

She dropped the leatherbound volume that she'd been clutching in the hands wedged between them. The book tumbled, almost unnoticed, to their feet. Reaching up, she wrapped her arms around his neck. Her touch was cool on his heated flesh.

Mitchell wanted her touch. He needed her touch. But he needed far more than the innocent caress she was giving the cord at the back of his neck, or the feathery brushing of her fingers through his hair, or the way she made the faintest impression circling his ear.

He needed her hands on him.

Badly.

"Torey," he breathed heavily into her mouth, beseeching her, "touch me."

"I am touching you," she murmured against his lips.

He backed off an inch or two, certainly no more, and stared down long and hard into her eyes and then repeated the request. "Touch me. Please."

"How?"

"As if you wanted me."

"I do want you."

Honestly spoken.

"Where?" she finally asked as if the word had been stuck in her throat for a minute.

Mitchell's gut tightened. "Touch me here." He placed

a hand on his chest just above his heart. "And here."
He moved lower, stopping in the general vicinity of his
ribcage. "And here." His palm came to rest on his ab-
domen.

Without a word of argument, without another word,
Torey granted his wish.

First, she ran her hand along the slope of his shoulder,
down the entire length of his arm all the way to the very
tips of his fingers, and then back up again.

The second time she made a detour and leisurely
trailed her fingers across the expanse of his chest, hesi-
tating when she encountered the hard nub of a male nipple beneath his denim shirt, then curiously going in
search of the other.

He shuddered.

She splayed the fingers of both hands, covering as
much of him as she could, then deliberately and slowly
caressed him—it was, oh, such sweet torture—from his
shoulders to his chest to his ribcage and finally to his
waist, where she paused.

They both were well aware of the aroused state he was
in. It was there between them, unmistakable, indisputable, substantial, undeniable, rigid.

Rigid?

Hell, he was as hard as a rock.

Did he dare ask her to touch him *there*?

Mitchell knew he couldn't say the word. Instead, he
decided to return the favor. Raising both his hands, he
brought them down gently on Torey's shoulders and
then, at an excruciatingly slow pace, traced the outline
of her figure.

His explorations told him that she had a lovely body:
trim, firm, slightly muscular, yet soft and supple in all
the right places. He realized that he wanted to see her

naked, that he wanted to touch her in ways—and in places—that he would have to be content to only dream about under the circumstances.

Mitchell's hands were resting on her hips when the library door suddenly opened below them.

Torey's eyes flew to the oversized clock on the fireplace mantel. "Six-thirty!"

Shit.

"Iain and Miss Fraser," he announced, suddenly annoyed with her, annoyed with them, annoyed with himself.

She still had the amazing presence of mind to correct him. "Iain and Alice."

Mitchell turned his back to the brass railing and the vast library room below, grabbed a large, thick tome from the nearest shelf, opened it somewhere in the middle—where didn't matter—and held the book strategically in front of him. It wasn't much in the way of camouflage, but it would have to do.

Never judge a book by its cover, he mused sardonically as he stood there.

Torey quickly bent and retrieved the volume on Queen Victoria that she had been studying when he had first approached her.

They were both reading industriously when Alice Fraser's familiar voice rang out. "Ah, there you two are!"

Mitchell glanced over his shoulder without turning around. "Is it six-thirty already?"

"We'd lost track of time," Torey added unnecessarily.

"It's six-thirty on the dot," Alice confirmed without even bothering to consult her watch.

Iain MacClumpha followed the woman into the library and called up to them. "How did your search go?"

Mitchell tossed the question right back to the Scotsman. "How did your search go?"

Alice was all smiles. "We found one!"

"Where?" Torey asked, excited.

"In the picture gallery along that wide hallway leading to the Prince of Wales wing."

"I know the place," Torey said.

Mitchell, of course, didn't have a clue what they were talking about; he was just grateful they were talking. It took a man's body a few minutes to adjust to a sudden change in 'climate.'

"It's a bloody big plate hangin' on the bloody wall," Iain said, half complaining and scratching his head as if he hadn't quite figured out yet what it was intended to be.

"It's a commemorative plaque," Alice clarified. "The Prince must have presented it to Torey's great-great-grandparents when he was a guest at Storm Point during the summer of 1871."

"Imagine that," Mitchell said, deadpan.

"Have you found anything?" Alice reiterated.

Torey glanced down at the book in her hands, read for half a minute—no more—then looked up, eyes bright with excitement and declared, "I believe we have."

"We have?" Her claim surprised Mitchell.

"Listen to this." Then she began to read. " 'Queen Victoria was very fair, with a clear, high-colored complexion. Even in old age she never lost her grace of movement, which gave the impression that she moved on wheels. But she is believed to have lamented on at least one occasion: "we are rather short for a queen." ' "

Mitchell waited for the punch line. It was soon apparent there wasn't one. "So?"

Torey shoved the biography back onto the bookshelf

behind her. "Short, in this particular instance, equates to small. We're looking for a small queen."

Alice Fraser actually appeared to comprehend her cryptic meaning. "Of course. Why didn't we think of it before?"

"Well, for one thing," Torey said as she brushed by him and started down the circular staircase, "neither of us play."

"Play what?" Mitchell quizzed, following her. He was halfway down the stairs before he realized he still had the blasted book in his hand, and he no longer had any need for it.

"Neither of you lasses play what?" Iain MacClumpha piped up, not understanding what was going on any more than Mitchell did.

"Chess." Torey spelled it out for them. "Neither Alice nor I play the game of chess."

"A lot of people don't play the game of chess," Mitchell felt compelled to point out to her. He plunked the weighty tome down on the first table he came to.

"Do you remember what drawer it was stored in?" Torey asked her secretary and friend as both women made a beeline for the far corner of the library and the Vanderbilt desk.

Alice gave it serious consideration. She stopped dead in her tracks and shut her eyes. Then she opened them again after a moment and recited: "Right-hand side. Second drawer down."

"You're a marvel," Torey said.

Alice blushed with pleasure. "I try."

"Here it is!" Torey exclaimed, taking out a small, ornately carved wooden box from the second drawer down on the right side of the desk.

They all gathered around and waited while she worked the tiny clasp and opened the lid.

"It's a miniature chess set." Mitchell leaned over to take a closer look. "Well, I'll be," he declared.

"What'll you be, laddie?"

He ignored The MacClumpha and straightened. "The white queen is obviously Victoria herself."

"Actually she's the white king," Torey corrected him. "The white queen is Albert, her prince consort. Gladstone, who served four separate terms as prime minister and whom Queen Victoria loathed, is the black king. If you study all the various pieces, the chess set becomes a fascinating commentary on the political history of England during that era."

"More important for our purposes, it means we've found another Victoria," Mitchell said pragmatically.

Torey was visibly pleased with herself. "Now we have five in our possession."

"Six," Mitchell corrected.

"I count five." She ticked them off on her fingers. "The garden statue, the painting, the bronze figurine, the commemorative plaque, and the chess piece."

"There's one more," he told her.

"One more?"

She was a clever woman. Would she figure it out for herself? "One you haven't thought of."

Torey frowned. "What is it?"

He shouldn't tease her. "Not what. Who."

"All right. Who is it?"

"You."

That made her take a step back. "Me?"

"Yes. You, dear cousin, are the sixth Victoria."

Chapter 10

"He's asked you to return to Scotland with him, hasn't he?" The question came out of nowhere.

Torey should have known that Alice would have it figured out by now. Her personal secretary, friend, and confidante wasn't blind and, indeed, she saw far more than most people.

She braced herself. "Yes. He has asked me to return to Scotland with him . . . for a few weeks, anyway."

There was a heartbeat, then two.

Alice Fraser placed the stack of mail on the study desk, as she did each weekday morning, picked up the top envelope, and neatly and efficiently slit it open with the blade of the ceremonial *sgian dubh* that had once belonged to the first Andrew Storm, and which, for the past fifty years, had served as a letter opener. She finally glanced up and gave Torey an appraising look. "Are you going?"

"I haven't decided."

There was another pause of twenty or thirty seconds while Alice scanned the contents of the letter she held in her hand. "When does he want an answer?"

"Today."

That brought the woman's head up with a snap. "Today?"

"In fact, this afternoon. He'll be here in about an hour," Torey said to her.

"So soon—" Alice murmured, slowly sinking down into the leather desk chair.

"Mitchell needs to get back home."

"I realize there's no reason for either of them to linger any longer than is necessary," Alice reflected in a rare, pensive mood. She placed both of her capable hands on the edge of the desk, pushed herself up—it was almost as though the effort took more energy than she possessed, however—and went to stand at the study window. "But so soon," she repeated in a whisper.

"We've searched this house high and low for an entire week, and we haven't found a trace of another Victoria," Torey reminded her.

"And the six—" Alice turned toward her for a moment. "Well, the five we have located are packed up and ready to be shipped back to the Isle of Storm."

Torey joined her and, standing side by side, the two women gazed out at the overcast day. There was no delineation between sky and water. The sky was gray. The water was gray. Even the air was gray this morning; the fog had yet to burn off. Maybe it wasn't going to.

"If I do decide to go to Scotland, I thought we would try to follow Mitchell and The MacClumpha within a week or so, giving ourselves just enough time to pack our bags and make the necessary arrangements on this end."

"We?"

"Not that many arrangements need to be made. Dickens and the staff can see to everything here, of course."

Torey laughed lightly. "Sometimes I think dear old Dickens believes it's his house, anyway. It probably has something to do with the fact that he's actually lived at Storm Point longer than I have. He was under-butler, you know, ten years before I was even born."

"Yes, I know."

"I can remember hearing my parents quietly joking about it when they were certain Dickens couldn't hear them. My father would laugh and remark to my mother: 'We both know who the real master is around here, Marilyn.' And my mother—she was always wise about men, I realize now, especially the man she married—would pat his arm affectionately, or squeeze his hand, and declare, 'But you will always be my only lord and master, Andrew.' "

It was quickly apparent that Alice Fraser hadn't heard a word Torey had said.

Her companion repeated, "We?"

"We?"

"*We* are going to Scotland?"

"Of course, we." Torey reached out and placed her hand on the other woman's arm. "I never go anywhere without you, do I?"

"No."

"How could I?"

Alice didn't reply.

"You're absolutely essential to me. You know that."

Alice was.

"Well, why would I go off and leave you behind now?"

Unadorned lips scarcely moved. "I didn't realize you meant both of us were going to Scotland."

"Don't you want to go?"

It was a good thirty seconds before Alice Fraser said, "I hadn't thought about it."

"Would you prefer to stay here? Or in New York?" Although Torey couldn't imagine why anyone would want to spend the summer in Manhattan if they could avoid it.

"No."

"I assumed you wouldn't mind spending the rest of the summer on an island off the western coast of the Scottish mainland." It was time she quit assuming and simply asked. "Do you want to go to Scotland?"

Alice moved her head, but Torey couldn't tell if she was nodding her head yes, or shaking her head no.

"You could always take some time and visit the Frasers while you're in the general region."

"Clan Fraser was originally from Peeblesshire and East Lothian, but my people moved north in the time of The Bruce," Alice related as if the historical details were fresh on her mind and always on the tip of her tongue.

Torey tried a slightly different tack with her friend and companion, for Alice played both of those roles in her life as well as being her personal secretary and her right-hand everything. "I thought the change would be good for both of us."

Alice's pointed chin came up a fraction of an inch. "I suppose it would be."

"Frankly I'm tired of playing society hostess and charity fund-raiser, of attending endless gallery openings for the hottest new artist who needs my patronage or luncheons to honor one great humanitarian or politician after another, of doing all of the things—" she sighed deeply "—that as Victoria Storm I'm supposed to do."

"It's called burnout."

"Then I'm burned out, Alice." She made an attempt

at humor. "Even the idle rich deserve a break now and then, don't they?"

"No one works harder than you do," Alice stated staunchly. She would not hear ill of Torey even from Torey.

"Thank you, dear." She could always count on Alice. Which was more than she could say for most of the people in her life.

Alice turned and regarded her with shrewd eyes. "Why does Lord Storm . . . Mitchell . . . why does he want you to go back to Scotland with him?"

"I'm the sixth Victoria." Torey knew it sounded a bit crazy even as she said it. So she added, "Mitchell seems to be convinced that I'm the key to the whole mystery."

"Hmm."

"Does that sound crazy to you, Alice?"

Alice Fraser opened her mouth and closed it again at once.

Torey didn't even bother to take a breath before answering her own question. "Of course, it sounds crazy. Why wouldn't it sound crazy? This whole thing is crazy," she ranted.

She began to pace back and forth.

Alice moved out of her path.

"A century-old feud between two warring branches of the same family. One twin brother taking revenge on the other. Cheating. Stealing. Lying. A whole list of missing Victorias. A long-lost treasure that no one is even certain exists when you get right down to it. The whispered words of a dying man." Torey stopped pacing. "Mitchell's grandfather was probably delirious and spouting all kinds of nonsense at the end, poor man." She turned, planted her hands on her hips and looked directly at her friend. "There are all kinds of unanswered questions when it comes to this business, aren't there?''

"Yes, there are." Alice was Alice, however. She cut right to the heart of the matter. "I think there is really only one important question you have to ask yourself, Victoria Storm."

Alice almost never—maybe once in a blue moon—called her Victoria Storm. It always meant something serious, something important, something to take note of.

"And what is that?" she inquired, not at all certain that she wanted to ask.

"Are you in love with him?"

"With who?"

Alice raised one thin eyebrow and said, "With whom."

Torey blinked. "With whom, then?"

"I think we both know with whom."

She couldn't fool Alice. Not now. Not ever. Never had been able to. And she certainly couldn't stand there, look the woman straight in the eye and lie to her.

It came out as a whisper. "I'm attracted to him, yes."

"And you think you *may* be in love with him."

She threw her hands up in the air in the ultimate gesture of exasperation. "All right, I'm ready to confess. I may be in love with Mitchell Storm."

"Does he know?"

Torey paled. Dear God, she hoped not, she prayed not. "I don't think so. I just discovered it myself in the past day or two."

"He's not like other men," Alice pointed out.

"I know."

"He's a Scot."

"He's spent almost no time in Scotland until the past few months when his dying grandfather begged him to return home."

"Believe me," Alice said, and she was deadly serious, "he's a Scot right down to the heart and soul of him."

"What if he is?"

"He's not only a Scot. He's the chieftain of one of the oldest and fiercest clans in all of the Western Isles."

"I thought all clans were once fierce."

"They were. They had to be. They were born fighting for survival: the Norse, the English, even each other."

"You're saying some of them still are?"

"Yes."

Torey arched one brow in a knowing fashion. "Mitchell already warned me about that."

"About what exactly?"

"He told me that a true son of Scotland lived and died by the sword," Torey said uneasily.

"It's true."

"He claimed that in his heart and soul," she struggled to keep her voice even, "every Scotsman's a warrior."

"I believe it to be true," Alice said, folding her hands together in front of her.

Torey felt the color rising sharply in her face. "I said, 'Forewarned is forearmed.' "

Alice frowned. The skin around her mouth was taut. "What did he say?"

Torey's heart was pounding, and her palms were damp. "He said there wouldn't be any warning."

"The man was telling you the truth."

Her heart beat even harder. "I know."

"They will do whatever it takes to get what they want or what they need," Alice said quietly.

"I know that, too."

"And, knowing all that you know, you're still willing to go with the man."

"I am."

"Then you, Victoria Storm, are a true Scotswoman."
Alice seemed both proud of her and afraid for her at the
same time. She must have felt compelled to put in one
last cautionary word, however. "Do you know what he's
called by his own clan?"

Torey shook her head. "I know he has a long list of
fancy names and titles."

"I'll give you the name that means the most to Mitchell Storm, at least according to The MacClumpha, and
The MacClumpha should know. The name that strikes
the greatest fear into the hearts and souls of other men.
For Mitchell's official title is 'The Chief of the Name,
Clan, and Family of Storm.' ''

"That doesn't seem particularly frightening to me,"
Torey said after not the slightest hesitation.

"For a thousand years and more, from the time of
Conn of the Hundred Battles and the ancient Dalriadic
kings, from the days of William Wallace and The Bruce
and Rob Roy MacGregor, from the battle of Stirling
Bridge in 1297 and Bannockburn and Pinkie and Glencoe
and even the bloodbath of Culloden, the man bearing that
title has also been known simply as 'The Storm.' ''

What was she going to do about Mitchell Storm?

Torey posed that question to herself for the umpteenth
time as she headed out the side door of Storm Point and
hiked across the perfectly maintained lawns.

But not in the direction of the ocean as might be expected.

This was not the time for a leisurely stroll along the
beach. A stroll along the beach included stopping to kick
off her shoes so she could walk barefoot in the sun-
warmed sand.

It meant tarrying to pick up a random and unusually

pretty seashell here and there along the way, perhaps slipping it into her pocket until her pockets became filled.

It might entail pausing and staring at length out at the sameness and yet ever-changing nature of the ocean, or to listen to the rhythmic waves as they washed ashore, one after another.

No, a stroll along the beach was the perfect choice for relaxation, for gaining peace of mind, for finding inner serenity, but it wasn't the place for decision-making.

And she didn't head in the direction of the formal gardens, either. They were too neat and tidy and orderly for her present disheveled frame of mind. And the colors and fragrances of the informal gradens would be too distracting.

There was only one place Torey could go when she had to do some serious thinking.

She took off in the opposite direction from the house and headed toward what she had fondly called since her childhood 'The Hundred-Acre Wood.'

In reality, her woods were a small grove of deciduous trees with a few orchard varieties of fruit-bearing cherries and apples mixed in, the occasional overgrown lilac, a wild, rambling wisteria and the odd patch of lavender, a stand of protective fir trees, and something akin to an English hedgerow.

But deep in the woods, there, in the center of the hodgepodge, was *her* tree.

It was old.

Very old.

No one seemed to know precisely how old, but it was older than any other living thing in the area. It had massive, contorted branches and a gnarled trunk that had grown too close to the ground and had essentially divided into three separate trunks.

Her tree had thick, green leaves in the summer that turned a brilliant shade of scarlet in the fall. Her tree was home to countless creatures: birds, squirrels, even the occasional owl. She had heard him 'who-whoing' one night when she had dozed off and been forced to find her way home in the dark.

There was a natural formation, no more than five or six feet off the ground, and easily reached if one knew precisely where to locate the toeholds.

Torey knew, of course.

The seat provided by nature was the perfect spot to sit and watch the world go by—such as the world was in The Hundred-Acre Wood. She always felt safe with the solid tree at her back and her legs stretched out along a neighboring branch or left to dangle over the edge if she wished. There was enough leafy camouflage in the summer that she could hide there and never be seen, never be found.

This was Torey's secret tree.

Only a handful of people—her parents, who were now dead; Dickens, out of necessity; and of course Alice, a kindred spirit who was wise enough to never go there herself—knew of its location or even of its existence.

This was her place.

And it was to her place that Torey came now, today, troubled, indecisive, thirty years old and still drifting, wondering how life and other people's expectations of her had somehow gotten in the way.

For some time now Torey had realized that she was living someone else's life.

Was it her mother's?

Marilyn Storm's life had been cut tragically short by cancer at the age of forty-five. That had been nearly a decade ago and Torey still mourned and missed her mother.

Was it her father's?

Andrew Storm IV had dedicated himself to the same ideals, principles, and goals as all the Andrew Storms before him: preserving the family name and the family fortune for future generations. He had given his life for the cause, suffering a fatal heart attack just two months after his wife's premature death.

Was it her parents'?

She lived in the same houses where they had lived, surrounded by the same furniture, the same paintings, even the same butler. She carried on the charity work begun by her mother, the financial empire created by her father.

She moved in the same social circle her parents had moved in, saw the same people, still dated off and on the same man—dear, dependable Peter—that they had hand-selected for her.

She was living a life that fulfilled other people's, especially society's, expectations of her.

Wasn't it time for her to live her own life?

Except Victoria Storm had no idea what her own life was, what it could be, what it should be.

"There's still time to find out," she murmured as she stuck the tip of her shoe into the first toehold, grabbed a branch, and swung herself up into her sitting place. She made herself comfortable, as she had a hundred—a thousand—times before over the past twenty-odd years.

She went through the ritual, which involved affectionately patting the thick trunk of the tree with her hand and saying just loud enough for her and the tree to hear: "Hello, it's me. It's Victoria."

She was almost certain the tree heard her and answered with its own kind of welcome.

Then Torey leaned back, rested her head against the smooth spot where the bark had worn away years ago and reached up to touch the chain and locket hanging around her neck.

Today, as she sometimes did—and always in private, although she couldn't have said why—she carefully opened the antique locket and gazed at the face inside.

It was a miniature portrait of a young woman. Well, her head and shoulders, anyway. She had long, fair hair: blond with perhaps the merest suggestion of red to it, especially in the sunlight, or so Torey had always imagined.

Her skin was ivory and her eyes blue-green in color. She was pretty but not necessarily beautiful, although that could have been more a deficiency of the artist's skill than that of his subject's features.

Torey didn't know who the young woman was. She didn't know her name, or her age, or where she came from, or what had happened to her. The girl's hair was braided and then looped over each ear. That, and the style of the artist's brush strokes, told Torey the tiny painting was old, possibly quite old.

She had found the locket in a dust-encrusted case in the bottom of an old trunk in a back room of Storm Point where no one went and no one even seemed inclined or interested in keeping clean.

Six or seven years old at the time, Torey had been feeling a little lonely. But she developed a sense of instant kinship with the young woman inside the locket, almost a spiritual connection. Other children had their invisible playmates; Torey had her secret friend. In fact, on more than one frightening or dangerous occasion Torey had decided the young woman might be her guardian angel.

And so she had claimed the locket as her own. And it had been hers ever since. It would always be with her, right there, hanging from the gold chain, resting next to her heart.

"Ah, tree," Torey said with a heart-rending sigh as she caressed its smooth branches. "I will miss you. I wonder if you will miss me."

She looked up, then, and gazed out through a natural opening in the leaves.

He was early.

She watched him hiking across the grassy meadow that led to the woods. He walked as if he knew the way, and yet she knew that Mitchell Storm had never been here before.

She could see the wind playing with his hair—every now and then he reached up and impatiently brushed it out of his eyes—and the long-legged, lilting gait to his walk.

He came closer.

Her heart was pounding, but her heart—and she liked to think her tree and her secret friend—knew, too.

She had her answer.

Mitchell came closer still.

And whispered words passed Torey's lips. They were the words of Robert Burns, altered ever so slightly to fit the occasion. Surely the great Scottish poet and romantic would not mind too much, under the circumstances.

Torey murmured so softly that only she and the tree and her secret friend could hear, " 'But to see him was to love him, love but him, and love forever . . .' "

* * *

"Well, what happened?" The MacClumpha demanded to know the instant Mitchell walked into their suite of rooms at Storm Point later that same afternoon.

"What happened when?"

"Don't play games with me, laddie. We both know what we're talking about here."

Mitchell supposed they did.

He blew out his breath and said, "I'm not playing games, Iain. I'm tired."

The Scotsman scowled. "I won't even ask why a healthy young man in his prime is tired at five o'clock in the afternoon."

"Well, I'll tell you why," Mitchell said, turning back. "I'm tired because I can't seem to get any sleep."

"You miss Scotland."

He shook his head and said dryly, "Somehow I don't think that's the reason."

"Then it's the lass."

He didn't give any response. None was required, in his opinion. The comment hadn't been worded in the form of a question.

"It *is* the lass."

"It could be," he mumbled, taking out his suitcase and beginning to throw his things into it.

"You're not happy."

"Not particularly."

"What did the lass say?" The MacClumpha didn't wait for an answer. "She must have told you nay."

"As a matter of fact, she said yes."

Iain brightened. "Then why the long face?" He followed with a frown. "You didn't have to use your charms on the lass, did you?"

"No." Mitchell tossed his jeans into the open bag. "Not that it's any of your bloody business."

"Whether you like it or not, everything about you is my bloody business."

The MacClumpha took their kilts and neatly laid them out in preparation for their journey tomorrow. They would arrive home in traditional dress, the way The MacClumpha and certainly The Storm were expected to appear.

It was some time before Iain spoke again. "Did you have to make her any promises to get her to come?"

"She would have come, anyway."

"Then you did make her promises."

"Two of them," Mitchell admitted.

"Are you going to tell The MacClumpha what they are?"

Sure. Why not? There was certainly no reason why he couldn't tell Iain.

"The first was easy enough." Mitchell threw himself down into a chair and propped his feet up on the footrest. "One I think you'll like and approve of, as a matter of fact."

"Don't keep me in suspense. What is it?"

"My first promise was that she can bring Miss Fraser—Alice—along with her."

Iain was suddenly very busy with their belongings, but not before Mitchell saw the quickening color and the quickening interest on his friend's face.

"Seems reasonable enough," he said gruffly. "After all, the lass and Alice are bosom companions."

"Yes, they are."

"What was the second promise?"

Mitchell folded his hands together, intertwining his fingers, and brought them to his mouth. Absently, he began to chew on his fist.

"Is it that bad?"

His expression was vacant. "No."

"Is it expensive?"

"It won't cost me so much as a pence."

"Then what is it that has you so troubled?"

"I've promised her a tree."

The MacClumpha froze. "A tree?"

Mitchell nodded his head. "A tree."

"Any particular type of tree? An oak? An elm? An alder?" Iain racked his brain and came up with several more varieties. "A cedar of Lebanon, perhaps, or an avenue of limes?"

Mitchell shook his head. "Just a tree."

"We've got plenty of trees on the Isle of Storm," he reassured Mitchell.

"This must be a tree that she can climb up into and sit down comfortably on—by the hour if she so desires—and without being disturbed."

"Ah—" Iain MacClumpha got a knowing smile on his craggy features. "I understand."

Mitchell glanced up. "You do?"

The MacClumpha had the final word on the subject. "The lass wishes for a *boo'er*."

"A *boo'er*?"

"A bower," the Scot translated.

Mitchell sat up. "Of course, she wants a place that is hers, a place that she can call her own."

And he would make certain that Torey got her wish.

Chapter 11

"Where the devil is the man?"

Sylvia Forbes sat back in the richly upholstered velvet armchair before the fire in the drawing room, raised the glass of fine sherry to her lips, and repeated, with far more forbearance than she was feeling, "I told you, Roger. He has gone to America."

Roger Forbes sniffed in that indignant manner as only Roger could, and voiced his complaint. "I don't see why he would go gallivanting off to the States when he was expecting guests. I've never heard of such a damned fool thing."

Sylvia looked at Roger. The man was far too handsome for his own good, which she believed had resulted in a certain deficiency in his character, a fact which, naturally, she had *not* kept to herself. The object of her attention paused, muttered under his breath, nudged at the end of a large ember in the open fireplace with the toe of his black dress shoe, and watched as the sparks flew up the massive chimney.

Even on summer evenings a fire was often required within Castle Storm, according to the housekeeper, Mrs.

Pyle, although perhaps more to ward off the damp than the chill.

Roger Forbes helped himself to another drink from his absent host's excellent selection of liquors. "I suppose Storm's lack of good manners must have something to do with the fact that he wasn't really to the manor born."

"Of course he was," Sylvia immediately contradicted the idiotic comment from her stepson.

"I thought his parents—or his mother, anyway—were foreign," he ventured.

"Quite the opposite is true, I can assure you." Sylvia had done her homework thoroughly. "As a matter of fact, his mother was the youngest daughter of the Duke of Carron."

"A bloody duke's daughter. Well, I'll be."

Sylvia intended to set the record straight for Roger here and now. "Mitchell Storm can directly trace his lineage back a thousand years and more to the ancient rulers of these isles. It doesn't get much more 'to the manor born' than that."

"Well, he seems like a foreigner to me."

"He seems like a man who has traveled widely and lived in a number of exotic locales around the world."

"He's uncivilized."

"He's cultured, sophisticated, well-educated, and speaks at least six languages." She took another healthy swallow of her sherry. "Which is a damned sight more than you managed to learn before you were kicked out of Cambridge."

Roger's cookie-cutter good looks became tinged with color; whether out of anger or embarrassment or a little of both, was difficult for her to tell. "That was twenty years ago, Sylvia."

"I have an excellent memory as you well know," she

stated, reminding him in a not-so-subtle fashion that she recalled any number of things about him that he would just as soon she'd forget.

Or had never known.

Sylvia rather enjoyed the hold she maintained over Roger. It made him agreeable on occasions when she desired him to be agreeable. It usually encouraged him to civility, and it provided her with a certain power. She was a woman who enjoyed having power over men.

And women.

Roger got *that* tone in his voice. She recognized it instantly. She disliked it intensely. "I seem to recall a few facts about you, as well, my dear Sylvia."

She attempted a bluff. "Behave yourself, Roger."

"I know a thing or two about you from twenty years ago that you, no doubt, might prefer to forget, stepmother."

She absolutely detested the word stepmother, and he damned well knew it.

Roger laughed; it was an unpleasant sound. "For instance, despite your lies to the contrary, despite all the expensive herbal treatments and in spite of the very fine way in which you have managed to preserve your figure—and I can vouch for that one, myself." He sauntered closer to her chair, leaned over the arm and lazily drew an imaginary line with the index finger of his right hand across the considerable cleavage revealed by her evening dress. "Despite all of your efforts, I know for a fact that you are fifty-five years old."

"That was uncalled for, Roger," she cried out, dramatically, as if he had wounded her in some manner.

The truth was Sylvia had been sixty-three on her last birthday. But that was, perhaps, her best-kept secret of all.

"So was the crack about Cambridge," he countered.

"I'm sorry," she murmured, knowing when it was to her benefit to apologize and back off.

"Apology accepted," he said after a moment. "But doesn't it still seem odd to you?"

"What?"

"The fact that we show up here at Storm's invitation and discover that he has recently left for a week or two in the States."

A Mona Lisa smile appeared on Sylvia's perfectly made-up face. "Perhaps."

"Why you conniving little—" Roger stopped himself from saying the last word on the tip of his tongue, chortled in the back of his throat, and slapped the back of the overstuffed armchair between them. "You are the sly one, Sylvia."

"I have no idea what you're talking about," she said, lying through her teeth.

Lying was a particular talent of Sylvia Forbes's and one that she had mastered—no, one that she had perfected—long before she had met the late Mr. Forbes and become the second Mrs. Forbes.

In her youth, she had been plain little Ruby Moore, sometime actress, sometime exotic dancer, sometime . . . well, sometimes just about anything and everything.

Roger latched onto the possibility that had, apparently, just occurred to him. "Mitchell Storm never actually invited us for a visit, did he?"

"Not in so many words," she admitted.

"So the lord of the castle is going to return home and find he has unexpected houseguests, and he'll be too polite, or too bowled over by your audacity, to throw us out on our arses."

"Possession is nine-tenths of the law."

Roger circled the chair and came to a halt in front of her. "What are you up to, Sylvia?"

"I'm just trying to find a way to escape London in the heat of summer."

"And while everyone else who is anyone else in society is sailing at Cowes. . . ."

"We've decided to skip Cowes this summer. All that sun and all that wind and all that water isn't any good for my complexion. We're just a teensy-weensy bit early for the shooting in Scotland, that's all," she said as if she had rehearsed her answer for anyone who might ask within the next several months.

"I don't believe you for a minute, you sly bitch," Roger muttered, reaching from behind her chair and thrusting his hand down the front of her dress.

"Stop it!" She slapped at his hand.

He laughed nastily. "Why?"

"I don't like being pawed."

He laughed again. "Of course, you do. As a matter of fact, you love it."

She decided not to pick another argument with him. "Someone might walk in on us," she said instead.

"The servants won't come unless we beckon them. Besides, they're trained to knock."

"Nadine."

"Nadine is always late for dinner."

"I don't mean that," Sylvia said, disposing of his groping hand and diverting his attention by bringing up his stepdaughter and her step-granddaughter through marriage.

Well, it was all through marriage. She wasn't blood-related to Roger either, for that matter. She had simply married his father long after Roger's mother had died.

Roger's forehead creased into an unattractive maze of

wrinkles for a forty-year-old. "What about Nadine, then?"

"She's young and beautiful and—"

"Not too bright," he finished, gulping his drink and returning to help himself to another. "Nadine's mother was the same way when I married her: sweet and trusting and not too bright. Simplemindedness must have run in the family."

"Naive or unworldly is the preferred term."

Obviously he wasn't the least interested in semantics. "As I said, what about Nadine?"

She answered him only indirectly. "Mitchell Storm has everything. Well, almost everything," she conceded. "All he lacks is a vast fortune and a wife."

Roger snickered behind the rim of his glass. "Sounds like he lacks a bloody lot to me."

"That is why he has gone to America."

"To find a wife?"

"Good heavens, no. He's gone to find a fortune."

"How would you learn something like that?"

"I haven't wasted my time since we've been here . . . unlike some people I know. I had a long chat yesterday with the housekeeper, Mrs. Pyle. It seems that Lord Storm is calling upon his American cousin: one of the richest women in the United States, if not in the world." Sylvia took another sip of the expensive sherry, savoring every drop. "The wife will come next."

"Don't you think you're a bit long in the tooth for Lord Storm, old thing?"

"Don't be vulgar, Roger." That was like commanding the tide not to come in. "I have my heart set on Nadine marrying Mitchell Storm."

"Good God."

"She would become a countess."

"And being the step-grandmother of a countess would be very useful to you in society."

Sometimes Roger wasn't as dumb as he appeared.

"Of course." She would simply make certain that the emphasis was on the relationship, and not the word grandmother. "Mitchell Storm's titles are old and highly respected. He is, without a doubt, the most eligible bachelor in the entire realm."

"So that's your little scheme."

"In fact," she went on as if she hadn't heard him, "I think it's time you remarried as well, Roger."

"Me?"

"Yes, you. You were married once before, to Nadine's mother," she said needlessly.

"I'm of the school of thought that every woman should marry, and no man," he said, paraphrasing, no doubt, some famous quote he had once heard.

"Yes, I think it's time. I'll have to keep my eyes open and find you a suitable wife," Sylvia plotted. "Someone with money and position. She can be pretty, too, of course. But not too pretty."

"What about us?" Roger inquired.

"What about us?" she repeated, blinking.

He made a vague movement with his hand. "You know—"

"I'm afraid I don't know."

He lowered his voice to an intimate level. "I'm talking about sex."

Sylvia patted his hand as if to say he'd always been a good boy. "I don't mind sharing you with a wife, if you don't mind sharing a wife with me."

For a moment or two Roger Forbes seemed uncertain whether Sylvia was teasing him or actually serious. Then he laughed—it was a particularly vulgar sound—and said, "You are naughty, Sylvia."

Yes, she was naughty.

Even naughtier than Roger could imagine.

They didn't think she knew anything.

They thought she was stupid.

She had once heard her father—her stepfather; they weren't related, thank God—refer to her as a stupid cow.

She had cried for two days. Then she had realized that Roger was the stupid one.

She wasn't clever, perhaps. But she wasn't dumb, either. She was smart enough to know the difference.

Besides, she kept her eyes and ears open, and her mouth shut. She heard things. She saw things. She even spotted things: open letters left on a desk, telephone messages scribbled on a pad of paper, old photographs and new ones, too.

And she remembered it all.

She knew about them: her grandmother—who wasn't really her grandmother—and her stepfather.

He had married Mummy when Nadine was twelve and then Mummy had died, and her grandfather had died the following year, and then there had just been Sylvia and Roger and her in what had once been her grandfather's house; the one person she had always loved, the only home she had ever really known.

They had ruined it, of course.

They had sold most of the furniture she had grown up with and replaced it with modern sofas and tables. They filled the house with clever society people and she had never been good at small talk. She usually retreated to her room when Sylvia was throwing one of her parties; which was frequently.

They did it.

She could hear them in the middle of the night when they thought she was sound asleep and it was safe to sneak down the corridor from *her* bedroom to *his*.

She had seen them once, doing it in the loo: Sylvia's white thighs parted and Roger standing between them, thrusting into her. Sylvia's breasts had jiggled in time to the pumping of his even whiter and hairy backside.

Her step-grandmother had made pathetic little mewing sounds and Roger had breathed heavily, sweated heavily, and groaned, biting his lips apparently to keep from making an even louder and more obscene sound when he had finally come.

At first she had thought it was disgusting.

But only at first.

Then she had decided it was funny and she'd had to cram her fist into her mouth to keep from laughing out loud and giving herself away.

Sylvia was a liar.

She had lied about the cost of her new dress when Roger asked to see the bill.

She had lied about the new employee who served as butler, chauffeur, and all-around servant at what used to be her grandfather's house in town. Sylvia pretended not to be able to stand the sight of the man. Yet she had seen Sylvia kissing him in the pantry one afternoon, her hand grabbing his crotch.

And she lied about her age.

She lied about everything.

She had even lied just now to Roger about why they were here on the Isle of Storm.

Nadine slipped away from the door—it had been left ajar only an inch or two, but an inch or two was enough. She silently retraced her steps back down the hallway.

She stopped, turned, put a pretty and vacant smile on her pretty and vacant face and walked up the corridor, making sure the heels of her shoes clicked noisily on the floor.

Then she knocked, just to be certain they'd heard her, and entered the drawing room.

Chapter 12

"The name's Ned," the man informed them as he opened the rear passenger door of the automobile and, with a motion that could only be described as both a polite bow and a grand sweeping gesture, coaxed Torey and Alice into the vintage Rolls-Royce.

"I'm—"

"You're Miss Victoria Storm and the lady with you is Miss Alice Fraser," Ned announced, seeming rather pleased with himself for having jumped the gun and anticipated the introduction.

"How—?"

"Every living soul within fifty miles knows who you two ladies are. It isn't every day of the week that we get Americans visiting these parts," he bragged.

"I dare say they don't," Alice murmured in an aside to her as they settled in.

Their driver replaced his tam-o'-shanter. He had removed his cap upon greeting them as they had disembarked from the train only moments before.

" 'Course we get more and more visitors in Scotland every year from the States," he said. "They're all searching for their Scottish—roots, I believe the word is."

Then he slammed the door shut after them and went to see to their luggage.

Torey and Alice could clearly hear, through the closed window of the ancient Rolls, Ned bellowing in his Scottish burr. "Hey, Murdo, get a move on it, laddie."

Murdo, tall, thin and seemingly bone without muscle, was struggling under the weight of their suitcases.

"Lord Storm expects these ladies to be on the last ferry out this evening and arrive at the castle in time for dinner."

Once the luggage was stowed—it seemed to require a great deal of animated discussion and three separate attempts in order to get it all to fit properly in the boot—they were finally on their way.

Torey leaned forward slightly from the back seat and inquired discreetly of the gentleman behind the steering wheel, "Excuse me, sir." The "sir" was in deference to his age; he was seventy if he was a day. "Did you say your name is Ned?"

"That's me. Ned. Just Plain Ned. No 'sir' about it," he chattered as he started the engine.

Ned drove off from the train station through a small, picturesque village until he came to an intersection.

It was two country roads crisscrossing in the middle of nowhere, as far as Torey could tell.

There wasn't another car or truck—were trucks called lorries here in Scotland?—or a vehicle of any kind in sight. Or, for that matter, a bicycle or a horse or even a human on foot.

Nevertheless, Ned slammed on the brakes, craned his neck to look both ways, first to the left and then to the right, snatched off his cap with the traditional pompon in the center, scratched his head, replaced his tam, then turned down the road clearly marked with a sign that read: THIS WAY TO FERRY.

Once the Rolls-Royce was lined up waiting to go aboard—there were perhaps a dozen cars ahead of them in the queue for the ferry—Ned resumed his conversation right where he'd left off a half hour before. "No doubt you ladies will be meeting Young Ned, as well, while you're visiting the Isle of Storm."

"Young Ned would be your . . . ?" Torey allowed him to finish the sentence.

"Son." The man nodded. "Young Ned's the oldest of five." He nodded again, his pompon bobbing slightly. "All boys."

"You and your wife must be very proud to have five sons," Torey remarked, not knowing what else to say.

Ned glanced in the rearview mirror and announced, "You'll be meeting Old Ned, too."

"Old Ned is your . . . ?"

"Father."

"Of course," said Torey.

"My, what a great of number of Neds you have in your family," observed Alice, without any marked change in her tone of voice or her facial expression.

Ned chuckled and lightly whacked his palm on the steering wheel several times. "We've got more Neds than you can shake a stick at, misses."

Since Ned—Plain Ned, as he had referred to himself—appeared to be in his early seventies, Torey couldn't help but wonder just how old that made Old Ned.

She cleared her throat. "Your father must be a gentleman of some advanced years."

Ned wrinkled up his face into a grimace, took a gander at her in the rearview mirror, and, raising the volume of his voice a decibel or two, said, "Pardon, miss? I'm afraid I didn't hear the question."

It hadn't really been a question.

Torey raised her voice slightly and hoped that Ned could hear her. "May I ask how old your father is?"

"Old Ned's getting up there."

"I imagine he is."

"Must be ninety-two now." Their sometime driver rubbed the back of his neck, inadvertently sending his cap flying forward and partially down over his eyes. "I take that back." He adjusted his tam. "Dad was ninety-three on his last birthday."

"Ninety-three," Torey repeated, impressed.

"You mustn't hesitate to talk to Old Ned about his age. He's very proud of his years."

"He should be."

"Why, there isn't anything about the history and legends of the Clan, or Castle Storm, or the Isle of Storm, or the whole of the Western Isles, for that matter, that Old Ned doesn't know better than any soul . . . any living soul, that is."

The queue of vehicles began to file onto the ferry. Ned put the Rolls into gear and they followed in turn.

"You can get out and stretch your legs for a wee bit, ladies, if you have half a mind to," he told them. "We have two other islands to stop at along the way, so it will take us nearly another hour to reach the Isle of Storm."

It was like something out of a dream.

At first Torey thought it might be a mirage, or a mere figment of her imagination rising up from the dark silver-blue waters, or a dream, a long-past dream.

There were phantom mountains in the distance. They

were all shadow and mist, without form, without substance. Surely they weren't real.

They couldn't be real.

The sky was that rare and breathtaking shade of pink and yellow and colors for which there was no description, created by the setting sun as it slipped for a moment behind a strata of wispy clouds.

Then the sun broke through in a burst of pure light illuminating the island and the great, towering fortress built upon its crest.

All was suddenly turned to gold.

There was a shimmering golden island afloat in a shimmering golden sea with a shimmering golden castle at its center.

It was like something out of a dream.

"There's Young Ned now, coming at us in a great rush," pointed out his father as they drove up into the courtyard of Castle Storm.

Young Ned, fifty and hair already graying, was out of breath. He went straight toward his father, knocked on the window of the automobile with his knuckles, and announced the minute the window had been lowered even partway down, "Lord Storm needs to see the young lady immediately."

"Which one? I have two young ladies with me," Ned said, forever endearing himself to Alice Fraser.

Young Ned had his orders. "You're to take Miss Fraser inside and Mrs. Pyle will show the lady to her rooms. I'm to escort Miss Storm directly to his lordship."

"Doesn't make sense," Ned said, shaking his head and, once more, dislodging his tam-o'-shanter.

"Doesn't have to make sense to us," his offspring stated.

"True enough, Young Ned. True enough." Ned opened his door and climbed out from behind the wheel while Young Ned saw to the ladies. Then he said to his passengers, "You heard the lad as well as I did. I'll take Miss Fraser to the housekeeper, and you, Miss Storm, are to go directly to Lord Storm."

"If you'll follow me, then miss, it's this way," Young Ned said, fingering his own cap and one very similar to his father's.

"Of course," Torey replied. She'd find out soon enough, no doubt, what this business was all about. "Lead the way."

They circled around the huge tower of Castle Storm, cut between passageways so narrow that they had to walk single file, and finally came to a door that looked out over the sea.

Torey paused for a moment, wanting to enjoy the view.

"Please, come along, miss," urged Young Ned, "or it'll be my head for sure."

She assumed it was merely a figure of speech.

"Are you married, Ned?" Torey inquired as they cut down a remote corridor.

"Young Ned," he quickly corrected. "And I certainly am."

"Do you have any children?"

He nodded his head. "Three sons and three daughters."

"Are any of them named Ned?"

He chuckled and stuffed his cap into the pocket of his trousers. "Only one of the boys."

Torey chuckled along with him. "Of course. Your oldest son, no doubt."

"Yup, my oldest is Ned."

She wondered what in the world they called him to differentiate between his Ned, Young Ned, Plain Ned and Old Ned. She had to ask. "What do you call him?"

"What do I call who, miss?"

"Your oldest son."

"Just Ned."

"Doesn't that get confusing for your family?"

He seemed puzzled by her question. "No."

"But all the men in your family have the same name."

Young Ned opened a door, stood back gallantly, and waited for her to enter before him. "There's Just Ned, that's my oldest. There's Young Ned, that's me. There's Plain Ned, that my father. Then there's Old Ned, my granddad. We don't have any trouble keeping it straight, miss." He closed the door behind them. "But I suppose we're used to it."

"By the way," she asked, peering ahead of them, "where are we going exactly?"

"The earl's bedroom."

"Did you say the earl's bedroom?"

"I did, Miss Storm. Ever since Castle Storm was built—well, at least since this wing was added in about 1371—this has been the private room or bedroom of the laird."

Torey noticed the walls appeared to be several feet thick in this section of the castle. Judging by the depth of the windows—which would have been added at a later date, presumably when the likelihood of enemy attack had disappeared, or, at least, had diminished greatly— some sections of wall must have originally been five or six feet thick.

Castle Storm was a veritable fortress.

"Here we are now, miss." Young Ned knocked at the door at the end of the corridor.

There was a muffled "Enter."

Young Ned turned the great hand-carved wooden knob, opened the door, ushered Torey into the room, quickly backed out, and closed the door behind him.

Mitchell strode into the sitting room from what was obviously the bedroom beyond. He was dressed in a traditional kilt, but he had yet to button his dress shirt, or add a tie, or put on an evening jacket.

He still hadn't taken time for a haircut, Torey noticed.

His hair was even longer than before. It fell in dark brown waves that tempted her to take a brush to it, then muss it up again on purpose, just so she could brush his hair a second time.

Mitchell was still intently involved with his shirt cuff. He appeared to be struggling with a button or a cuff link.

Torey used those few moments before he looked up to enjoy—to savor—the very sight of him. He was a magnificent man.

And she was in love with him.

Mitchell glanced up at that exact moment. "You're here." It was neither enthusiasm nor censure she heard in his voice; it was pure and simple relief.

"I'm here."

"And Alice?"

"Alice is here, too."

"Mrs. Pyle will be showing her to her rooms and getting her settled, I imagine."

Which was where she would like to be and what she would like to be doing as well, Torey almost blurted out.

"I know you'd like to be doing the same."

So, he could still read her mind.

"Traditionally, on the first evening of their arrival, we excuse guests who have traveled long distances from dressing and joining us for dinner downstairs," he explained. "They have the option of taking a tray in their private rooms."

"But—"

"But tonight I need you and Alice to join us in the formal dining room."

Mitchell was on edge; Torey could feel it.

"Why?" she asked.

An expression of irritation crossed his handsome face. "There are other guests present in the house." There was the briefest of pauses. "Unexpected guests."

"Unexpected as in uninvited?"

He nodded.

She bit the corners of her mouth against the temptation of a smile. "I know what that's like."

Mitchell had the good graces to appear somewhat chagrined. "I'm afraid this isn't quite the same situation."

Torey laughed. "Ah, then you haven't put your guests to work as waiters at your party."

"This is no laughing matter, Torey," Mitchell said as he began to pace the floor.

"I can see that."

He halted and made one more frustrated attempt to deal with the cuff links at his wrists. Then he threw his hands up in exasperation. "Bloody things."

"Let me help you," she volunteered, deciding it was time to come to his rescue. "You obviously need my help."

His eyes widened with appreciation. "That's it exactly. How did you guess? I do need your help."

She finished his sleeves and looked up at him. "It wasn't hard to figure out, Mitchell. You've been fussing with your shirt since I walked into the room."

"My shirt?"

"Yes, your shirt."

His frustration began anew. "I'm not talking about needing help with my shirt."

Well, he had needed her help with it, whether he liked to think so or not.

A woman did what a woman had to do.

Torey remained calm and serene, and asked in a similarly calm and serene manner, using simple words and simple sentences, which always seem to work best when a man was upset, "Something is bothering you. You need help. You're asking for my help."

"That's it exactly," he exclaimed.

She'd thought so.

"What is the problem, Mitchell?"

He began to pace again, up and down the floor of his sitting room. "I can't get rid of them."

"You mean your uninvited guests."

He moved his head affirmatively. "They had already finagled their way into the house, and into the good graces of my housekeeper and staff by the time The MacClumpha and I arrived back home a week ago. And they don't seem the least bit inclined to leave anytime soon."

"In other words, they won't budge, huh?" Torey shrugged and pushed her hair back from her face. She'd had a similar problem once with the Deweys.

Dreadful people, the Deweys.

She asked Mitchell outright, "Do you want them to leave?"

He nodded his head vigorously. "Yes. They're nothing more than acquaintances and bloody bores at that."

"There are worse things."

"I knew you'd understand, Torey. It does get worse." It suddenly occurred to Mitchell that he was forgetting his manners. "Would you like to sit down while I fill you in?"

"No, thank you. We've been sitting most of the day: first on the plane, then the train, and then the car that met us at the station. I think I'll stand."

The man was obviously too keyed up to sit down himself.

He explained as he continued to pace, "There are three uninvited individuals who have taken up residence at Castle Storm: A fifty-something society matron named Mrs. Forbes; her stepson, Roger Forbes; and a kind of unrelated—from what I can gather—step-granddaughter named Nadine."

"I suppose you can hardly claim that you don't have room for them," she said, tapping a fingernail against her lips and recalling the size of the castle as they'd driven up into the courtyard.

"The grandmother is pushy. The stepson is obnoxious, and the granddaughter is a sweet, simple girl—and I do mean simple."

Torey was beginning to get the feeling there was more to this tale than Mitchell was coming out and telling her.

"Go on," she urged.

He drove his fingers through his hair in a gesture she had come to love. "I think Mrs. Forbes has me earmarked."

"Earmarked for what?"

"Not for what. For who."

The light dawned. "For Nadine?"

He stopped pacing. "For Nadine."

Her heart skipped a beat or two. "Is there something wrong with that?"

Mitchell suddenly exploded in anger. "Christ, nothing beyond the fact that I've scarcely exchanged more than two words with the girl ever, or the fact that she's eighteen or nineteen years old and practically young enough to be my daughter.''

Torey stood and listened.

''Or the fact that I have no interest in Nadine whatsoever. But I don't want to intentionally hurt her feelings, either. I feel sorry for the kid. That's all.''

''Not exactly grounds for matrimony,'' Torey agreed.

''When I do choose to marry it won't be to a girl like Nadine Forbes, who has a step-grandmother and a stepfather that I can't stand to be in the same room with for five minutes.''

''Well, you do have a valid point or two why this particular marriage would never work.''

''Or three or four or a bloody hundred,'' he growled.

Torey wondered what Mitchell wanted from her.

''I need a favor.''

''From me?''

He nodded.

So, that was it.

''What kind of favor?''

He rubbed his large, graceful hands together. ''At dinner tonight I would really appreciate it if you would give the impression that you're here on approval.''

Torey stiffened. ''What kind of approval?''

She could almost hear the wheels churning in his handsome head. ''To see if you like Castle Storm and the Isle of Storm. To determine if you would want to live here on the island.''

Oh, boy, what was she getting herself into now?

''Why? Am I supposed to be thinking of buying it from you?'' Torey inquired.

He regarded her with incredulity. ''Good God, no.''

''Then what?''

Mitchell Storm raised his eyes heavenward; he appeared to be asking the Almighty for patience. "You are supposed to be thinking of marrying me."

"Marrying you?"

"These are not subtle individuals, Torey. They just won't get it otherwise."

"Marrying you?"

"Trust me, a charade is the easiest way of dealing with people like the Forbeses."

"Marrying you?"

"Yes. Marrying me."

Chapter 13

"I understand that congratulations are in order, Lord Storm," Sylvia Forbes purred like a feline—a pampered and preened and overindulged feline—the minute Mitchell entered the drawing room for drinks with his guests before dinner.

Mitchell wasn't rude, but he wasn't exactly polite, either.

He simply was.

"Thank you, Mrs. Forbes." He helped himself to a Scotch whisky, a double shot in a large glass, no water, no soda, no ice. He deserved a drink, and something told him he was going to need one before this evening was over.

"Sylvia, surely."

"Thank you, Sylvia," he said with indifference, wondering all the while how in the hell he was going to get rid of the woman, her stepson, and her step-granddaughter.

"Congratulations?" echoed Roger Forbes, who, Mitchell noticed, had already helped himself to a glass of his finest and who apparently did not have access to the same gossip network within Castle Storm as his stepmother.

"Yes," Sylvia Forbes said with all apparent good wishes, but she didn't fool Mitchell for a second—the words contained pure venom. "It seems that our host has recently become engaged."

Roger Forbes's overly handsome brow creased in puzzlement. "Engaged?"

"Yes. Engaged as in the step one takes before one decides to enter the state of holy matrimony," his stepmother explained unnecessarily as she slinked across the drawing room and made herself comfortable in Mitchell's favorite chair.

"It must have been a very recent engagement," Roger said, failing to offer his own congratulations.

"It was," Mitchell replied without elaborating.

Just how recent they would never know.

"You met while you were in America, I believe," commented the elegant woman with the champagne-colored hair, the champagne-colored skin, the champagne-colored dress.

"My fiancée is an American," he agreed, taking a healthy swallow of undiluted whisky.

It burned all the way down.

Sylvia sipped daintily at her glass of sherry. "And the woman is a cousin of yours, I understand."

Mitchell shifted his weight restlessly from one foot to the other and back again.

Where was Alice?

And where was The MacClumpha?

And where in the hell was Torey?

"A cousin?" repeated his uninvited female guest.

"A distant cousin," he finally answered vaguely as he paced back and forth in front of the fireplace.

"How very cozy to keep it all in the family," the felinelike creature said smoothly.

With a look that had been known to make lesser men tremble in their shoes, Mitchell speared the woman with his eyes. "How cozy to keep all of *what* in the family, Mrs. Forbes?"

She sputtered for a moment. Then she made an inconclusive gesture that seemed to encompass the drawing room, the 1812 wing, the entire castle, the gardens, the island, most of Scotland, and a good portion of the world beyond.

It was at that fortuitous moment the door to the drawing room opened and in walked Alice Fraser.

Mitchell turned. He heaved a sigh of genuine relief. "You're looking very lovely tonight, Alice."

"Thank you, Mitchell."

And she was.

Alice Fraser was wearing a long silk dress that seemed to emphasize the natural rosy hue to her complexion and the golden highlights in her otherwise undistinguished brown hair.

Her hair was brushed back from her face and swept up into a barrette that looked suspiciously like real diamonds.

On loan from Torey, perhaps?

Alice also appeared to be wearing makeup. Just enough to bring out the best in her features: her eyes and her smile.

Mitchell wondered if Iain MacClumpha had anything to do with Miss Fraser's . . . with Alice's efforts at a transformation.

Roger Forbes, who was already on his second very large glass of madeira, looked from Mitchell to Alice and back again to Mitchell, and said, "Well, aren't you going to at least do the honor of introducing us to your fiancée, Storm?''

''Of course, I'd be delighted to when—''

At that moment Mitchell heard a footfall just outside the door of the drawing room.

He knew it was Torey.

Then the door quietly opened and she swept gracefully and effortlessly into the room.

Mitchell smiled.

Torey had outdone herself tonight.

She was ravishing in a simple but elegant designer gown. The dress fit her perfectly in every way. The style showed her unequaled figure to advantage. The color seemed to capture and emphasize both the green and the blue in her eyes, and the porcelainlike quality to her skin. Her hair was arranged in a style that created the perfect frame for her features.

She looked like a million dollars.

She looked like several million.

''Mrs. Sylvia Forbes ... Mr. Roger Forbes ...'' Mitchell was taking genuine pleasure, he realized, from the circumstances in which he found himself. In fact, he decided to savor the moment. ''May I present Victoria Storm, my cousin and my fiancée?''

It was Roger who muttered under his breath, very softly but very distinctly, ''Shit.''

They didn't know she could hear them talking.

But she could.

Something had gone wrong.

Very wrong.

Something had not gone according to their plans.

They had lowered their voices as soon as they had come upstairs tonight, shutting the door to *her* bedroom completely and tightly so no one could hear them, but she always found a way to listen—and to see—and she knew they were arguing.

"You're an ass, Roger," Sylvia cried out softly.

"So are you," he threw right back at her.

Then he gave her a playful slap on the backside. It must have stung a little, but *she* didn't seem to mind. In fact, Nadine suspected that her "grandmother" rather enjoyed the occasional spanking.

Roger bent over, unsteadily, and pressed his mouth to the back of Sylvia's dress. "Well, you've got a nice ass to kiss, anyway."

"How could you?"

"How could I *what*?" he demanded to know, slurring his words, standing up.

Roger had had too much to drink again. The signs were all there: the slurred speech, the swaggering attitude, the slightly unsteady movements of his hands, his unbridled interest in sex.

He always tried to get between Sylvia's legs when he'd had too much to drink.

"How could you do the things you did and say the things you said tonight in front of Lord Storm and that ravishing creature he has made his fiancée?"

"She's a looker."

"She is a beautiful young woman."

"At first you thought it was the other woman, the rather more ordinary woman, now didn't you, Sylvia?"

She sniffed. "I had my hopes."

"It would have made the whole thing so much easier if it had been Alice Fraser."

"Yes, it would have made it easier."

"Of course," Roger pointed out, "looks aren't everything."

"No. They aren't," she said, looking back over her shoulder at him with a sarcastic smile on her aging face.

Grandmother always looked older in certain light.

"So what do we do now?" Roger wanted to know.

Sylvia Forbes got that expression on her face. It was one that Nadine had seen before.

She knew what it meant. It meant that her step-grandmother had another plan up her sleeve.

"Believe me," the woman proclaimed as she allowed Roger to paw her breasts. "There isn't an engagement made that can't be broken."

Chapter 14

"Believe me, Torey, there isn't an engagement made that can't be broken," Mitchell assured her as she marched into his private sitting room the following afternoon.

"You said I was supposed to be thinking about marrying you." She pointed her index finger at him. "You didn't say one word about an official engagement."

"There is a very thin line between considering marriage to a man and being engaged to him."

"You're splitting hairs, Mitchell."

He seemed disinclined to argue with her. "It was a last-minute decision." He licked his lips. "I was desperate."

Torey raised an auburn eyebrow into a questioning arch. "A great big man like you intimidated by one gray-haired little old lady, her annoying stepson, and a young girl." She planted her hands on her hips. "What's wrong with this picture?"

He scowled. "What gray-haired little old lady?"

She didn't mean to be catty, but the truth was, after all, the truth. "*Magna est veritas et praevalebit.*"

Mitchell translated almost instantaneously: "Truth is mighty and will prevail."

"So will gray roots."

"Ah . . . Mrs. Forbes dyes her hair. She wouldn't be the first woman—or man, for that matter—who has tried to appear younger than they are."

"And I certainly wouldn't hold it against her if she would behave herself, otherwise," Torey stated.

"She isn't behaving herself?"

"Let's just say that Sylvia Forbes and subtlety are unlikely to be mentioned in the same breath—ever."

"What has the woman been up to?"

That couldn't be amusement on his face, Torey thought.

"At breakfast this morning—and I noticed you managed to absent yourself quite nicely, by the way."

"I decided to take breakfast early with The Mac-Clumpha. We had a great deal of business to see to on the estate."

It was a reasonable answer.

"Well, I had a most fascinating conversation with Mrs. Forbes over bacon and eggs and something called *sulfock* on the subject of inbreeding and its unfortunate consequences," she informed him.

Mitchell coughed.

"I told Mrs. Forbes that I knew nothing about sheep or their breeding habits and that she should take up the matter with you."

Mitchell laughed out loud.

Torey wasn't amused. She was curious, however. "By the way, what is *sulfock*?"

"You don't want to know."

"Why don't I?"

"Sometimes ignorance is bliss."

"Very rarely. What is it?"

"Don't say I didn't warn you." He took a breath. "It's an acquired taste."

"Mitchell—"

"It's traditionally served with bacon and eggs."

"I know that."

She waited.

"*Sulfock* is a black pudding made with pig blood."

Torey felt the blood drain from her head. "You shouldn't have told me," she said accusingly, pressing her hand to her stomach.

"I did warn you."

"But I didn't believe you. Why didn't you tell me that like *haggis*, it's best not to know exactly what one is eating?"

"You know about *haggis*, then."

"Mrs. Forbes described it while we were in the middle of breakfast."

"She is naughty."

"She is insufferable." Torey could feel the heat rising in her cheeks. "At lunch—which I noticed you also managed to be absent from—"

"The MacClumpha and I were out in the fields checking on the sheep."

" 'The sheep are in the meadow; the cows are in the corn,' " she paraphrased the old nursery rhyme.

"We don't raise cattle on the island."

"Well, after luncheon Sylvia took me aside for a tête-à-tête. She said as a woman of more experience and a few years, and since she had heard that I was both motherless and fatherless—indeed, I had scarcely a living relation in the world except yourself, of course—she felt it was her duty to warn me about you."

Mitchell's head came up sharply. "Warn you about me?"

"Yes. She claims that you want to marry me for nefarious reasons. Three nefarious reasons, as a matter of fact."

"Naturally, you're going to tell me what those three supposedly nefarious reasons are."

"Naturally." She ticked them off on her fingers one by one. "The first reason you want to marry me is for my money. I have a great deal of money, she understands, and you need a great deal of money, she has heard. In fact, did I know that the roof leaks?"

"I told you about the roof."

"Yes, you did."

"Go on." He didn't seem to be enjoying this part of the story as much as he had the earlier recitations of Scottish fare.

"The second reason is revenge."

"Revenge?" That seemed to leave him confounded.

"Mrs. Forbes knows a great deal about Clan Storm. The woman has done her homework thoroughly. She was acquainted with a surprising number of details concerning the falling-out between the twin brothers over a century ago."

"The woman is a damned snoop," he swore as he crossed the sitting room to the bookcase and stared at the books inside. Torey didn't think he was actually seeing them. He was seeing red.

"Revenge. That is the most ridiculous reason, in this day and age, I have ever heard for marrying someone." He went to the window and looked out. It gave him, she could see from her vantage point, a clear view of the stone ramparts and the battlements overlooking the sea. "What was the third reason?"

Torey wasn't sure she wanted to tell him what Sylvia

had divulged as the third and most degrading reason for his wanting to marry her.

He turned. "What was the last reason?"

She mumbled, "Base animal attraction."

He frowned. "What?"

"Sexual attraction."

"Well, at least Mrs. Forbes was right one out of three times."

"What is that supposed to mean?"

He spelled it out loud and clear. There was no room for misunderstanding. "It means that if I were going to marry you it would certainly be based on a mutual sexual attraction."

"Mutual," she burst out.

Mitchell raised one hand. "Let's not start telling each other lies at this stage of the game."

"Is it a game?"

"You know what I mean. We are attracted to each other and there is no reason to deny it to ourselves or to each other."

Torey decided not to comment further on the subject. Besides, she knew he was right.

Then she spotted something familiar propped against the wall of the connecting room beyond the one they were in—the laird's bedroom, according to Young Ned—and went to investigate. "What are you up to?" she inquired.

Leaning against the wall was the painting of Queen Victoria they had brought from the study at Storm Point. Next to it was the large, commemorative plaque discovered in the Prince of Wales wing, and on a small table nearby sat the bronze figurine and the chess piece. Every Victoria was there except the piece of garden statuary;

due to its size and weight, it was still in transit from the States.

Mitchell took in a breath and released it. "I'm trying to put the pieces of a puzzle together." Then after a period of silence, he said, "I'll bet you're clever at puzzles."

Torey smiled to herself. "Is that your own peerless way, Lord Storm, of asking me if I'll help you solve this one?"

His entire face brightened. "Would you mind?"

"Of course, I wouldn't mind." Silly man. "Tell me what you know so far."

He invited her to take the chair comfortably situated in front of the grouping and moved another seat over beside her for himself.

She gave him a sidelong glance. "What have you been doing?"

"When?"

"Since you brought this collection of Victorias back to Scotland with you over a week ago. Have you been sitting here staring at them every night?"

Mitchell nodded his head, leaned forward from the waist, rested his elbows on his knees, drove his hands through his hair in utter frustration, and announced, "I'm not a stupid man, Torey."

Of course he wasn't. He was considered brilliant, in fact. "I'm well aware of that," she told him.

"Well, I feel stupid."

How was she to respond to that? "I guess we all feel stupid at times."

"But I can't even seem to get to the fifty-yard line with this one," he stated.

"Fifty-yard line?"

He eyed her. "It's a football term."

"That's right. You played football, didn't you? For the University of Texas."

He nodded. "In this case, what I'm saying is that I seem to be getting nowhere fast."

"In other words, you don't have a clue."

"Oh, I have clues." He motioned toward the menagerie. "They just don't make any sense."

Torey decided it was time to take a logical approach to the problem. "Let's start at the beginning and take it step by step. You're attempting to locate a long-lost family treasure."

"Yes."

"Are you even certain that such a treasure exists?"

"No."

She stifled a groan of dismay. "We will, for the sake of argument, assume there is a long-lost treasure. Do you have any idea what form it's in?"

Mitchell's handsome brow creased. "Form?"

"Physical form. For example, is it a historical artifact? Or precious gemstones? Perhaps jewelry? Or an original manuscript? Rare coins? Holy relics?"

"I don't know."

Torey didn't wish to add to Mitchell's already obvious distress. She concluded on a hopeful note. "Well, considering the distinguished ancestry and the notable importance of Clan Storm throughout history, it's possible, even probable, that the treasure could be in any one or in several of those forms."

"It could, couldn't it?"

"Certainly it could." She sat back in the chair he had provided for her, crossed one leg over the other, reached for the gold chain around her neck, wrapped it around her index finger, and stared at the collection gathered in front of her.

One minute passed.

Then another.

After some minutes of silence—Torey would have estimated five or ten minutes if she had cared to guess how long it had been since they'd last spoken—Mitchell asked her, "What are you doing?"

She unraveled the chain from around her finger and murmured, "Thinking."

He closed his mouth again.

She finally took a deep breath and exhaled. "What first gave you the idea that a Victoria was the key?"

Mitchell shrugged. "Common knowledge."

"Common knowledge?"

"It's always been known within the family."

"Then why didn't your grandfather or your great-grandfather or any of the other Earls of Storm who came before you try to find the Victoria and the treasure?"

"They did," he said simply.

"Which of them?"

"All of them."

"And they all failed to find it?"

"And they all failed to find it."

That did not bode well. "Please tell me again the exact words your grandfather said to you on that last day."

Mitchell seemed to have them memorized. "He pulled my head down and said very clearly: 'You must find the treasure. The key is in America. Go to America and bring back Victoria.'"

Quietly, and without any disrespect meant to the late William Storm, Torey said, "Were they the words of a delirious and dying man? Or a final message given by a man who felt compelled to pass on the quest to the next generation?"

"Those are the same questions I've asked myself over and over again," Mitchell admitted.

"What do we know?" Torey rubbed her eyes and repeated softly, "What do we know?" She raised her head and stared straight ahead. "We know there was an auction. We know that a number of family heirlooms were bought up by agents of Andrew Storm and shipped to America."

Mitchell voiced the opposite query. "What *don't* we know?"

"We don't know why your grandfather assumed or knew the key was in America." Torey glanced around his bedroom without looking for anything specific. "Why wouldn't the key be here in Scotland, on the Isle of Storm, in Castle Storm itself?"

Mitchell blew out his breath.

She turned and looked directly at him. "Do you ever get these feelings?"

Was this one of those trick questions women liked to ask men, Mitchell wondered as he stared right back at Torey.

"What kind of feelings?" he finally asked.

"Gut feelings."

She had no idea the feelings he got in his gut and in several other parts of his anatomy when she looked at him with those incredible blue-green eyes of hers.

"Do you mean like basic instincts?"

"Sort of."

He was obviously barking up the wrong tree. He snapped his fingers together. "Feminine intuition?"

"Kind of."

"A feeling of déjà vu?"

"I think everyone has experienced a feeling of déjà vu at some point in their lives, don't you?"

That wasn't it, then.

Mitchell tried again. "Premonition?"

Torey caught the tip of her tongue between her teeth. "That's closer to what I mean. But it's more a sense of right and wrong about things." Here she stopped herself and clarified, "I don't mean a moral sense of right and wrong." She uttered a sigh and seemed to give up trying to explain it to him.

He suddenly understood. "You're talking about a feeling, a knowing, a sense of rightness and wrongness when it comes to things, to people, to places, even to events."

"Yes," she said, concentrating on her hands.

Mitchell hadn't really studied her hands before.

He did so now.

They were slightly small, fine-boned, long-fingered, perfectly formed, yet somehow they gave the impression of being . . . capable, that was the word. He realized he wouldn't mind in the least putting himself quite literally into this woman's hands.

He made himself look away. "What is it you have this gut feeling about?"

"It's what I don't have a feeling about."

Now he was more than a little confused. "Would you mind running that by me again?"

Torey made a gesture that was meant to encompass the assorted Victorias in front of them. "I don't have a feeling of rightness about any of them."

A muscle in his face started to twitch. "Translation?"

"I don't feel any of these objects are the Victoria you're looking for, Mitchell. I don't think any of them are the key to you finding your treasure."

That wasn't what he wanted to hear.

She appeared anxious. "Do you think I'm crazy?"

"Not any more than the rest of us mere mortals," he muttered, half in jest.

"Does it sound . . . *odd* to you?"

"You mean the fact that you sometimes get these special feelings?"

Torey nodded and avoided his eyes.

"Are you kidding?" Mitchell turned halfway in his chair, took her by the shoulders and forced her to look at him. "Do you know what it's called in Gaelic?"

Her head moved slowly from side to side, followed by a whisper. "No."

"Well, I'll tell you—and I have to warn you that my pronunciation stinks—it's referred to as *taibhse* or *Da-Shealladh*, which literally means the 'two sights,' or 'second sight.' " Mitchell went on. "This is a country that still believes in good omens and bad omens, lucky days and unlucky days, ghosts and fairies, the foretelling of events, especially unhappy or tragic ones. Hell, having the gift of the 'sight' used to be so common in Scotland that every clan and township had its official *filed* or seer." He released his grip on her. "Why, only recently The MacClumpha was bemoaning the fact that I don't appear to possess the 'gift.' He claims it would come in real handy sometimes."

Torey seemed heartened by what he'd related to her, but she added a disclaimer, "I could be wrong about the Victorias, of course."

"You could be."

But he didn't think so.

And he didn't think she did, either.

Torey stood and stretched, arching her back slightly. They had been sitting for longer than either had evidently realized. "Where does that leave us?"

Mitchell's stomach growled. "Hungry."

She laughed. "Hungry?"

He checked his watch. "We'll be late for tea."

"And we certainly wouldn't want to miss the opportunity to spend another meal *en famille* with Sylvia Forbes and her assorted offspring."

Mitchell didn't detect so much as a trace of sarcasm in Torey's tone of voice, but it must have been there.

"We could always have tea for two sent up," he said with a twinkle in his eye.

"On second thought, we mustn't ignore your guests," she quickly countered.

"They aren't my guests."

"By the way, remind me sometime to share my feelings with you concerning Nadine."

Mitchell changed his mind; he wasn't that hungry. In fact, he was fast losing his appetite. "Let's take the long way around to the drawing room," he suggested.

The long way around led them down an ancient, and at one time secret, staircase, along a row of gunloops, which he explained to Torey had been part of the castle's earliest defense systems, past some of the thickest and oldest sections of the castle walls and through a wooden door that opened up onto a private garden.

"This is lovely," Torey exclaimed to him when she saw where they had ended up.

Mitchell hadn't been in the secluded garden in weeks, in months. He had forgotten how lovely and how private the spot was. "Yes, it is," he agreed.

Torey strolled under a natural arbor created by an impressive wisteria. "I wonder how long the garden has been here."

"A long time," he volunteered.

Her mouth turned up at the corners. "That long?"

"Maybe even longer."

They walked past a garden bench recessed into a brick archway. It was large enough for two.

No more.

No less.

Torey paused. "A love seat, do you think?"

Mitchell raised and lowered his shoulders in a shrug. "Maybe."

"Maybe more than one laird, in his time, came down the same way we did, and met his ladylove here in secret," she concocted.

A secluded garden. A beautiful and desirable woman. A woman he hadn't had to himself in far too long. A woman he wanted . . . badly. It was enough to give any man ideas, Mitchell Storm had to admit to himself.

He took a step toward Torey.

At that same instant she glanced over his shoulder, saw something or someone behind him, propelled herself toward him and said in an urgent tone, "Kiss me, Mitchell."

Chapter 15

So he kissed her.

Without hesitation. Without a single reservation on his part. Without even asking why she was suddenly insisting that he kiss her.

He pulled Torey into his arms and took her mouth eagerly, hungrily, demandingly with his own. He emptied his head of every other thought and filled it with thoughts only of her: the soft compliance of her lips, the sweet intoxication of her taste, the scent that was hers alone and that always eluded him when he tried to pin it down.

He never wanted to come up for air. He would live and breathe through her breath. He would survive by eating and drinking what she offered him as sustenance.

Mitchell knew he must touch her. He had to. His hands moved from her waist to her ribcage and he was about to cover her breasts when she pushed at his chest.

"Nadine," came out on a breathless whisper.

"Not now," he muttered.

"Nadine," she repeated.

They could talk about Nadine another time.

"Later," he insisted.

"She's watching us," he was informed.

"Christ," Mitchell swore against her lips.

They both seemed to realize instinctively the wisdom of not allowing Nadine Forbes to know that they were aware of her presence.

"Where is she?"

"Window."

"Which floor?"

"Third."

"Direction?"

"West, I think."

The west wing, of course.

"Alone?" he asked.

"I believe so." Followed by, "Yes."

"Tell me when—"

"She's gone."

"Are you sure?"

Torey paused, nodded her head ever so slightly, and then exhaled. "I'm sure."

"Don't look up," he instructed. "Wrap your arms around my waist, rest your head on my shoulder, maybe go up on your tiptoes and nuzzle my neck every now and then. We're going to slowly make our way to the love seat."

Torey had the sense not to ask why.

They reached the stone bench recessed into the castle wall and sat down side by side. The vegetation that grew up and around the area created a natural canopy and enclosure.

They could see out.

No one could see in.

"Are you certain nobody can see us?" was Torey's first question once they were settled.

"Positive." They had been visible only when they'd been out in the open.

"What was she doing at the window?"

"Watching us." He didn't like it. Not one bloody damned bit. "My question is why."

Torey said matter-of-factly, "I know why."

That took Mitchell by surprise. "You do?"

She nodded her head. "That's what I was going to mention to you sometime about Nadine. It may have originally been Sylvia Forbes's idea to snare you as a husband for her step-granddaughter, but I believe the girl has plans of her own."

"What kind of plans?"

"The same as Sylvia's," Torey said in a half whisper. "She intends to become your wife."

"Still?"

"Still."

"But I'm engaged."

Torey appeared to be biting her tongue. "Somehow I don't think that matters to Nadine."

"What are you trying to tell me?" Most of the time Mitchell believed that he understood why people did what they did, but this situation frankly had him baffled.

Torey drew a breath and spoke slowly. "The girl has developed a crush on you, Mitchell."

"The girl doesn't know the first thing about me, I've told you that before."

"It doesn't matter."

He wanted to swear a blue streak but settled for a vehement, "Good God!" in the end. Then he inquired, "Do young women still have crushes on older men?"

"This one does."

He moved his head from side to side. "It doesn't seem very likely to me."

"Trust me on this one," Torey said dryly.

"That feeling?"

She shook her head. "Plain old feminine intuition."

"All right, I'll trust your feminine intuition." Mitchell sat back deeper into the shadows created by the wall and clinging vines. "Now I understand why you insisted I kiss you."

"Do you?"

"We've got to find a way to let the girl down gently, not hurt her feelings if we can help it, and by seeing us kissing each other she'll soon get the picture and give up her fantasy."

"You think so?"

"Don't you?"

"Not if Nadine is obsessed with you and the idea of becoming the next Lady Storm."

"That is illogical."

"You're expecting logic in a situation where logic will have very little, perhaps nothing, to do with the outcome. Thoughts may be logical. Actions may be logical. Emotions are *not* logical, Mitchell."

He leaned over and dropped a kiss on the end of her perfect nose. "You are an amazing woman, Victoria Storm."

She seemed taken aback by the sudden compliment.

When she didn't say anything—and Mitchell wasn't certain what one would say under the circumstances—he went on. "Have I told you how much I admire you?"

"No."

"Have I mentioned that I have the utmost respect for you?"

"No."

"I like you."

The slightest hesitation on her part. "I like you."

"You have a fine mind, a quick wit, and an understanding heart, Torey. Those qualities are rare in any human being, let alone in a young woman with your wealth and beauty.''

She swallowed with some difficulty. ''Thank you, Mitchell.''

''You're welcome.'' He inched closer to her on the stone love seat. ''I enjoy kissing you.''

''I . . . ah . . . enjoy kissing you, too.''

''How much?''

Her eyes flew to his. ''How much?''

Mitchell nodded. ''How much do you enjoy kissing me?''

She hemmed and hawed and finally sputtered, ''I don't know quite how to answer that question.''

''On a scale of one to ten, then.''

She still wasn't getting it.

So he expounded on the subject. ''One on the scale being you don't mind kissing me but you have, say, a thousand other things you'd rather be doing.''

''And ten?''

Here it went.

Mitchell tried to sound nonchalant, yet sincere, and definitely not melodramatic. ''Ten being my kiss has become the very breath of life for you. In fact, you would rather die right now than ever go again without my kiss.''

She was silent.

He said at last, ''You don't have to answer, of course.''

She knew the answer, of course.

The question was did she want Mitchell to know it, as well? Perhaps it was time he did.

Torey opened her mouth and heard herself say in a husky voice, ''Kiss me, Mitchell.''

''Here?''

''Yes.''

"Now?"

"This minute," she insisted.

"Any ulterior motives?"

"Not a one."

"Then why?"

"For the pure pleasure of it. Because I like kissing you. Because I've missed kissing you. Because I want you to kiss me. Because I desperately need for you to kiss me."

So he kissed her, and this kiss was not like any kiss they had shared before. It began red hot and heated up from there. It started as lips and teeth and tongues and they wound up with their hands all over each other.

Buttons were fumbled with.

Skin was exposed.

Torey felt her bra pushed aside and his lips searching for her nipple. He found one, licked it, rolled his tongue around it, drew it deeper and deeper into his mouth where he suckled her until she could feel the erotic tug all the way down to the tips of her toes.

She found herself quivering, actually shaking with the force of her own sexual arousal, and reached for him. Her fingernails made small, sharp scrapes across the muscles of his chest, searching and finding one hard male nipple. She pinched it—not particularly gently—between a thumb and finger, and felt him shudder.

The zipper of his pants caught halfway down. Mitchell swore under his breath until Torey managed to coax it to the bottom.

His penis sprang free.

He was hot and heavy in her hand, yet his skin was smooth and silky and sensitive to the slightest touch. She touched him tentatively at first, then carefully, then with that singular mix of feminine curiosity and unleashed female passion.

"Torey—" Mitchell sounded as if he were in pain, but loving every second of it. "God help me."

She saw the tiny beads of perspiration break out on his forehead. She saw the taut line to his mouth. She heard the quickening of his breathing. She even felt the fast, hard beat of his heart. Then she realized his racing pulse was right there in her palm.

His hand was on her knee, slipping under her skirt and sliding up her leg until he encountered the inevitable barrier.

"Damned panty hose!" His curse was half frustration and half irony at the ridiculous situation in which he found himself.

"There's nothing to them. They rip easily," she promised against his mouth.

He grasped a small handful of the transparent material and jerked. They both heard the resulting tear.

Then his hands were on her silk panties, inside her silk panties, and his palm was intimately pressed against the intimately placed curls.

"Are you red here?" he murmured, twisting a tiny strand around his finger.

Torey felt the rush of heat to her face—her entire body was on fire; she was burning up—but she still found the presence of mind to answer him. "Auburn."

Then he seemed to realize how damp she was, how ready she was, how her body had already anticipated what might come next . . . what would inescapably come next.

Mitchell slid his finger into her, and Torey heard an astonished gasp.

It was her own.

He withdrew, slowly, deliberately, pausing purposely to stroke the sensitive nub of female flesh and to listen for—and then savor—the moan that spilled forth involuntarily from her lips.

"Mitchell, I can't—" came the breathless plea for . . . what?

"Yes, you can."

He thrust two fingers into her and waited for the slight internal adjustment for size. Then he drove them in and out of her body again and again, his mouth on her mouth, his mouth on her shoulder, his mouth wild on her bare breast.

Torey found herself grasping him tighter and tighter, her hand moving up and down his smooth shaft seemingly of its own volition. The outcome seemed certain.

Then it began.

That inevitable journey.

Her breath caught somewhere in the back of her throat. Mitchell's name was on her lips, but her lips wouldn't move. She felt her body start to convulse around his hand, and she was suddenly delirious and half-dizzy with the thrill of it all and more than a little overwhelmed by what was happening to her. She couldn't have stopped it now even if she had wanted to.

She didn't want to.

Then Torey became aware, on some elemental level, that Mitchell was facing the same inevitable and climactic dilemma.

"Torey, I can't—" he muttered fiercely.

"Yes, you can," she assured him, her heart filled to bursting. "You're in good hands."

And then she took him past the point of no return and plunged straight over the edge. . . .

In the end, they did not make it downstairs to the formal drawing room that afternoon to join the others for tea.

Chapter 16

"Can you swim?" Mitchell inquired the next afternoon as they met at a prearranged time and place—two o'clock sharp by the old iron gate, which dated from the late fifteenth century, just this side of the path that wended its way down to the sea.

Torey was watching him closely, head cocked. "Why do you want to know?"

"Don't worry," he reassured her. "I don't have any ulterior motives for asking."

She flashed him a frolicsome grin and said, "Too bad."

Two could play at *that* game. "On the other hand," Mitchell came back, "our outing could always wait for another time."

"Outing?"

He held up his hand, studied first the palm at some length and then the back. "I always try to keep a promise."

"What promise?"

He had a reason for being deliberately oblique. "A promise I once made to you."

"When?"

"If I tell you when," he said, his dark brows drawing together, "I'll give the secret away."

Torey planted her hands on her hips and glowered at him. "Has anyone ever told you, Lord Storm, that you're something of a tease? Now I'm here at two o'clock sharp as you instructed. I'm dressed in blue jeans and an old sweater—"

That brought an immediate response from Mitchell. He reached out, ran his hand along the sleeve of her pale pink cashmere sweater, and repeated, hooting, "*Old* sweater?"

Torey's bottom lip protruded marginally. "Well, I didn't actually have an old sweater with me, so I thought this one would do." Determinedly, she went on. "I'm wearing sneakers . . . as you ordered. I've brought along my sunglasses and a protective hat . . . as you ordered." As if to prove the last two of her points, she slipped on a pair of dark glasses and plunked a very practical and completely non-Toreylike khaki canvas cap down on her head.

Mitchell sank his teeth into his tongue. Yet he still had to clear his throat and take a deep breath before he could inquire, "Where did you get the hat?"

Her chin came up. "I borrowed it from Alice."

He should have known.

"Are you ready, then?" he asked.

"I'm ready."

He took her hand and they started down the pathway toward the sea. "I have something I want to show you."

"What is it?"

"It's a surprise." Then he suddenly remembered. "You never answered my question."

"What question?"

"Can you swim?"

"Of course I can swim." Then she proceeded to go on at some length. "I'm like a fish in the water. Why, I'm told that I could swim before I could walk. Every summer since I was born has been spent living at the seashore. I was on the girl's championship swim team at Miss Porter's for four years running and I took the ninth grade honors for the breaststroke, as well."

"I guess the answer is yes," he concluded.

"The answer is yes," she said and sniffed.

"In that case, Miss Storm, it's safe for you to come with me," he announced.

"Where are you taking me?"

Mitchell stopped and pointed at a spot not far from the water's edge. "There."

"There?" She took off her sunglasses and squinted in the direction he was pointing. "*There* is a very small wooden dock with a very small skiff moored alongside," she observed, unimpressed.

"We need the skiff to get where we're going."

" 'Curiouser and curiouser,' " she murmured.

"I have something I want to give you."

That brought a husky laugh from her. "I've heard that one before and rather recently, I think."

She meant yesterday. Yesterday in the garden. Yesterday when they had given to each other and taken from one another: joy, satisfaction, fulfillment.

Mitchell decided to play it straight. "I'm serious, Torey. I have a present for you."

Her lovely face lit up. "Will I like it?"

He hadn't expected that reaction. "I think so." He kicked a stone out of the way. "I hope so."

"I've always liked presents. I don't get them very often." She got a pensive expression on her face and a wistful tone in her voice. "Most people don't know what to give me."

"Why not?"

She shrugged and didn't seem to care in the least that she looked rather more than a little ridiculous in an expensive cashmere sweater and a cheap canvas hat. "I suppose because they think I'm one of those women who already has everything."

A natural assumption.

"If I do receive a present it's usually the type that cost a lot of money but took absolutely no thought on the part of the sender."

"Ah, the generic gift."

They were reaching the end of the pathway when Torey said, "It truly is the thought that counts, isn't it, Mitchell?"

"Yes, it is."

"I'll get the mooring," she quickly volunteered, untying the single secured rope while he stepped into the rowboat and settled himself on the seat between the oarlocks.

Then she nimbly hopped aboard.

With the tip of one oar, Mitchell pushed off from the dock. Then he grabbed the other oar in his hand, braced his feet against the bottom of the skiff, and put his arms, shoulders and back into the job of rowing.

The key, of course, was to establish a rhythm.

Up.

Down.

Forward.

Back.

Slice through the water, little splash, no splash.

Begin again.

The physical exercise felt good. Damned good. The

sun on his back felt good, too. And the slight breeze; just enough to keep him comfortable. And the sound of the seagulls screeching overhead and the taste of salt in the air.

And being here, now, with this woman . . . that felt especially good.

It was a perfect summer day in the Western Isles. The sky was a piercing blue, and without a single cloud in it. The sea was calm and serene. It was one of the reasons he'd waited until this afternoon to do what he had to do.

"By the way," Mitchell added as he put even more energy into his rowing, "this is *Barbara Allen*."

He saw Torey's eyes blink open behind her sunglasses. She hadn't said a word since they'd left shore. She, too, had been basking in the sunlight and the perfect weather.

"Hm?" came the lazy response.

"I said, this is *Barbara Allen*."

To his amazement, in a sweet, soprano voice Torey began to sing softly and utterly unself-consciously. " 'In Scarlet town, where I was born, there was a fair maid dwellin', made every youth cry well-a-way! Her name was Barbara Allen.' "

"That's the song that inspired me to call her *Barbara Allen*," he informed her.

Torey eyes opened wider. "Who is Barbara Allen?"

"She is," he said with a jerk of his head. He didn't want to lose his rhythm.

"She?"

"Our mighty seagoing vessel," he proclaimed.

Mitchell could see Torey's mouth working. "You named your skiff *Barbara Allen*?"

He nodded and kept rowing.

"When?"

"The summer I was twelve going on thirteen."

"The summer you visited your grandparents here on the Isle of Storm," she recalled.

"That's right. I told you I had free rein of the place. Well, I found this old rowboat, patched her up, gave her a coat of paint, got her a couple of new oars—the original oars were long gone—officially christened her *Barbara Allen* and she became mine."

It was a moment or two before Torey said, "Your grandfather kept her for you all these years."

Mitchell's throat tightened. "I found her in one of the boathouses after he'd died."

"He must have known how much she meant to you," she said, her voice dropping to a soft murmur.

"I guess he did."

"He must have hoped that one day you would come back to the Isle of Storm."

He had.

William Storm had told him over and over again in those last few months they'd had together that the hope of Mitchell returning had often been the only thing that kept him alive.

"My father viewed the island as a prison. I never did," he confided to her as the small boat skimmed along the surface of the water. "Maybe it was because as a young man he'd never been anywhere or done anything. Or maybe he simply wasn't cut out for the demanding life of a Scottish laird." Mitchell sighed. "All he ever wanted was to get away from here and explore the big world outside."

"And your mother?"

His mother had been a beautiful, ineffectual woman of no great intelligence. But she'd had a good heart, and she'd loved him.

"My mother loved my father. She went wherever he

went." Mitchell slowed his tempo. "But I think it always broke her heart a little not to come back."

Her voice was so low he barely heard it over the quiet sea. "And you?"

"I'd spent my whole life wandering. I had no roots. I had no hometown. Hell, I didn't even know what country to call my own. When I returned to Scotland and the Isle of Storm last year I knew I was home at last. I knew I had finally found my place in the world." Mitchell put his head back for a moment, took in a deep breath and filled his lungs with the smells of his native land. "This is who I am, Torey. This is where I belong."

Mitchell was trying to tell her something important.

Torey had seen the look in his eyes as he'd rowed the skiff across the loch, looking back at his home. He loved this place: every hill, every rock, every crag of the Isle of Storm; every stone, every timber, every leaking roof tile of Castle Storm itself.

And that was as it should be.

"The water is so clear, I can almost see the bottom of the loch," she murmured, leaning slightly toward the right side of the boat and trailing her fingers along the silvery surface.

"Just watch out for the fairy-seals," Mitchell warned her.

"And what, pray tell, is a fairy-seal?"

As the skiff glided toward their destination, Mitchell related, "Once upon a time—"

"So, this story actually begins with 'once upon a time,' " she teased him.

"I'm just telling the tale to you as it was told to me twenty-five years ago by Old Ned. *That* Old Ned is long gone now, of course, and another Old Ned, his son, has taken his place."

"There are a great number of Neds on your island as Alice and I have discovered."

"It runs in the family."

She was ready to listen.

Mitchell began. "Once upon a time the Celtic fairy folk of Scotland lived in underground caverns or sometimes knolls, and entered this world through cracks and fissures in the rocks. Now, the nastiest sort of fairies were the ones who would steal human babies right out from under their mother's noses and leave a changeling in its place. The other fairy folk were impish, at worst, but they had amazing powers and they could do almost anything, so it served the Scots well to keep on good terms with them."

"I'll just bet it did."

"Anyway, the fairy folk preferred to marry humans, so they would take the form of a seal and swim from island to island looking for the right mate."

Torey was fascinated by the folklore. "A seal?"

He nodded. "The story goes that on an island not far from here, a fairy-seal woman came ashore one day looking for a mate. She took off her seal-skin and instantly became a beautiful woman. A very beautiful woman. The kind of woman who could make any man fall in love with her."

"Did a human male fall in love with her?"

"Yes. And soon after, they were married."

Torey strained toward him. "Then what happened?"

"Years passed. They lived happily. But the sad day came—a day that came inevitably for all fairy folk who married humans—when the woman was forced to put her seal-skin back on. She immediately became a creature of the sea once more and plunged into the crashing waves, never to be seen again on this earth.''

Torey looked past him, over his shoulder. ''That was a lovely fairytale, Mitchell, but I think there's something important you should know.''

''About what, sweetheart? About you? About me? About us? Surely it can wait until another day.''

''No, it can't wait.''

He heaved a sigh. ''What is it, then?''

''There's a big rock directly ahead of us,'' she said urgently, ''and if you don't do something in the next second or two we're going to crash right into it.''

Warned in the nick of time, Mitchell managed to bring them safely ashore. He maneuvered the skiff into a secluded cove and secured the mooring line around the same boulder that had been there a quarter of a century ago when he had been a young boy out exploring with his first boat.

''I'd nearly forgotten about this place,'' he confessed to her.

''What is it?'' Torey asked.

''Officially it's called an islet.''

''In other words, it's a very small island.''

''That's about the size of it.''

''It's a wonderful place,'' Torey said, looking inland at the grove of trees, which pretty much constituted the entire land mass of the islet, along with a few rocks, several large boulders—including the one they'd very nearly run into—and a small meadow of wildflowers primarily in purples, yellows and pinks. ''Does it have a name?''

''Not that I know of.''

"Everyone and everything should have a name," she told him in a perfectly serious manner.

"Then you can name this islet whatever you like."

"I'll have to give it some thought, naturally. A name isn't something one wants to rush into."

"Take all the time you want." Mitchell took in a fortifying breath, held it for a moment and then released it. "It's yours."

"What's mine?"

He gestured. "This is."

Torey didn't sound certain. "You're giving me an island?"

"A very small island."

She went silent. "I don't know what to say."

"You don't have to say anything. There is, however, a reason why I'm giving you this particular island," Mitchell informed her, taking her by the hand and urging her along toward the grove of trees.

It stood majestically in the center.

The diameter of its trunk was larger than many a small cottage's. There were dozens upon dozens of branches, perhaps hundreds of them, twisting up and out and down and in every conceivable direction; contorted, misshapen boughs forming odd shapes and creating every manner of natural canopies and shelters.

Torey stood there.

Mitchell was getting nervous. "That day in Rhode Island, I promised you a tree, remember?"

"I remember," was all she said.

"I always keep my promises."

She didn't say a word.

Mitchell stuffed his hands into the pockets of his jeans and shuffled his feet in the leaves and organic matter at the base of the giant tree. "No one knows how old this tree is."

She stood and stared.

"Hundreds of years old, anyway."

She was still silent.

"It's even thought by some historians that Robert Burns visited this islet in 1787 while he was a guest at Castle Storm. The story goes that he stood under the tree's heart-shaped boughs—" Mitchell pointed up at what could loosely be termed a rambling heart-shaped grouping of branches "—and composed one of his poems."

She spoke at last. "Which one?"

"They claim it was 'Ae Fond Kiss,' " he said.

She shook her head.

Mitchell quoted what he could recall of the Burns poem:

> *But to see her was to love her,*
> *Love but her, and love forever.*
> *Had we never loved sae kindly,*
> *Had we never loved sae blindly,*
> *Never met—or never parted—*
> *We had ne'er been brokenhearted.*

*   *   *

"He gave me a tree," she called out to Alice, in the adjoining room, as she sank down even deeper into the warm bathwater.

"Well, he did promise you one."

Torey put her head back against the porcelain tub. "Robert Burns composed poetry under the heart-shaped boughs of this tree over two hundred years ago."

"That is impressive."

"It's a very old tree. Possibly even an ancient tree.

And there were strange marks carved deeply into its trunk.''

''What kind of marks?''

Torey shrugged her bare shoulders and blew the soap bubbles from her hands. ''They looked a little like a V and an M.''

''That seems odd.''

''That's what I thought. Mitchell suggested I ask Old Ned. Apparently Old Ned knows everything there is to know when it comes to Clan Storm, Castle Storm, or the Isle of Storm. I thought I would visit the old man to-morrow.''

''Good idea.''

She spread a wet washcloth across her face. ''Would you like to come along?''

''Can't.''

Torey smiled and sat up in the old claw-footed Vic-torian bathtub. ''The MacClumpha again?''

A slight hesitation on Alice Fraser's part. Then, ''Yes.''

When there was no more information forthcoming on the subject of Iain MacClumpha—and she did try to re-spect Alice's privacy—Torey went on. ''Did I tell you that the tree stands in the center of a small, lush island?''

''No. How lovely.''

Torey sighed. ''Mitchell gave me the island, as well.''

That got Alice's undivided attention. ''My word.''

''Yes, my word.''

A minute later. ''I hope you thanked the man.''

''So do I.''

She had been so overwhelmed that she wasn't certain what she had said or done for some time after they had landed on the islet. She only remembered clearly that she had gone to the great tree as they were leaving, touched one of its branches and whispered: *It's me. It's Victoria. I'll be back.*

Torey raised her voice. "It's the most wonderful gift anyone has ever given me, Alice."

"I imagine it is, my dear."

"It's the most wonderful gift any man could give any woman," she murmured, sinking down into the warm water again.

"Perhaps," said Alice Fraser quietly from the adjoining room.

Chapter 17

"Ceud mile failte," said Old Ned as he proudly ushered her into the small sitting room of his cottage. "That is the traditional Gaelic greeting and it means 'a hundred thousand welcomes.' "

"Thank you, sir," Torey said, politely.

"Not sir. Just Old Ned will do."

"Then will you call me Torey?"

"Don't know if I can do that, Miss Storm, but I might slip up every now and then and refer to ye as lass." There was a twinkle in Old Ned's eyes.

An ancient dog, no purebreed but he looked to be part sheepdog, came lumbering up to Torey, wagging its tail and nuzzling her hand, seeking its share of her attention.

"And who is this?" she inquired, bending over to give the dog an affectionate pat on the top of its head.

"That be Old Toby. We've been together a long time, Old Toby and me," the elderly man told her.

"I've brought you a few things from the cook at the castle," Torey said, indicating the basket she was carrying over her arm. "Mrs. MacGrubb made me promise to tell you that she's included several of your favorite tea cakes."

"Cook never forgets to send Old Ned his *dundee*," he stated, obviously pleased. He accepted the basket with a surprisingly steady hand for a man Torey knew to be ninety-three years old. He glanced at the clock on the modest mantelpiece above the fireplace and observed with a tinge of disappointment, "Too early for tea."

Lunch had only been an hour ago.

"I'm afraid it is." Torey had almost forgotten the rest of the cook's message. "A choice bone or two, and some kitchen scraps, are wrapped in old newspaper and packed in the bottom of the basket for Toby."

Old Ned nodded as if completely satisfied now. "Cook never forgets Old Toby, neither."

The elderly gentleman motioned her to one of two cushioned rocking chairs situated in front of the hearth, facing the fire, although there was no fire lit on this fine August afternoon.

Old Toby followed, tail swishing back and forth, and when they sat down, he curled up at his master's feet.

Apparently Old Ned felt age had its rank and privileges. He didn't beat around the bush. He came straight to the point. "So, lass, are ye going to become the bride of The Storm?"

"The Storm?"

"The laird himself."

Mitchell, of course. Her tongue suddenly was tied in knots. "I . . . ah . . ."

"Ye love him," came the unadorned statement. "That's plain as the pretty nose on yer pretty face."

"How in the world—?"

"Old Ned still has eyes to see with and ears to hear with, ye know," he advised her. "The Storm took ye out in his skiff yesterday. Took ye to the island, didn't he?"

There was obviously no reason to try to argue otherwise with Old Ned. "Yes. He did."

"Old Toby and I beheld ye two walking back together, coming up the pathway from the small dock, all lovey-dovey like." He smacked his lips together several times and slapped his bony knee with delight. "Ye love him."

Torey sighed and fingered the lace doily looped over the arm of the rocking chair and secured underneath, she noticed, with a rusting safety pin. "Yes, I love him."

Old Ned nodded with contentment. "It will be a fine day when the two warring branches of Clan Storm are reunited at last in name and in love. That will be a fine day, indeed."

She didn't have the heart to tell Old Ned that he would never live to see that day.

"When The Storm and I were on the island yesterday, he showed me a huge tree."

"The Rabbie Burns tree," the old man said knowingly.

"That's the one. I understand some historians believe that Robert Burns wrote at least one of his finest poems there."

"So they say."

"We also saw two strange marks carved deep into the trunk of the old tree." Torey folded her hands in her lap and tried not to fidget. "I was wondering if you knew what the marks represent."

"Old Ned knows," he stated, rocking back and forth.

She swallowed. "What are they?"

He took the roundabout way to answering her question. "Ye see, lass, a long time ago the tree had a different name."

"It did?"

"Yes."

Her elderly host continued rocking to and fro. It was a soothing sound, a comforting sound, and Old Ned was in no hurry. What was the sense in hurrying at his age? Torey supposed she would feel the same way when she was ninety-three.

She decided to broach the subject from a different angle. "How old do you think the tree is?"

"Don't think, lass. I know."

She attempted to keep calm. "You know its age?"

Old Ned nodded in rhythm with the motion of the rocking chair. He raised a knobby arthritic finger and pointed to his head. "It's all in here. Passed down from generation to generation, from father to son, from one Old Ned to the next."

She knew about the tradition of oral storytelling in the Isles. "Has the information been written down?"

He shook his head.

"What if something should happen to the Old Ned?" The thought more than dismayed her. "All would be lost."

"Nay, lass, it would still be here," he consoled her, tapping his chest just above his heart. "But we were speaking of the tree. We know it was there—although no' the giant it is today, of course—when The Bruce fought against the weak and despised Edward, son of Edward 'Longshanks,' at Bannockburn."

Torey realized that she definitely needed to brush up on her Scottish history.

"That would be 1314, lass."

She blinked several times in rapid succession and repeated, "1314." She quickly did the math. "That would mean the tree is at least seven hundred years old."

"That be about right."

Torey tried the direct approach again. "What was the original name of the tree?"

Again, Old Ned's answer was given by a circuitous route. "Ah, they say she was a fair and lovely lass. The only daughter of the chief of Clan Storm. It was her island and her tree. And when she fell in love it was there the lass arranged to meet her lad, though no lad was he. It became their tryst."

"The place where lovers met."

Torey still didn't know the young woman's name, but she also knew that Old Ned would get around to telling her in his own time and in his own way.

"Peculiar, and yet no' so peculiar when ye come to think of it," he said cryptically.

"What is?"

"Ye are called Torey."

"It's short for Victoria."

"That be her name, as well, lass."

"Victoria?"

Old Ned nodded. "Lady Victoria. That be the reason the tree was first called Victoria's Tryst."

"And it explains the marking on the tree that looked like a V," she murmured. "It was a V."

The old man's tone changed to one of complete disapproval. "The lad's name was from the Scotch, and meant 'the one who is like God.' Only it were a case of a misnaming for sure."

"He wasn't a good man, then?"

Old Ned's lips formed a thin, tight line. "He wasn't the man for such a lass as she."

"What was the name of the man that Lady Victoria of Clan Storm fell in love with?"

He told her in a word. "Michell."

Surely it was too much of a coincidence.

Torey struggled to keep her voice even. "V and M. Victoria and Michell."

"Theirs is a tragic tale of love and betrayal, Miss Storm," Old Ned related as he picked up a small, sharp knife and a chunk of rough wood from the table at his elbow and began to carve. "I always like to work when I tell my stories."

Were they no more than Old Ned's stories? Or was it truly part history and part legend passed down from one storyteller to another for hundreds, perhaps even for thousands, of years?

Torey watched the elderly gentleman for a few minutes, amazed by the steadfastness of his hand and the acuteness of his eyesight as he made detailed and intricate cuts in the wood.

"What are you carving?" she inquired, genuinely interested in what he was doing.

"It's a face, lass."

"Whose face?"

"The face hidden in the wood."

He held the fragment of a small branch toward her so she could get a better look. It was just a piece of old wood, undoubtedly picked up off the forest floor. No more than twelve or fifteen inches in length and three or four inches in width, its only distinguishing mark was an interesting knot on the surface.

"First I must find the right knot," he explained. "Then I study the grain and the texture of the wood and the shape of the knot itself, until I can read the story that the face tells. I remove only the wood that has kept the face concealed."

"That's fascinating," she admitted.

"Traditionally the carving should be hung at the highest point in a man's home."

"Why?"

"To protect him and his family." He peered at her. "The face is a powerful talisman that protects against all evil."

A handy thing, no doubt, to have in any home.

Old Ned continued to work his knife as he talked. "Theirs was a tragic tale of love and betrayal," he said, picking up where he'd left off earlier in their conversation.

"Lady Victoria and Michell's?"

He bobbed his head. "Some of what I am about to tell ye is history, and some is legend, and some has been lost forever to the memory of man."

Torey only hoped and prayed that enough of the story remained.

"It was a time of war for independence in Scotland. There was always a need for strong fighting men, men with their own armor and horses, men with half a mind and money to wage battle against the English. Into this time and place, rode a great warrior knight, Michell, and his small band of fellow knights."

"Where had he come from?"

Old Ned shrugged. "No one knew for certain. Some claimed that he was a member of a distant sept of Clan Storm, who had gone off to fight in the Holy Land and had only recently returned to Scotland. Others said he had been on the run for several years from the Pope himself, in Rome, and from Philip of France."

"Why would he be on the run?"

"It was rumored that Michell had once taken the vows and been among those who called themselves the Knights Templar."

"The warrior monks who fought in the Crusades," she said thoughtfully.

"By now, the Knights Templar were no more. Most of them had been burned at the stake and their vast wealth supposedly grabbed up by the greedy French king."

"So, whoever Michell was, he returned or escaped here to the Isle of Storm."

"That he did, lass." Old Ned kept chatting and carving, stopping every now and then to study the piece of wood more closely. "Some said that Michell and his men brought a great treasure with them. Some even hinted that it was the wealth of the Templars smuggled out of France before the last Grand Master was executed."

"So there was a treasure."

"Could be fact or it could be legend, lass. But the betrayal was true enough."

"Whose betrayal?"

"His." Old Ned paused in his carving and after a moment, added, "And hers."

"What happened?" Torey asked, needing to know.

"The warrior knight made a mistake. He believed that the lady's love for him was stronger than her loyalty to the clan."

"And he was wrong," Torey ventured softly.

"This island has always been a natural fortress. If a man wanted to conquer it, he would need the help of someone who knew all there was to know about the Isle of Storm: from the number of fighting clansmen within its walls to the secret entrance in the seagate."

Torey suddenly understood. "Michell wanted Lady Victoria to betray her own people."

"That were the right and the wrong of it, lass."

"And she didn't, of course."

"There is no betraying the clan."

"Once of Clan Storm, always of Clan Storm."

"I see you comprehend. Lady Victoria did, too. But she paid a mighty price."

"What was the price?"

"Her immortal soul. And the life of the man she loved."

Torey realized her mouth had dropped open. "Lady Victoria killed Michell?"

"As surely as if she had stabbed a dagger through his heart." Old Ned blew on the wood carving and she watched as the shavings dropped onto the front of his shirt.

Old Toby clattered to his feet, whimpered once or twice and rested his head on Torey's knee. Without a word she reached down, scratched behind his ear, and patted his head.

"Ye've made a friend there, Miss Storm."

"I've always liked dogs," she said simply.

Out of the blue came, "Have ye seen the stone steps not far from my front door?"

"Yes." Torey had noticed the impressive and large square stones set into the hillside as she'd approached Old Ned's cottage that afternoon.

"Did ye happen to see the small chapel at the top of the hill?"

"Yes. I did."

Old Ned seemed satisfied with her answers. He nodded and said, "That be her chapel."

"Her chapel?"

"Saint Victoria's."

"Who—?" She stopped herself. "Lady Victoria became Saint Victoria."

"She was canonized in the fifteenth century. Long after the events that took place here, of course." Old Ned held the wood carving up to the sunlight that was streaming in the sitting room window and made a sound that could only be described as recognition. "Ye should climb to the chapel. She's there, you know."

"Saint Victoria?"

He made a motion with his head that told her yes. "She had the chapel built at the very top of the hill, and every day she climbed the stone steps to spend hours on her knees in prayer. She had her tomb already prepared, as well, and when she died, she was laid to rest before the window overlooking the sea and the Stones."

"The stones?"

That seemed to startle the old man. "Ye've not seen that side of the island?"

"Not yet."

"Then ye've not see the Stones."

"No. I haven't."

"Did no one ever tell ye about the Standing Stones?"

She shook her head.

"The waters be treacherous on that side of the island," he said, and it was a dire warning to her. "At low tide, ye can almost walk across on foot, and ye could certainly ride across mounted on the back of a horse. But the tides are unpredictable. They have a mind and a will—and some say a spirit—of their own. The currents that flow through the channel are strange and powerful, as well. A man could be caught unaware and dragged down into the watery abyss before he had time to draw his last breath."

Torey shivered. "What did she do?"

"Lady Victoria knew what her beloved warrior knight intended, that he planned to conquer or kill her clansmen and claim the Isle of Storm as his own. She promised to help him. She even revealed the time of the low tide on that moonlit night—knowledge which all of Clan Storm possessed but would never give to an enemy. Michell and his knights rode confidently into the shallow waters. No one knew of their approach. They moved with stealth and cunning. They could almost taste the victory that would soon be theirs. It appeared the crossing to the island would be a quick and safe one.''

''But it wasn't.''

Old Ned agreed. ''Lady Victoria climbed to the top of the hill, to the very spot where she had her chapel later built, and she stood at the summit and she watched.''

Torey's voice was suddenly strangely hoarse. ''She watched the tide come in.''

Old Ned nodded.

''She watched as the man she loved was caught in the overpowering currents and swallowed up by the sea.''

Old Ned kept nodding his head.

Torey was stunned. ''Michell and all of his men perished as she stood there and watched.''

''Legend or no, it is said that as he disappeared beneath the onrushing tide, she called out his name one last time. Then she ne'er spoke another word for as long as she lived.''

It was a minute or two, maybe longer before Torey could bring herself to ask him. ''How long did Lady Victoria live after Michell was . . . drowned?''

''Fifty years.''

Torey's hand flew to her mouth. ''Dear God, fifty years.''

''For all of those many years she devoted herself to caring for the sick and infirm, the destitute and the dying. She was a kind and giving woman, with a gentle touch and a good heart. But she had taken a vow of silence and she kept it.''

''She became a nun.''

''In her own way. She cut off her long, lovely hair,

said to be both yellow and red, the colors of the setting sun as it slipped behind the isle each evening. She wore only plain, coarse clothing. She lived in a small, spare room with only a straw pallet on the floor and an earthen jug for drinking and washing. She ate the simplest food and very little of it. And she climbed those many stone steps each day to pray in the chapel for forgiveness— forgiveness for Michell and for herself.''

Torey's voice grew stronger with each word. ''I'd like to see Saint Victoria's chapel.''

''I would gladly take ye myself, lass, but my knees gave out for climbing last year. Old Toby will go along and keep ye company.'' Old Ned rose from his rocking chair. He glanced down at the piece of wood in his hand. Then he held it out to her. ''The face has revealed itself. This is for ye, lass. It will stand vigil against evil and keep ye safe always.''

Torey was touched by his gift. ''Thank you.''

The old man walked with her as far as his front gate. The stone steps were directly on the other side of the gate and the garden wall that surrounded the cottage. The tiny chapel was visible at the top of the steep hill.

''I saw her once,'' he suddenly declared.

''Who?''

''Saint Victoria.'' Old Ned reached down and patted his dog. ''She was there at the bottom of the stairs, on her knees, her head bowed in prayer.''

Torey wasn't about to insult the old gentleman by contradicting him.

''Each year on the anniversary of Michell's death— and her betrayal of him—Lady Victoria climbed those steps one by one on her knees as a form of penance. It was on just such an anniversary day that I saw her. She turned and looked at me for a moment—with kindness,

I like to think—and then she up and vanished."

Torey was silent.

"You'll find her altar and her tomb up there, overlooking the sea," he told her.

"The very spot where he drowned." It was a statement, not a question.

Old Ned pursed his lips. "Sometimes at low tide ye can catch sight of the Stones."

"The Stones?"

"Legend tells us that Michell and his men were transformed into great stone pillars as they died."

Torey gazed up toward the chapel. "And so she watches over him still."

"In life and in death, and now for all eternity."

Torey looked back to the elderly gentleman. "Thank you for the talisman."

"Ye be welcome, lass."

"I'll go up to the chapel now."

"Old Toby be going to keep ye company."

She reached out and placed her hand on his for a moment. "May I come visit you again?"

"Ye are always welcome, lass. Next time come for tea and we'll have some of my favorite *dundee*."

Torey started up the stone stairway. She paused and turned to wave to Old Ned. But he had already turned his back and begun the short walk to his cottage door.

Old Toby had stopped with her. He whimpered as if to ask whether they were going up or down.

"Come on, Old Toby," Torey said, reaching down to give him a friendly rub around his neck. "Let's climb all the way to the top, all the way to heaven itself."

Chapter 18

The outside of Saint Victoria's chapel was roughly hewn gray stone. It was the same gray stone that had been quarried for the steps Torey had just climbed from Old Ned's cottage to the summit of the hill.

The unrelenting starkness of the stone was relieved by the roses that rambled up its walls, clung to its crevices, and tumbled down again in a riot of color: brilliant scarlets and canary yellows and even Torey's personal favorite—pale pinks.

The inside of the chapel was smaller than Torey had expected it to be. There was a plain stone altar set against a plain stone wall with a plain stone cross placed in the center of it.

At the opposite end of the diminutive chapel there was a plain stone sarcophagus situated facing a large, low, open window that overlooked the sea below.

At the foot and on either side of the tomb stood life-size sculpted marble figures, depicted wearing long, flowing robes that covered their heads, faces, bodies, hands, even their feet.

Torey recognized what the statues were from the large

number she had seen in the Burgundy region of France. The figures were called *pleurants* which meant "weepers," and they were the eternal mourners placed at the tombs of important people.

The cowled and faceless figures were a little unnerving, Torey found. She was suddenly grateful for the cheerful afternoon sunlight streaming in the open doorway of the chapel and through the open window, and for the comforting presence of Old Toby who waited faithfully just outside the entrance.

The only color inside St. Victoria's chapel came from the stained-glass windows, two along each wall. They were magnificent. Large with intricate designs and rich, bright colors, they were truly works of art from long-ago artisans.

The first window showed two knights sharing a single horse. There were words in Latin that Torey wasn't able to decipher, but there was a small brass plaque under the window frame, imprinted in modern English, identifying the year, the artist believed responsible for the work, and a brief explanation.

She read aloud from the plaque: "Two knights sharing a single horse was the emblem of the Knights Templar and represented one of their original vows: the vow of poverty. However, by the late thirteenth century these warrior monks had become the bankers to all of Europe and as powerful as kings."

Torey studied the stained-glass image for some time and then moved on to the next window.

The second window was a rendering of a single warrior on the back of a magnificent dark steed. The man was dressed in full battle armor and wielded a great silver sword in one hand and carried a small, ornate box in the other. There was a ribbon of Latin winding along the bottom of the scene.

The plaque underneath stated that the knight's name was unknown. There was an inscription, however, from Proverbs, 11:28: "He that trusteth in his riches shall fall."

Curiouser and curiouser, Torey reflected thoughtfully as she then moved across to the two stained-glass windows on the opposite wall of the tiny chapel.

The third window was a depiction of the crest of Clan Storm: a raised hand with a bolt of lightning grasped in its palm. There was also the traditional sprig of cranberry: the clan badge that was worn on each man's cap. The clan motto was etched in Latin beneath the crest. *Nemo me impune lacessit:* No one assails me with impunity.

"No one attacks me without punishment," Torey murmured aloud in more understandable English.

She knew the clan motto would become, one day, the motto of Scotland itself.

Stopping in front of the last of the four windows, Torey studied the narrative scene on the wall in front of her. The design was far more intricate in this piece of stained glass than in the others and not as easily, nor as quickly, understood.

The picture showed a young woman climbing a long stairway that seemed to ascend from earth all the way up to heaven, complete with a band of winged angels waiting for her at the summit.

Torey felt as though she should recognize the young woman, but she couldn't quite place the face.

In addition, several of the glass panes had been left blank and the illustration on this fourth window appeared incomplete. At the bottom of the frame were several wise aphorisms: "Do not hold as gold all that shines as gold."

Followed by another admonition: "The richest of heaven's pavement is trodden gold."

Torey sighed and made her way across the tiny chapel to the tomb of Lady Victoria. She paid her respects and said a short, silent prayer. When she opened her eyes again, it was then Torey noticed the huge stone slab that had been used for the lid of the tomb.

She reached up and traced the design on the stone. One side was clearly the coat of arms of Clan Storm. She recognized the symbols from the stained-glass window. There was an ornately carved "V" for Victoria, as well.

Whatever had been on the other half of the stone had long ago been partially chiseled away. But Torey could still make out the faint outline of a warrior on a horse and the letter M.

Victoria and Michell.

This had been their marriage stone. The stone that was to have been set above the front door of their home after their wedding. The wedding and the marriage that never took place.

Yet, here it was sealing the top of Lady Victoria's sarcophagus, obviously at her request and certainly with her knowledge. Old Ned had told her that the tomb had been prepared some years before Victoria's death.

Whatever else may have happened in her lifetime, Victoria of Clan Storm had always loved her knight, Michell.

Torey turned and stood at the chapel window, then gazed out at the scene her namesake had chosen for all eternity.

The view was beautiful, but the location precarious. Directly outside the window was a narrow ledge, then a straight drop of several hundred feet to the rocky cliffs and treacherous waters below.

Looking out across the causeway, Torey could clearly see the legendary Standing Stones halfway between the safety of the mainland and the Isle of Storm.

As she stood at the window and watched, the tide began to come in. She had no idea how long she remained there, but she suddenly realized that the Standing Stones were quickly becoming submerged and that tears were streaming down her face.

Suddenly Torey understood.

Not on an intellectual level, but an emotional one. Not with her mind, but with her heart and soul. She knew now what Lady Victoria had felt as she had stood on this very spot and watched her beloved drown, knowing that she was the cause of his death, knowing that she had no choice, knowing that she was breaking her own heart.

For she would never see him again.

Torey wept.

She wept for Lady Victoria and Michell.

She wept for Mitchell and herself.

She loved Mitchell Storm and yet like her namesake, she, too, was likely to have her heart broken. She would leave the Isle of Storm soon and she would never see the man again.

Grasping the talisman from Old Ned in one hand, Torey reached up for the familiar security of the locket around her neck. She held it in her palm and felt its comforting warmth against her skin.

There was something she was missing. There was something she should see and understand that she wasn't seeing or understanding. There was something she should know that she didn't.

It was on the tip of her tongue.

She was concentrating so intently that Old Toby's growl from the doorstep barely registered with her.

Out of her peripheral vision Torey thought—surely it was her imagination—that she saw one of the *pleurants*, one of the cowled figures, moving toward her.

Then someone—or something—gave her a hard shove toward the window of the chapel, the window that opened up onto the rocky cliffs and the perilous waters far below.

Torey tried to save herself from falling. She opened her mouth and heard herself scream one word: "Mitchell!"

Chapter 19

His blood ran cold.

One minute Mitchell was leisurely making his way up the hill toward the old chapel, the next he was taking the stone steps two, maybe three, at a time.

He had clearly heard his name.

Then came a second scream of sheer terror. "Mitchell!"

His blood ran ice cold.

It was Torey.

Something was wrong.

The way she had called his name said it all. She was in danger . . . or frightened to within an inch of her life.

As the chapel came into view, Mitchell thought he glimpsed a robed and hooded figure slipping around the corner of the building and into the shadows, but there was no time to investigate now.

He ran the rest of the way. He reached the door. It was standing ajar. He braced himself against the door frame, one hand on each side, let his eyes adjust for an instant to the difference in light and then quickly scanned the interior of the tiny chapel.

Torey wasn't there.

His eyes flew to the open window.

Suddenly he felt his guts twisting into knots the size of boulders. Dear God, he intoned. Please, God, no.

Then he spotted the swish of a golden brown tail *inside* the window and the flutter of a skirt *outside* the window and just the tips of her fingers around the stone window frame.

Old Toby.

Torey.

She was in perilous danger if she was hanging on to any part of that narrow ledge.

He was across the room in a split second. He said her name softly so as not to startle her. "Torey, honey, are you there?"

The answer came. "Y-yes."

He leaned out the window and there she was, back flattened against the chapel wall, one hand grabbing the corner of the building, the other keeping a precarious grasp on the window frame, face white as a sheet, eyes squeezed tightly shut.

He had to think fast.

Mitchell turned and braced his lower body against the inside wall. "I'm going to lean out the window and wrap my arm around your waist as far as I can reach. On the count of three, I want you to open your eyes. Don't look down. Just let go of the grip you have on the chapel with your left hand, turn, and throw yourself toward me."

Torey made a sound halfway between a moan and a cry.

"I promise I'll catch you, sweetheart. I'm here now. We can do this together."

There was a barely perceptible nod of her head.

Mitchell realized that his heart had stopped beating.

His breathing was nonexistent. His brain was emptied of every rational thought but the primitive survival mechanism needed for what he had to do within the next four or five seconds.

Nothing else mattered.

Nothing but Torey and the need for bringing her to safety.

Time was running out. He braced his feet. He bent forward from the knees and leaned out the window.

He licked his lips and spoke softly but clearly to her. "I'm going to reach for you now. Remember on the count of three, open your eyes and push yourself toward me."

Dear Jesus, this better work.

Mitchell reached for her. "One."

He got his arm almost around her waist. "Two."

He hoped she didn't panic. "Three."

Torey's eyes flew open. She stared straight ahead for a fraction of a heartbeat. Then she turned her head, looked directly at him, and propelled herself into his arms.

Mitchell caught her, wrapped both arms around her, pulled her in through the window, staggered back safely against the wall of the chapel, and held on to her for dear life.

He would never let her go again.

Neither of them knew how long they stood there, arms around each other, clinging to one another.

At some point Mitchell realized his body was covered with sweat, that his lungs had begun to take air in and out again, and that his heart had been jump-started.

Apparently he was still alive.

Torey had been shaking, trembling, quaking, when he'd first pulled her in through the window. Gradually, and it could have been five minutes or ten minutes or an hour later, he realized she had finally gone still in his arms. Then he felt the small heaving in and out of her chest and he realized that she was crying.

She had a right to cry.

She'd just had the fright of her life.

This was no time for words or questions or even answers. They would come soon enough. This was a time simply to hold and to be held. And, so, that was what Mitchell did.

Finally even her tears started to cease. He detected a small hiccup and then Torey slowly raised her head from his chest and looked up into his eyes. Her face was still damp and her voice came out tentative and hoarse. "You came."

"I came."

"How . . . ?"

"I was already on my way."

She turned and glanced toward the window. Then quickly looked back at him. "I thought—"

"I know," he crooned soothingly, pressing his mouth to her forehead. "But it's all over now. You're safe."

"You saved my life."

He'd had to.

Was she ready for a question?

"What happened?" he asked.

Torey licked her lips as if she were suddenly parched. She wrinkled her brow and appeared to be trying to put the pieces together. "I was walking around the chapel, studying the stained-glass windows, and finally I decided to stop here and gaze out at the sea and at the Stones. I was thinking about Lady Victoria and Michell."

Torey must have meant Saint Victoria, but she could always explain that part to him at a later date.

"I was watching the tide come in."

"The tides and currents are particularly treacherous in that channel," he said.

"That's what Old Ned had just told me."

"Old Ned knows things no one else knows."

"That's where I was before I came up to the chapel. I was visiting Old Ned at his cottage and he was telling me the history of Saint Victoria and this place."

"Go on."

"I remember I was crying."

Mitchell noted that she didn't explain why.

"I have a vague recollection that Old Toby growled and then I felt something shove me toward the open window."

Mitchell scowled. "Something or someone?"

She swallowed hard. "I thought it was one of the *pleurants* at her tomb." She swallowed again. "Could I have imagined the whole thing?"

"I don't think so."

"Why not?"

"Because I saw someone bolt from the chapel as I came running up the hill."

She shuddered. "Who?"

Mitchell shook his head. "I don't know. The figure was wearing a hooded robe."

"Why?"

"I don't know." But he was going to find out if it was the last thing he did.

There was a whimper from somewhere down around their knees and then a damp nose tried to nudge itself between their bodies.

"Old Toby," Torey murmured and went down on her haunches and put her arms around his neck. "Dear Old Toby." She kissed the top of his head.

Mitchell found himself envying the sheepdog.

"I'm going to look around for a minute. Would you like to sit down on the step right outside the door?"

There were shadows under and in her eyes. "I'd rather wait for you right here."

"All right."

Mitchell made a quick inspection of the chapel. There wasn't much to see and frankly there didn't appear to be anything out of the ordinary. Then he spotted something on the floor on the other side of the sarcophagus and leaned over to pick it up.

"That's mine," Torey spoke up.

"It's a piece of carved wood."

"A gift from Old Ned."

"I see." He handed it to her. Then he stood, feet planted apart and studied the small room with a critical eye. "There's nothing here."

"Not now," she said quietly.

He nodded. "Not now."

"Can we go?"

"Of course. Let's get you back to the house and fix you a cup of Mrs. Pyle's famous tea."

"What's famous about it?"

"The 'wee dram of whisky,' " he informed her. Then he patted the ancient dog on its head and said, "C'mon, Toby, it's over. Let's all go home."

"Son of a bitch, Iain, somebody tried to kill her this afternoon," Mitchell swore, pacing furiously back and forth from one end of the Hunt Room to the other, stopping only long enough to slam his fist down on a thick, wooden trestle table. The sound reverberated throughout the entire two-story, vaulted-ceilinged chamber, bouncing off the walls, the mounted stag heads, the spears and lances, the ancient crossbows, the long bows and arrows, and the various other accoutrements of hunts long past.

Iain grunted.

It was spelled out for him in detail. "Someone attempted to push her out of the window of the chapel and onto the rocks below. She would have been killed in the blink of an eye if she hadn't somehow miraculously caught hold of the ledge."

The Storm's face was white with rage.

The MacClumpha had never seen him in this emotional state before. He couldn't remember ever seeing Storm's grandfather, the old earl, this angry, not even when he ranted on about his errant son and daughter-in-law.

The Storm was earning his name today.

Iain MacClumpha knew what his job was and he did it well. Better than most . . . he knew that, too. "You're angry, my lord, and you have every right to be. But now is the time to put your anger aside and make your plans."

Mitchell halted in front of a large gun rack that covered nearly half a wall, took a series of deep breaths, stood there for a minute or two without speaking and then turned to Iain and said, calm as you please, "You're right, of course."

"You say you saw someone in a hooded robe running away from the chapel," Iain confirmed.

The Storm nodded his head.

"Was there anything, anything at all, to tell you if it was a man or a woman?"

The Storm considered carefully and then shook his head. "I was too far away at the time." He said as an afterthought, "If it was a man, I would hazard a guess that he wasn't the size of you or me."

That wasn't much help, Iain concluded. There were

fewer than a handful of men on the island that even approximated his size or The Storm's. That left hundreds of possible suspects.

" 'Know thy enemy,' " The MacClumpha said aloud.

"Who said that?" Mitchell inquired.

Iain arched a shaggy eyebrow in the direction of the laird. "You did, laddie."

The word "when" formed on the younger man's lips.

"Back in the States when we first arrived at the lass's mansion," came the prompting.

"Everyone is an enemy until they prove themselves to be a friend," Mitchell murmured, repeating his own pragmatic philosophy.

"That's about the size of it."

"We trust no one but ourselves."

"No one."

Mitchell Storm's determination was like tempered steel. "I'm not going to take a single chance. Someone must keep an eye on Torey or be with her every minute until this business gets sorted out," he stated uncompromisingly.

"It will be done."

"We'll take turns standing watch. Twelve hours on. Twelve hours off."

Iain made a suggestion. "There is someone else I know we can trust to do her part."

Mitchell smacked himself lightly on the side of his head. "Of course, Alice Fraser."

"She loves Torey like a daughter. She'll protect the girl with her own life if she must."

"Will you fill her in?"

"I'll fill my Alice in."

A raised brow. "So, that's the way the wind blows, does it?"

"Aye, that's the way it blows."

"I'll go check on Torey. Alice is with her now, but I'll send her along to you in a few minutes."

Iain MacClumpha stood in front of the Hunt Room door, scarcely realizing that his shoulders nearly filled the available space from side to side and his height from top to bottom. "You think you know who it is, don't you, Mitchell?"

A dark head nodded. "Yes. I know who it is."

"Why not kick the whole bloody lot of them out of the castle?" he suggested.

Dangerous eyes narrowed to deadly black slits. The voice was without inflection. "Better to know where the enemy is. Better to have the enemy where you can see him. Better that the enemy doesn't suspect that you suspect him."

Iain felt a shiver ripple all the way down his spine. This man was surely The Storm if any man ever had been.

"I won't give the enemy a second chance. If he harms her, he'll pay the price."

They all thought she was stupid.

But she wasn't.

She might not be clever, but she wasn't stupid, either.

She was quick. She had always been able to race like the wind, run like a gazelle, slip in and out of places, small places, narrow places, places that went unnoticed by others.

She was learning the castle and its countless secrets and secret places by heart. She probably knew more about it than anyone. Certainly more than her beloved.

He was tall and handsome and, at the moment, very angry.

225

Angry men were dangerous.

She would keep away for a while. Away from him. Away from her. Away from them all.

She would know when it was safe to come out again. She always did. She always had.

Until then she would put a pretty, vacant smile on what vile Roger called her "pretty, vacant face," and wait.

And watch.

And plan.

She was very good at waiting and watching and planning. She would know when it was time, the right time, and what she should do.

Hadn't she known with Mummy?

She wondered if Roger intended to slink into her grandmother's room tonight and crawl into bed beside her and roll over on top of the old lady, spread her legs and thrust himself into her until they were both covered with sweat and the sheets were twisted around their ankles and the bedcovers and pillows were half strewn all over the floor, making a terrible mess of the lovely room.

If he did, she would sneak into her favorite hiding place and watch them.

It would give her something to do while she waited.

It wasn't the right time for the other. She was smart enough to know the difference and she could wait.

Chapter 20

"What are you doing?" Torey inquired as she walked out of the adjoining bathroom and into her bedroom.

Mitchell was sitting on the opposite side of the room, in an overstuffed chair beside a reading lamp and a table stacked with leatherbound books. "What am I doing?" Each word was said slowly and clearly and with perfect enunciation.

He was obviously stalling.

She repeated the question in the same careful manner. "What are you doing?"

"Reading," he claimed, grabbing for one of the books, flipping open to somewhere in the middle and beginning to read.

"Mitchell, what are you doing here?"

He gave her a semblance of a smile, but it never even made it past his mouth. "Standing guard."

"Standing?"

He glanced down. "Sitting guard."

"Why?"

"We took a vote."

"Who is we?"

"Alice, The MacClumpha, and me."

"Did you win or lose?"

"That depends on your point of view."

That brought a raised auburn eyebrow.

"We all agreed that I'm the one who should be watching over you at night."

"You mean like a guardian angel?"

He hemmed and hawed. "Something like that."

"Or, perhaps, more like a bodyguard?"

Mitchell's face lit up. "That's it. Like a bodyguard."

"Guarding my body."

He nodded.

"Keeping me safe from harm."

He nodded again.

"Is all of this because of what happened earlier today at the chapel?" she asked.

He was innocence itself. "All of what?"

"Well, I have noticed that either you or Alice or Iain is always by my side. One might even say that you three have agreed not to let me out of your sight."

"Yes."

She shuddered. "Then you think whoever attempted to shove me out the window will try again."

"He didn't *attempt* to shove you out the window, Torey, he did shove you out the window. You simply didn't fall onto the rocky cliffs below the way he had planned." Mitchell blew out his breath. "I don't want to frighten you any more than is necessary. But, yes, I think the culprit will try again."

"Why would anyone want to kill me?"

"I don't know."

She pulled her bathrobe more securely around her. "It's not that I'm naive, Mitchell. When you've grown up in the kind of family I have, security is always an issue. My parents tried to be discreet about it, but I sensed that there were eyes frequently watching me to make sure I was safe. I knew there was always the threat of kidnapping and being held for ransom because of the Storm name and the Storm wealth. I knew to be careful about strangers. And about friends, for that matter.'' She opened her arms wide and let them fall in a classic gesture of defeat. ''But here on the Isle of Storm was the last place that I expected to find myself feeling threatened.''

He drove a hand through his already tousled hair. ''If I had thought for one moment that you might run into a problem here, I would never have invited—''

She cleared her throat.

He corrected himself. ''I would never have insisted that you come to Scotland.'' He muttered half under his breath. ''I thought it would be safe. It should have been safe.''

Torey walked to the chair and placed a hand on his shoulder. ''Quit beating yourself up about it. It's not your fault. You couldn't have foreseen any of this.''

Whatever *this* was.

''It's late,'' he announced, with a glance at the clock on the bedside table.

''Is that a hint?''

''You've had an exhausting day. I think you should be in bed.'' It was more than a suggestion on his part, but less than a command.

She agreed. But how he expected her to sleep, under the circumstances, was beyond Torey.

She put it into plain and simple words. ''You mean, take off my bathrobe, climb into that lovely antique bed over there that probably dates from the seventeenth century—''

"Sixteenth," he interjected.

"—From the sixteenth century, pull up the covers, punch my pillow once or twice, close my eyes, and then just drop off to sleep while you spend the entire night sitting in that chair watching me?"

"Keeping watch over you."

There was a subtle difference, she realized. But this was not exactly a time for appreciating subtleties.

"It won't work," she stated.

"Why not?"

"Because I'll feel guilty that I'm lying down and sleeping in a perfectly comfortable bed, and you're spending the night sitting up wide awake in an uncomfortable chair."

He frowned. "Is this chair uncomfortable?"

In a word: "Yes."

"Why didn't you say something to the housekeeper or the butler or to any of the staff? Or even to me? The chair will be replaced by another one first thing in the morning."

Torey heaved a sigh. "That is not the point I'm trying to make here, Mitchell."

He was solemn. "I know."

Torey didn't know if she wanted to laugh or cry. "What am I supposed to do?"

He gave her a sidelong glance. "Pretend I'm not here."

That did make her laugh out loud. "Pretend that *you* of all people, that *you* of all men, aren't in my bedroom?"

He began his lecture with, "It's a matter of self-discipline. It's the mind taking control and precedence over the body."

"Mind over matter?"

"Yes. You simply get into bed, close your eyes, and imagine yourself somewhere else."

"Where?"

He gave it some thought. "Your tree back home."

Suddenly there were tears in her eyes. She quickly made a swipe at them with the back of her hand.

He wasn't fooled. "Did I say something wrong?"

She shook her head but didn't trust herself to speak.

His voice grew softer and went deeper in tone. "Are you homesick?"

She shook her head again and still couldn't speak.

"Aren't you going to tell me what I've said or done wrong, sweetheart?"

"It isn't anything that you've said or done wrong, Mitchell," she assured him, turning to the bedside table and plucking a tissue from the box. She wiped her face. He would want to know. She might as well tell him. "The fact you suggested that I imagine my tree back home means you understand."

"Understand what?" He didn't appear the least bit confused. "That your special tree represents a kind of security to you, a safe place, a haven?"

"Yes."

"Didn't anyone else understand that?"

She shook her head. "Not when I was a child. I think Alice does now, but Alice has only known me as an adult."

"Alice Fraser is a good woman," he stated.

Torey nodded and wiped her nose. "I'm going to miss her more than anyone knows."

"Miss her?"

She gave a knowing little feminine laugh, the kind that always tended to bug men because they never quite got it. "Somehow I don't think Alice Fraser will be returning to the States with me."

Mitchell got a confounded expression on his handsome face. "You've fired her?"

Torey hooted. "Fire Alice? I'd rather cut off my right arm. Heavens no, I mean The MacClumpha, of course."

"Alice and Iain."

"Alice and Iain," she repeated.

"So, that's what he meant this afternoon when he called her 'my Alice.' "

"That's what he meant," she verified.

"I knew but I didn't know. Well, I'll be," he said and thumped his knee.

"Well, I won't be," she said. "My loss is your gain." She tossed the used tissue in the wastebasket, walked over to the window, and pulled open one of the heavy drapes that had already been drawn for the night. "I can't think of anything I could want more for Alice than to find the right man to spend the rest of her life with." She sighed. "I think she's as surprised as anyone that it's happened to her."

"Iain is probably in something of a state of shock himself."

"They're perfect together."

Mitchell didn't echo her comment in a meaningless fashion. He seemed to actually give the matter its due consideration. Then he said, "They are perfect for each other."

"If we had a bottle of champagne handy, I think I'd toast our friends right now," she said, allowing the drape to fall back into place.

"A bottle of chilled champagne and two champagne flutes can be arranged in a matter of minutes," he pointed out.

Torey shook her head. "Perhaps another time. When the lucky couple have made an official announcement."

Mitchell sat up straighter in the chair. "It's getting late."

"You said that before."

"You should be in bed."

"You said that before, too."

"I'll tuck you in."

"You *didn't* say that before."

"I just wanted to see if you were paying attention."

Of course, she always paid attention when he spoke . . . almost always.

Mitchell got the strangest look on his face. He pushed himself up from the chair and headed straight toward her bed. Hands on hips, a puzzled expression on his handsome features, he stood there and gazed at the very top of the massive wooden headboard. "What in the hell is that?" he demanded to know.

Torey followed his stare. "That is my face."

He turned and glanced over his shoulder at her. "What do you mean your face?"

"It was a gift from Old Ned."

That didn't seem to explain much to Mitchell.

"Old Ned carves faces from odd bits and pieces of wood. Or I should say that he discovers the face hidden within the wood."

Mitchell made a face. "That doesn't explain what it's doing hanging from the top of your bed."

"Old Ned told me that the tradition is to hang the carving from the highest point in a man's house, because the face is a powerful talisman," she explained.

"Against what?"

"Evil, of course. The face will stand vigil against all evil."

"Do you really believe that?"

She shrugged. "I promised Old Ned." She looked straight at him. "I always keep my promises."

Mitchell suddenly leaned over and gently gathered her in his arms and held her to him. It was very much like what he had done that afternoon in the chapel after her brush with disaster. He buried his mouth in her hair and murmured, "Oh, God, Torey."

"What is it?" came out muffled against the front of his shirt.

"When I think of what a close call it was today." Then he didn't—or couldn't—say anything for several minutes.

"I know," she murmured, now being the one to offer him comfort and reassurance.

"I was so afraid for you," he admitted at last. "And I was afraid for myself."

What if she had fallen at that moment and ended up at the bottom of the channel? She would have gone to her death never having known what it was like to love or be loved by the man she was in love with.

She wasn't going to get everything she wished for or wanted in this life. Torey had acknowledged that to herself some years ago. But, surely, something was better than nothing.

"I'd better get back to my chair and *sit* vigil," Mitchell said with a crooked smile.

"I have a better idea." She went up on her tiptoes and caressed the side of his handsome face. There was a slightly unshaven texture to his jaw; it scraped her palm—heaven knew what it would do to her skin—but Torey found that she didn't care.

"A better idea?"

"Why don't you keep vigil right here?" She patted the mattress beside them.

"You mean share the bed with you tonight?"

There was nothing coy in her manner or in the way she spoke to him. "That's exactly what I mean."

"I don't think that would be a wise idea."

"Do you always do what is wise?"

Mitchell had once asked her that same question. And she had answered that she tried to.

He gave the identical reply. "I try to."

"And who is to say, Mitchell Storm, what is wise and what is unwise?"

He suddenly looked tired. He'd had one hell of a day, too, Torey realized, and there had been, perhaps, too many words spoken between them already.

It was time to be direct. "I want to sleep with you, Mitchell. I want to curl up beside you in that big bed and sleep next to you all night long. I also want you to take me in your arms and make love to me."

The man's voice grew softer, almost caressing her with his words. "I may not say the things you need to hear, but you know that I want you," he declared.

Men had always *wanted* her. That wasn't what she needed, what she wanted to hear from this man, but she would make peace with herself later. There would be plenty of time for regrets, then, too.

"I want whatever you have to give to me . . . even if it is some nameless passion."

"My passion is anything but nameless," he came back with quickly. "It is very definitely named Victoria."

Torey went into his arms and it was like coming home.

His kiss, his touch, his taste, the feel of him was familiar and yet thrilling. She remembered it well and yet she was learning it all over again.

She began with the buttons down the front of Mitchell's shirt and discovered her hands were shaking. She couldn't manage to get them through the buttonholes.

"Let me try," Mitchell insisted, and then found he could do no better and ended up tearing the shirt from his own back.

Her bathrobe was easy. One slender silk cord tied around the waist. One tug on the loose knot and it floated on gossamer wings to the floor at their feet.

Mitchell kicked off his shoes. They went flying halfway across the bedroom. His socks followed.

She was standing there in a diaphanous silk gown of pale pink.

He was left in a pair of jeans.

And when Torey unbuttoned them at the waist and eased the zipper down, she discovered that's all there was. He wasn't wearing a stitch underneath.

She smiled seductively as she inched the zipper down as far as it would go. "Is it something with you Scotsmen?"

"Is what something with us Scots?" he repeated, drawing in his breath when she tugged on his pants and they began their descent to the carpet.

"You never seem to wear any underwear?"

Mitchell gave her a wicked grin and declared, in a rather bad imitation of a native Scottish burr, "We Scots like to be prepared on a moment's notice, lass."

"Well . . . and I can see that you are prepared, laddie," she teased, depositing his pants down around his ankles.

Mitchell stepped out of his blue jeans, gave them a nudge with his foot and stood in front of her at attention.

"Good Lord!" Torey couldn't keep herself from exclaiming.

Mitchell glanced down. "What?"

"You're—" She swallowed hard.

"Is something wrong?"

He waited.

"You're magnificent," she said.

He beamed.

Mitchell reached out and quickly dispensed with her sheer nightgown; it slipped to the floor and joined her bathrobe in a forgotten, silky heap. Then he stood there and looked her over from head to toe, as she had so recently and so thoroughly done with him, and announced, "You are perfect."

It was exactly the right thing to say to her at that moment. She could use all the self-confidence, Torey realized, and, indeed, all the bravado, that she could muster.

She licked her lips. "I have something to tell you."

Mitchell swept her up in his arms, deposited her in the middle of the big bed and stretched out alongside her. "What is it?" he asked, nuzzling her neck.

She laughed and it came out as a raw sound and as anything but amusement.

He propped himself up on one elbow and gazed down into her eyes. "What is it, Torey?" he asked again.

"I'm really nervous," she blurted out.

"Why?"

"I don't think I'm very good at this kind of thing," she confessed, a little embarrassed and more than a little mortified that she had told him.

"What kind of thing might that be?" he inquired. Apparently it was a rhetorical question because he asked and answered all the questions, himself. "Are you afraid that you aren't any good at kissing? I know better. I've kissed you a hundred times and you have the mouth of an angel."

As if to prove his point, Mitchell bent down and

touched his lips to hers. It was a sweetly seductive kiss that quickly inspired her to thrust her tongue into his mouth, seeking more, always seeking more. They were both breathless by the time they broke it off.

"Are you afraid that you don't know how to touch a man? Believe me, I do know better. There was that afternoon in the secluded garden when your caress made me hotter and harder than I have ever been before in my life."

He took her hand and placed it on him. He was hot and hard. He was smooth and silky. She loved the feel of him. She loved touching him. She loved the idea that she excited him to the point that he had to make her stop or he would explode on the very next caress.

Mitchell's head bent to one breast while his hand traced a pattern from her throat to her other breast, deliberately grazing the nipple, down her stomach, around the inside of her thigh to end up at that sweet, aching juncture between her legs.

"Are you afraid you don't know how to respond to a man's touch?" he murmured, his own breathing changing, becoming labored, as he pressed his mouth to her breast, drew her nipple between his teeth, and nipped and licked and sucked even as he eased his finger between the damp auburn curls and slipped inside her.

Torey moaned aloud and instinctively lifted her hips off the bed, driving her breast deeper into his mouth, and causing his finger to thrust ever deeper into her body. She could feel the tiny convulsions begin, knew the moment when her heart seemed to cease its beating, sensed herself nearing the brink, and called out his name in that instant before she was catapulted over the edge. "Mitchell!"

Then he withdrew his hand, eased himself between her

legs, looked down into her eyes and thrust into her.

Her eyes flew open even wider and his name became a litany on her lips. "Mitchell. Mitchell. Mitchell."

"Stay with me, Torey." His thrust grew stronger, harder, deeper. "This is only the first of many, I promise," he said, giving a triumphant shout and exploding inside her.

She was taken by Storm.

Mind over matter be damned!

That was the last semirational thought Mitchell recalled having for the next several hours.

He finally lay back against the pillows and tucked one arm behind his head. He was momentarily satiated, downright happy, and tired, but it was the best kind of tired. He realized on some fundamental level that he had never felt better in his entire thirty-seven years.

There was definitely something to be said for good sex, great sex, the best sex he'd ever had in his whole bloody life.

And there was even more to be said for the woman stretched out beside him on the bed.

"You, my lord," Torey murmured, twisting her little finger in his hair, *that* hair, in an erotic pattern, "are a liar."

"A liar?" In what conceivable way, he wondered, could she consider him a liar?

She released the strand of dark pubic hair and chose another, making a small curl out of it. Realizing that it wouldn't stay in place without a touch of moisture, she leaned over him, took it between her lips, and moistened it with her tongue.

Mitchell felt his chest, and other significant parts of

his anatomy, begin to tighten in that old, familiar way. God, he couldn't be ready again already.

"A liar?" he repeated, telling himself, reassuring himself that she wouldn't be the death of him.

At least not yet.

Maybe not for years to come.

Blue-green eyes gazed up at him from the general region of his pelvis. "You told me that it was late and it was time for me to be in bed. That was nearly three hours ago," she scolded, with a quick consulting glance at the clock on the bedside table.

"I didn't lie," Mitchell felt compelled to point out to her. "You've been in bed the entire time."

Torey was stretched out on her stomach, legs raised, knees bent, ankles crossed, feet moving in time to some rhythm she heard only in her head. She rolled over onto her back, resting her head on his thigh, her hair brushing softly across a very sensitive place on his male anatomy, and stared up at the ceiling.

"You're right," she finally relented. "I have been in bed the whole three hours."

"Then an apology would be in order."

"I apologize, Lord Storm, you are not a liar."

"Your apology is accepted." Mitchell reached down and combed his fingers through Torey's mussed auburn hair. She had lovely hair: soft, silky, sweet-smelling. "On one condition."

"Why is there always a condition?"

"Because I say so. It's one of the privileges that comes with being chief of your clan."

She sighed and reached behind her head, only to discover an obstacle—a rather large obstacle, at that—in her path. "About this one condition . . ."

"Well, there is a penalty to be paid, of course."

''Of course.''

''Some kind of recompense that must be made.''

''Must?''

''Must. Surely you know what they say about the fighting men of Clan Storm?''

''I'm afraid I don't.'' She began to squeeze him, just a little here and there, up and down his shaft.

It was enough to drive a man to distraction.

''I'm afraid I've forgotten what we were talking about,'' Mitchell confessed to her.

''I was admitting my ignorance, until very recently, about the men of Clan Storm.''

''Then please allow me to fill you in, lass.''

Torey couldn't hold back the laughter that time. ''Yes, please do fill me in, my lord.''

Mitchell had a little surprise for the minx. He pushed the pillows aside and twisted around until his head was in the same relative position to her body as her head was to his.

He could feel her quiver when he took his first taste of her with his tongue, and the gasp of astonishment as he took it a step further and nibbled on the sensitive nub with just the edges of his teeth. And when he finally decided the time had come, he thrust into her, taking a long and hearty drink of the sweet libation she offered.

Torey awoke him again in the night, sat straight up in bed, and announced that she finally had the answer to the age-old question.

Mitchell pulled her down on top of him, took her in his arms and rolled over, kissing her all the while, caressing her until she was clinging to him, until she begged for him to come to her, arching her back and raising her body toward his erection.

Big deal, The Storm thought, his attention on more important matters. He had the answer to the age-old question, as well.

"God, you're beautiful in the morning," he murmured.

"It's not morning," Torey pointed out with a quick gesture toward the gray light coming in the windows.

"You're right. It's not morning and it's not night," he said in a low voice that sent strange shivers down her spine. "It's that time suspended between the two—the time when night creatures have crept away to their beds and day creatures have not yet awakened."

The timbre and rhythm of his voice captured her imagination as much as the words he was saying.

Then Torey remembered what she had tried to tell Mitchell last night before he had distracted her again and again. "I have something important to tell you," she said in preamble.

"What is it?" he asked, more interested in her at the moment than in what she was saying.

"I've found the sixth Victoria."

He kept on nuzzling her neck just at the spot that he knew made her shiver every time. "You're the sixth Victoria."

"No."

He opened his eyes. "No?"

"I've found the real one, Mitchell. I've found *the* Victoria that you've been searching for."

She had his attention now.

"Where is she?"

"Here."

"Here?"

Torey patted the chain and locket around her neck. "She was here all the time."

Chapter 21

"You've been wearing this locket around your neck since you were how old?" Mitchell asked her several hours later once they had dressed, eaten breakfast, and were on their own for the day.

"Six or seven years old."

"Who gave it to you?" His tone conveyed curiosity.

"No one."

"Where did you find it?"

It came back to Torey in bits and pieces. "I was bored. I decided to go exploring. There was this old trunk in an attic storage room at Storm Point where no one ever went. I suppose it was like the summer you discovered the portrait of the twins, Angus and Andrew, when you were visiting Castle Storm."

"The curiosity of children."

"Anyway, down under all the old lace curtains and outmoded evening gowns and stacks of vintage photographs, I found this dust-covered jewelry case. It probably hadn't been opened in a century."

Mitchell's brows congealed into a scowl. "Maybe not even since the original auction."

"That was my thought just this morning," she admitted.

"I interrupted you. Please go on."

"I can recall yet dusting off the case, looking it over from top to bottom, setting it down on the top of the trunk, and then gradually opening the lid. There, inside, nestled on a cushion of decaying red velvet was this locket. I took it out and held it up to the window. I remember the way the sunlight reflected off the gold. Then I realized that the locket had a small latch on the bottom. I released the latch and there she was. I felt as though I had discovered a wonderful treasure. And since no one seemed to want the locket—in fact, I convinced myself that no one else even knew it existed—I took it."

"Finders keepers, losers weepers."

"To this day, I believe the locket gave itself to me. I know I felt an immediate and special kinship with the young woman in the portrait. She became my secret friend."

Mitchell frowned a little and turned away. Then very slowly, he turned and retraced his steps. "What makes you think that the young woman in the locket is Lady Victoria?"

That was an easy question to answer. "I recognized her from the description Old Ned gave during his storytelling yesterday afternoon, and from her portrait in the stained-glass window of the chapel. Only it didn't hit me right away that's who she was."

"You probably had other things on your mind."

That was the understatement of the year. "I probably did," she agreed wholeheartedly.

Mitchell would have made an excellent attorney, she decided, as he inquired in cross-examination: "What makes you believe that this Victoria is *the* Victoria?"

Torey had been attempting to put the pieces of the puzzle together all morning. There were still a few pieces missing, but she was getting closer. She could feel it. She could *sense* it.

She held up one finger. "First, Lady Victoria lived during the right period in history."

"You know when the treasure dates from?"

"I'm pretty sure."

He gave a short, dry laugh. "How in the world did you discover that?"

"I looked and I listened, especially to Old Ned. The man has a wealth of information in that ninety-three-year-old brain of his. You told me so yourself."

There was a small, self-mocking smile on Mitchell's lips. "I did, didn't I?"

"Didn't you ever visit Old Ned?"

Mitchell gave a noncommittal grunt. "I suppose I did that summer, but he seemed to ramble on about romance and tragedy and lost love and things I doubt a boy of twelve or thirteen would have been interested in hearing."

"Lovey-dovey stuff."

"Yes."

"You said when your grandfather was dying he told you the key to finding the treasure was Victoria. You mentioned that it rang at least a distant bell with you at the time. Maybe you retained more of what Old Ned had rattled on about than you'd realized."

"Apparently not enough."

"Well, I was interested," Torey said after an interval. "So I did listen."

"What was the time period?"

"About 1314, give or take a year or two." She let that sink in.

"When did Lady Victoria live?"

Torey folded her arms over her chest. "She was born in 1297 and died in 1364."

"How did you learn that?"

"The dates are etched on her tomb."

Mitchell looked her square in the eyes. "Brilliant. Simple but brilliant."

"That's when I think it all began to make sense to me," she said, speaking as much for her own benefit as his. "I had this feeling."

"One of those feelings?"

"Yes, one of those feelings." She made a quick, involuntary movement with her hands. "I think the answer is down here in the locket and up there in Saint Victoria's chapel."

"Have you ever examined the portrait inside your locket under a magnifying glass?"

"No." It had never occurred to Torey.

"Have you ever pried the miniature out of its setting to see if anything is inscribed on the back?"

She shook her head. "I guess I wouldn't make a very good detective, would I?"

Diplomacy was exercised. "It might not be your calling."

"In other words, don't quit my day job."

He smiled and nodded. "A wise decision."

It was a moment or two before she thought to ask him, "Do you have a magnifying glass?"

"The library."

She reached for Mitchell's hand and pulled him toward the door. "I feel a sudden urge to be around books."

Hunched over a library table, lamplight shining directly onto the miniature portrait, they took turns peering at the locket under a strong magnifying glass.

Torey raised her head, stretched her arms and back, rubbed her eyes, and confessed, "I don't see anything unusual."

Mitchell, too, seemed to admit defeat. "Neither do I."

"Assuming that what we should be looking for would be classified as unusual."

Mitchell stared at her. "Brilliant but simple."

"That's the second time you've said 'brilliant but simple' to me today. I assume you mean it as a compliment."

"Believe me, it is," he stated with admiration. "The ability, the talent, to see the obvious where others do not is often brilliant. It is seeing with a clear eye."

"Are you saying that I see with a clear eye?"

"Yes."

"In that case, thank you. I think."

"Since we're not about to pry the portrait from its setting without the talents of an expert, this should be returned to its usual place for the time being," Mitchell informed her, hooking the chain and locket back around her neck.

She touched the locket tentatively. "Isn't it too important for me to be wearing now?"

"I think everything should stay as much the same as possible until we find the answers to our questions and until we discover who is behind the attempt on your life."

"Life goes on as before."

"Life goes on as before." Mitchell pushed his chair back, rose to his feet, sauntered to the library window and stood looking out.

Torey could see the fine drizzle coming down from where she sat.

He turned to her. "I think I'll go for a walk. Would you like to come with me?"

Torey nearly said no, then thought better of it.

So what if she got a little wet? She wouldn't melt, and she could always dry out later.

"Where are we headed?" Torey inquired as she sloshed along in a bright yellow mackintosh and a pair of "wellies" borrowed from one of the kitchen staff.

Mitchell paused on the front lawn—it was dotted with several dozen white sheep grazing on the lush green grass—put his head back and held his face up to the drizzle.

The rain in Scotland, especially the rain on the Isle of Storm, always seemed clean and somehow cleansing to him. Truth to tell, he loved the rain on his island.

"Wherever we end up," he finally said inconclusively. He glanced down at her. "Do you mind?"

Torey shook her head. "Those are often the best kind of walks," she said, skipping every now and then to keep up with his naturally longer stride and faster gait.

Mitchell deliberately slowed his pace. "Of course, I thought once we were out of sight of the house and any snooping eyes, we might double back and take a look inside Saint Victoria's chapel."

Torey rubbed her hands together in what appeared to be eagerness. "I assumed that had to be in the back of your mind. I mean, we've come this far and we're so near. This is no time for a leisurely stroll around the old estate." She looked up, paused and said, "Although it is a lovely place, Mitchell."

"Yes, it is," came his agreement. "Let's take the path to the left up ahead," he recommended. "I know a shortcut from there through the woods to the chapel."

"The chapel might be a bit dark inside on a day like this," she pointed out.

"That's why I have a torch stuffed into the pocket of my pants," Mitchell informed her.

Torey gave him one of those grins he was beginning to recognize. They always seemed to precede one of her so-called jokes. She did not disappoint him this time, either. "Is that your torch, Lord Storm, or are you just glad to see me?"

He put his head back and roared. It was several minutes before he could admonish her. "Remind me to discuss that with you at a later and more opportune time, Miss Storm."

She batted her eyelashes. "Discuss what?"

"This proclivity—one might even say this talent—you seem to have for double entendre and sexual innuendo."

"Why? Don't you like it?"

He gazed down at her with a wicked grin. "Quite the opposite. I love it." Then he wiped the grin from his face. "We're going to try to slip into the chapel unnoticed. Try not to be conspicuous."

"I'm wearing a bright yellow mackintosh and red wellies," Torey reminded him. "Under the circumstances, how inconspicuous do you expect me to be?"

"Then stay close to me and—"

"Try to blend in with the yellow roses around the doorway?" she suggested, only half in jest.

Without another word exchanged between them, they slipped around the corner of the small stone chapel and through the door, closing it behind them.

"It's cool and damp in here today," Torey said with a shiver that he concluded had nothing to do with the chapel being either cool or damp.

"No electricity. No heat."

"I noticed."

"The chapel has always been deliberately kept as it was originally constructed."

"Historical integrity."

"Something like that." Lack of funds to make improvements had also been a factor.

"Where do we start?"

Mitchell had been making his plans on the walk over. "By methodically taking this chapel apart stone by stone, stained-glass window by stained-glass window."

"I assume you mean figuratively."

"Since we only thought to bring one torch, we'll go over every inch together."

Torey contributed, "Two sets of eyes are better than one, anyway, I always say."

Mitchell had one stipulation. "You, however, will do us both a favor and stay clear—and I do mean clear—of that window."

After yesterday, he couldn't imagine that Torey would even want to get within a mile of the chapel, let alone the window. She had guts, this woman of his.

"What are we looking for?" she whispered as they began with the altar at the rear of the tiny church.

"I wish I knew."

"Ah, the proverbial needle in a haystack," said Torey with insight.

"We don't even know for certain that we're searching for a needle," he confessed.

Torey patted him on the arm and said with encouragement, "We're both very bright people, Mitchell. I'm sure that between the two of us we'll figure it out."

"Are you always this optimistic?"

"I like to think there is no such thing as insurmountable odds," she responded.

Mitchell explained his plan. It didn't take long. "We'll start here and employ the simple process of elimination," he divulged to her. "The altar appears to be a single chunk of solid stone. The cross is plain and solid stone as well."

"I think we can eliminate this area of the chapel from our list of possibilities."

"The walls are blocks of stone with nothing distinguishing except the stained-glass windows, which I suggest we tackle last."

Torey was in agreement and said so.

Mitchell flashed his torch at the ceiling. "Not much up there except wooden rafters and a bird's nest or two."

There was a soft sigh from beside him. "Where next?"

He looked down. "The floor."

"Is this going to require getting down on our hands and knees?" came the hesitant query.

"No," he assured her. "We'll just bend over as close to the ground as we can."

So they did.

A half hour later, their backs somewhat the worse for wear, they both straightened and concluded. "Nothing."

"The tomb of Lady Victoria is next on the list. I'll take the far end toward the window, both sides and the *pleurants*." Mitchell issued his orders. "You examine this end only."

A quick conclusion was reached. The only markings on Lady Victoria's tomb were her name and the date of her birth and death chiselled into the section Torey was scrutinizing, and the marriage stone that had been used as a cover for the sarcophagus.

Mitchell studied the marriage stone at some length. "This was apparently carved at a time when she expected to be married. I see the various symbols in the crest of Clan Storm and Victoria's initials. The gentleman's crest and initials appear to have been nearly obliterated from his side.''

''Because they never married.''

''Why was it called off?''

''He betrayed her. She betrayed him.''

''The same old story between a man and a woman, huh?'' It never seemed to change.

''At least her betrayal was for an honorable cause,'' Torey spoke up in Lady Victoria's defense. ''She did what she had to do in order to save Clan Storm.''

''What was the reason for his betrayal?''

''Money,'' she said contemptuously. ''Power. Land. All the usual things men are after. In fact, this particular one was after the Isle of Storm, itself.''

She had learned well apparently from Old Ned. ''When did all of this happen?''

''Sometime around the year 1314.''

''Now comes the real challenge,'' Mitchell said as he looked up at the stained-glass windows. ''You spent quite a bit of time here yesterday. Do you have any suggestions or observations?''

''As a matter of fact, I do,'' Torey told him. ''I noticed that the two stained-glass windows on the left side of the chapel appear to depict strangers, primarily warriors or knights. One plaque even states that the knight's name is unknown.''

Interesting.

''The windows on the right side, on the other hand, are very clearly associated with Clan Storm. One window shows the family crest and motto. The other is a narrative picture of Lady Victoria—who one day would become

252

Saint Victoria, of course—ascending a flight of stairs toward heaven.''

''The right and the wrong of it, huh?''

''That's the way it appears.''

''Which side do you suggest we start with?''

Torey chewed on her bottom lip for a moment. ''Let's start with Clan Storm.''

The stained-glass window with the crest of their clan seemed the simplest place to start, in Mitchell's opinion, as well. So that's where he started.

He recognized the crest: the hand grasping a thunderbolt. There was the traditional sprig of cranberry. He suddenly recalled seeing it on the shoulder of Torey's evening gown that first night at the costume ball. That night seemed a thousand years ago right now.

''And the clan motto,'' she said, reading a loose translation aloud: ''No one attacks me without punishment.''

''No surprises here,'' Mitchell told her.

''This window seems the most symbolic and the most complex,'' she told him as they moved on to the scene of the young woman climbing the stairway to heaven.

''You know she even looks a little like you,'' Mitchell said.

''Who does?''

''Lady Victoria.''

''I suppose there is some superficial resemblance. The hair. The eyes.''

Mitchell shook his head slowly. ''It seems like more than just her coloring. Too bad this window was never completed.''

''Yes. It is a shame.''

They moved across to the other set of stained-glass windows, examining first the one of the two knights on a single horse.

"The Knights Templar began their order by swearing poverty, chastity, and humility," Mitchell said knowledgeably. "They ended up rich, often lecherous, power-hungry, and eventually dead."

"This is the window I was telling you about," Torey said as they approached the last of the four. "This is the one that fascinates me."

"Why does it fascinate you?"

"Because I think I know the knight's name. Because I think that this window depicts the warrior that Lady Victoria fell in love with. I think this is the man who carved his initials into the tree alongside hers. I think this is the man who believed that she would betray her clan for him." Torey seemed almost reluctant to go on. "And this is the man she watched drown from the hilltop where the chapel now sits."

"What was his name?"

He could feel her taking a deep breath as if fortifying herself for what was to come. "Michell."

Christ.

Torey suddenly fell back several steps. "I think I see," she managed in a strangled whisper.

"See what?"

"The four windows shouldn't be viewed separately, but as a whole. Individually they each tell only part of the story."

She was right.

He knew it.

He *sensed*.

Mitchell was beginning to wonder if there might be something to this "second sight" thing, after all.

"Think out loud," he directed her.

Torey dashed from stained-glass window to stained-glass window as she condensed the story down to its essential form. "Strangers—experienced fighting men, indeed, knights—come riding into Scotland. There are those who believe they are associated with the vanquished Knights Templar. One knight is bolder, more brazen, more dauntless, and more determined than the others." She paused and mentioned in an aside to him, "By the way, have you noticed that you pay some slight resemblance to Michell?" Then she went on without waiting for denial or consensus. "The warrior knight's sword and armor and mighty war horse show that he has been in many battles. The inscription tells us that greed was his downfall."

Mitchell read the translation from the Latin aloud: " 'He that trusteth in his riches shall fall.' " He rubbed his chin and muttered, "I wonder what riches and where in the dickens he kept them—at least before his fall."

Torey said aloud, "Where would you keep your riches if you were a medieval knight?"

They stood and stared at the stained-glass window for a moment.

"Using the process of elimination," Mitchell proposed as he studied every detail of the colorful window.

"The box," they said in unison.

"It's the only place that makes any sense," he said.

"What is the box?" she puzzled.

"What does it represent?" Mitchell asked aloud.

"It must be the treasure the warrior knight supposedly brought with him, at least according to Old Ned's version of the story."

"I should have paid more attention to Old Ned."

"If the elderly gentleman turns out to be right about all of this, you owe him his favorite *dundee* at teatime every day for the rest of his life."

"It's a deal."

"But if there still is a box, where is it?"

"That is the question, of course."

Torey began to pace in her wellies and oversized mackintosh. The sight was really quite endearing, Mitchell thought.

"Where would I hide a box if I were going to hide a box?" she muttered.

"Inside another box," he answered off the top of his head.

They both turned and looked at the tomb.

Torey shook her head. "If the warrior knight Michell gave the box to Lady Victoria for safekeeping, she would have done something with it long before she died."

"Possibly." Mitchell thought about it. "Probably."

"The altar would be the logical choice, but as you say, it's solid stone."

"Where would I hide a box? I'd hide it inside another box," Torey chanted, as she walked around the chapel. Then she threw up her hands. "It beats me."

Mitchell went and stood in front of the stained-glass window depicting the warrior knight on horseback, great silver sword raised in his one hand, the ornate box tucked under the opposite arm. "A box inside a box." He turned and looked at Torey over his shoulder. "Do you suppose the box is shown symbolically or life-size?"

She came and stood beside him. "I don't know."

"Let's assume it's life-size. How big are we talking about?"

She held up her hands. "Perhaps no more twelve or eighteen inches in length, eight inches deep, perhaps the same in width."

"An accessible size."

"Yes."

"One might even say a common size."

"One might."

"And if one looked around this chapel, what would one see that was only slightly larger than what you've just described?"

"Only *slightly* larger?"

"Only *slightly* larger."

Torey turned in a slow circle. "Nothing," she concluded.

"Nothing?" he repeated. "Maybe you'd better look again. And don't make it more difficult than it is."

"I don't see anything," she wailed softly.

"As my history professor back at the university used to lecture us: 'Don't miss the forest because of the trees.' "

"Thanks," she said acidly.

"I'll give you a hint," he said.

"Please do."

"There are hundreds of them in the chapel."

The pale skin between Torey's auburn brows puckered. "Hundreds of them? There aren't hundreds of anything in the chapel—" Her voice trailed off. She quickly looked at Mitchell. "The walls. Hundreds of stone blocks make up the chapel walls."

"Bingo!"

Chapter 22

"We can't tear the chapel down block by block trying to find one that's hollow," Torey said in what she perceived as a reasonable tone of voice.

Mitchell gave her a stony stare. "Of course we can't."

She made a wild gesture with both her arms, the oversized mackintosh and wellies nearly tripping her in the process. "So how do you propose we go about trying to locate the right block out of all these blocks?"

What had she said only an hour before about there being no such thing as insurmountable odds?

She was a dunce, Torey told herself.

Mitchell stroked his jawline. Then he issued his orders. "Wait right here."

Opening the door of the chapel, he quickly glanced to the right and to the left, then hunched down to make himself appear smaller—a wasted effort, in Torey's opinion. Mitchell Storm was a big man and there was nothing he could do to conceal the fact. She watched him slip around the corner, and then disappear from sight.

He returned several minutes later, significantly wetter than when he had vanished, and with a sharp, metal object in his hand.

Her voice rose a little. "What's that?"

"A gardener's spike," Mitchell said succinctly.

He unbuttoned his damp jacket, shrugged out of the sleeves and shoulders, tossed it down, apparently without another thought, into a careless heap on the floor of the chapel. Then he proceeded to wipe the pointed tip of the spike off on the front of his shirt. It left a wide streak of dark brown mud across the blue denim.

"What is a gardener's spike?"

"The gardening crews drive them into the ground at the base of trellises and arbors to help secure the framework for rambling roses or wisteria or whatever needs extra support."

Torey found herself still in the dark. "What do you intend to do with that thing?"

"I'm going to use it to locate—if I can—a hollowed-out stone," he stated.

She didn't understand. "How?"

"It's the difference between an empty drinking glass and a glass filled with water."

She had obviously missed something. "What does glassware, empty or otherwise, have to do with this?"

He took a few seconds to explain. "If you tap your dinner fork, say, against the rim of a glass that's full or even half-full, it will sound entirely different than if you tap it against an empty glass."

"Of course." Now she got it. "You're going to use the metal spike as a kind of tuning fork and listen for a hollow sound."

"Well, maybe not hollow, but it should sound different if I tap on a solid block versus one that isn't completely solid."

Torey had to hand it to the man. It wasn't a bad idea. Mitchell began with the stone in front of him.

Tap.

Tap. Tap.

Tap.

Torey followed along directly behind him, bending her head—and, therefore, her ear—toward the wall.

"Try not to breathe so loudly," Mitchell tossed back at her over his shoulder.

Torey held her breath.

It was impossible, naturally, to hold her breath for more than half a minute or so. Almost as impossible, or improbable, as the process of elimination Mitchell was employing with the gardener's spike and the stone blocks.

"What about the blocks you can't reach?" she finally said, peering up at the ones near the raftered ceiling of the chapel.

"I'll cross that bridge when I get to it," Mitchell told her.

"We may have to come back another time with a ladder," she pointed out.

"We may have to," he agreed.

She wondered if he had any concept of how long it was going to take to tap even the stone blocks that were easily within reach.

"How long do you think this is going to take?" she inquired in hushed tones.

"Longer than I'd expected," he said, sounding a bit impatient.

That wasn't all she had on her mind, of course. "What if the box isn't even here?"

"Torey—"

Her name came out sounding like a warning.

"What?"

"Shhh!"

She persisted. "Why don't you at least start in the most obvious place?"

That got the man's undivided attention. "And what is the most obvious place?"

Plain as the nose on her face. Well, according to Old Ned, "plain as the pretty nose on her pretty face," and Torey decided she preferred the elderly gentleman's description.

"The stone block directly under the warrior knight's window," she stated.

"But—"

"Remember," she reminded him, "brilliant yet simple. Seeing with a clear eye."

Mitchell Storm could hardly argue with his own logic. "All right. We'll try the stone block under the warrior knight's window."

He bent over toward the stone. Torey was right there beside him. He tapped several times with the metal spike.

"What do you think?" he asked.

"Try it again."

This time he tapped considerably harder.

Torey frowned and suggested. "Try tapping the blocks on either side of that one."

Mitchell did. "I swear it sounds a little different."

Torey urged him on. "I say we go for it. After all, what do we have to lose?"

"You're right."

"*How* exactly do we go for it?" she asked, since it was getting down to the specifics.

"We have to find a method of extracting the stone from the wall," Mitchell explained.

"You mean we try to dig it out?"

"In a word, yes."

"With what? Our bare hands?"

"Not in the beginning. Later on it's hard to say what we'll have to use."

He was serious.

"Are we speaking of brute strength here?"

He nodded his head and gave every appearance of studying the stone block in front of him.

"Well, in case you hadn't noticed, Lord Storm, one of us is a little lacking in the brute strength department." She studied his broad shoulders. "I'm not sure even you are as strong as an ox."

"It's all a matter of mind over matter."

That drivel again!

He handed over the torch. "Try to keep the beam of light shining on that particular section of the wall."

That she could manage.

Mitchell took a Swiss army knife from his pants pocket—the man did seem to carry a surprising array of tools in his pants—and began to whittle away at the mortar wedged between the stone blocks. Chips flew off in every direction, creating a fine, gray powder.

It took time.

Considerable time.

More than once Torey had to ask for a short break from holding the torch. She flexed her arm and shoulder muscles and walked around the tiny chapel until she was certain she could return and hold the light steady again.

Once Mitchell had chiseled away at the outline of the stone block, he attempted to wedge the metal garden spike under one corner and use it like a lever. She realized he was trying to move the stone even a fraction of an inch. After all, *if* it was hollow, it shouldn't be as heavy as the other blocks.

It moved.

Not more than a fourth of an inch.

But it did move.

"This is going to take the patience of a saint," Mitchell grumbled under his breath.

But through patience, unadulterated male muscle, the sharp tip of the metal gardening spike, a little engineering know-how that Mitchell claimed he'd picked up somewhere in the islands of Indonesia, plain, old human effort, and sheer willpower, he managed to move the stone block two or three inches.

He stopped, leaned back against the chapel wall several feet from where he'd been laboring, raised one arm and wiped the sweat from his face with his sleeve.

"I can see a crack around the top of the block, an inch or two in from the edge," she said.

"A lid?"

"It could be a lid."

"We may both need to put some muscle into it now," Mitchell instructed once they were ready to start the next step in the extraction process.

"What do you want me to do?"

"Even if the stone is hollow, I won't have any way to judge how much it's going to weigh. I want you to provide backup, Torey. Literally. Turn around, plant your weight against my back and brace your feet against the stone floor."

"What are you going to be doing?"

"I'm going to try to move the stone block out from the wall until I can get an actual grip on it. Then I'm going to lift it and quickly set it down on the chapel floor."

"You could hurt yourself doing something like that, Mitchell. That block could weigh several hundred pounds."

"Yup, it could." He drew in a long, deep breath. "On the count of three."

"Why is it always on the count of three?" Torey mumbled, turning and placing her back to his.

"One."

Torey pushed her body harder against his.

"Two."

She took a deep breath and prepared herself.

"Three."

There was a single, audible grunt from Mitchell, then she was partially forced out of the way by the propulsion of his body, followed by a loud thunk as stone block landed on stone floor.

Torey immediately turned around, grabbed the torch from where she had placed it on the floor for safekeeping and shone its light on a spot at their feet.

Mitchell was breathing heavily. "Damned thing weighed more than I thought it was going to."

"Maybe it isn't hollow," she ventured.

"It's hollow all right. I doubt if two men could have lifted a stone that size, otherwise." He added as an afterthought, "Being hollow doesn't mean that it's empty, however."

She had been so intent on finding the box that she had nearly forgotten they were primarily interested with what might be *inside* the block of stone.

"We'll take it one step at a time," Mitchell reminded her. "I don't want you to get your hopes raised up too high. We don't know that there is a box—or anything else, for that matter—concealed within the stone. And we sure as hell don't know what's inside the box if there is one."

Enough talk.

"Shine the torch right here, will you, Torey?" Mitchell went down on his haunches, took his Swiss army knife and sliced along the sealed top of the stone block.

He had to repeat the process three or four times, cutting deeper and deeper on each round. Then the knife seemed to break through some kind of barrier. Again, using the metal spike and the knife in tandem, he attempted to pry one corner of the lid.

It wouldn't budge.

He tried again. "Come on, dammit," he urged.

"Come on. Come on," Torey repeated as if her voice added to his would help.

The corner of the lid moved slightly.

"It moved."

Mitchell kept working at it until he finally forced one end of the stone lid to crack an inch, then he slid it off the rest of the way.

There was a collective sigh of relief.

"You did it!" Torey exclaimed.

"Now let's see what I've done," he said, tempering his own enthusiasm.

They both peered down into the hollowed-out stone. Inside was a piece of cloth. Well, it wasn't exactly a piece of cloth; it was more like a fragment of animal skin.

"Seal," Mitchell said, hazarding a guess. "Probably skinned and treated with whatever was used for waterproofing in those days."

"Can you lift it out?" The suspense was killing Torey.

Mitchell reached down in the container and extracted the sealskin-wrapped package. It was tied and knotted with a length of ancient cord. He set the bundle down, and with a quick flick of his knife blade, cut the cord. Then he carefully began to unwrap whatever was underneath the centuries-old covering.

The protective animal skin fell away, and there it was on the floor of the chapel.

Torey went down on her knees.

"Why, it's beautiful," she exclaimed.

"It is beautiful," Mitchell agreed.

"It's the most beautiful box I've ever seen," Torey said in a voice filled with awe.

The box was very similar in size to what she had estimated earlier. Eighteen inches or so in length, perhaps eight inches in depth and the same in width. The top was slightly rounded.

It was primarily silver with some hammered gold accents. The top was inlaid with intricate patterns of mother-of-pearl and precious and semiprecious gemstones, primarily garnets and pearls, a veritable rainbow of topaz, and perhaps a spinel or two—what was once thought to be rubies but were not.

The sides, the ends, and even the bottom of the box were covered with finely drawn etchings. The scenes depicted ranged from great desert cities to grand palaces to pastoral settings that could have been of Scotland itself. It would take many hours of careful inspection to see all there was to see on the box.

"It's magnificent," Torey said simply.

"Yes, it is." Mitchell gazed into her eyes. "I don't see any lock on the outside. I think it's time we looked inside, don't you?"

Torey nodded. "I'm dying of curiosity."

"Now that you mention it," came a rather sardonic and scathing male voice from the doorway of the chapel, "I think we're all dying a little to see what's inside your precious box."

Chapter 23

He'd made a mistake.

A big mistake.

Mitchell Storm silently swore at himself and tried to think as quickly as he could on his feet, especially considering that he wasn't on his feet—he was down on his haunches like an animal. Not exactly the ideal position to be in when surprised by the enemy.

Especially when that enemy was clutching a particularly large and lethal revolver in his hand.

Bluff, man!

"What the hell are you doing here, Forbes?" Mitchell demanded to know. He had every right to be asking the questions and requiring the answers.

"Apparently the same thing you are, old boy. I'm searching for treasure," came the slightly amused reply from the handsome man at the doorway.

It was undoubtedly the one and only time Roger Forbes had had the upper hand since his arrival at Castle Storm with his stepdaughter and stepmother in tow.

"Somehow you don't seem quite so imposing or intimidating on your knees, Lord Storm," Roger Forbes observed, passing his tongue over his lips.

"I'm not on my knees," he snarled.

The deadly weapon was brandished by a soft, manicured, male hand . . . but the hand was surprisingly steady. "Then you'd better be sometime in the next five seconds, or the lovely Miss Storm will pay the price for your excessive pride."

Mitchell eased himself onto his knees.

Their unexpected visitor glanced at the ornate box between them on the chapel floor. "So, this is the treasure you two have been busy looking for."

"How did you know?" inquired Torey.

"I may appear to be something of a fool, or even at times a drunkard, but I assure you, Miss Storm, that I am not. I've been keeping my eyes and ears open."

Mitchell needed facts and he needed them fast. "Are you on your own, Forbes?"

"Good heavens, no, Lord Storm," came Sylvia's throaty laugh as she stepped into the tiny church behind her stepson. "Roger and I are partners in everything. Aren't we, dearest?"

"Yes, we are," Roger replied without looking around at the woman who came up to stand beside him.

They were both dressed for the weather in raincoats and sturdy walking shoes. It was certainly no accident that the pair had appeared when and where they did.

"By the way, it's currently coming down in buckets out there, Lord Storm. The very least you could have done as a thoughtful host," Sylvia admonished him, patting her damp and windblown coiffure, "is pick a day for dealing with all of this business when my makeup and hair wouldn't get ruined."

"My abject apologies, madam," Mitchell said to her with a dose of excruciating politeness.

"You see, Roger," she said, giving the handsome man

a sharp nudge with her elbow, "the aristocracy know how to behave like perfect gentlemen even under the most trying circumstances."

"As if you'd know one end of a gentleman from another," taunted her accomplice.

"That will do, Roger," Sylvia snapped. Then her voice dropped to a sultry purr, "So this is the treasure chest, is it?" She took several steps closer to the elaborately decorated box, but was very careful not to get too close, Mitchell noted.

Sylvia Forbes was not a stupid woman.

In fact, he had a strong hunch she was anything but. The woman was a survivor. And survivors usually had excellent instincts—they had to. Sylvia's appeared to be finely honed.

She looked straight at Mitchell and spoke to him as though they were the only two people present in the chapel. "I see you haven't opened the box yet."

"We were about to when we were rudely interrupted," he remarked as if they were sitting in the drawing room making casual conversation over a glass of dry sherry before dinner.

"Roger has no manners," she said, dispensing with discretion, as if she ever bothered with it, anyway. "But, believe me, my lord, the boy does have his redeeming qualities."

"I hate it when you talk about me as if I weren't standing right here in the same room with you, Sylvia," Roger complained bitterly.

"Then don't listen," she said to him sweetly.

Too sweetly.

"And I hate it when you call me boy."

"Don't persist in acting like a boy, then."

Mitchell wondered just how far and how long Sylvia

and Roger would go in exchanging insults. Would it be far enough and long enough to create a diversion so he could wrestle the gun away from Roger Forbes?

Unfortunately Sylvia foiled his plans.

"Let's not argue, dearest," she said in a conciliatory tone of voice. "This isn't the time or the place. Not when our thoughtful host is about to open the treasure chest and reveal to us why our visit to Castle Storm hasn't been a complete waste of time and energy, after all. Do proceed, Mitchell."

"Open the box," ordered Roger, flaunting the revolver in his possession.

Mitchell made one last effort to reason with the man. "You'll never get away with it, you know."

"That is where you're wrong, actually," Roger stated with confidence. "We will get away with it."

"Do you mind if I ask how?"

"Not at all." Roger Forbes made a motion toward the open window. "There will be a tragic accident. Two people will be found floating in the treacherous waters of the sound. I think the tide and the currents will cover any tracks left by Sylvia and me quite nicely, don't you?"

Mitchell sized up the space between the two of them and wondered how fast he could jump the sonofabitch.

"Don't even think about it," Forbes warned. "Now open the bloody box."

Mitchell reached over and slowly raised the lid.

It was just as he'd suspected . . . and feared.

"The box is empty." Roger Forbes's expression was one of disbelief, immediately followed by suspicion. "What kind of fast one are you trying to pull on us, Storm?"

"It's as much of a surprise to me as it is to you," he insisted, which was almost true.

Torey stared down into the box. "It's empty," she confirmed, stunned.

"I don't believe that you didn't know," Roger insisted, thoroughly infuriated.

"I'll wager that neither of them knew," Sylvia insisted from her position partway between her stepson and the pair on their knees. "Anyone with even half a brain or eyes to see can tell that they aren't acting. Especially the girl. She isn't any kind of actress, at all." She obviously meant Torey.

Roger snarled like a rabid dog. "How would you know, dearest Sylvia?"

She shrugged her elegant if damp shoulders. "I was once on the stage . . . in my youth."

"You never told me that before," her stepson said.

"I don't have to tell you everything, my dear boy," she claimed with a mocking laugh.

"Well, now what the bloody hell are we to do?" Roger demanded of no one in particular.

"I would suggest that you put the gun down and act like a rational human being," Mitchell advised. "There's nothing to be gained by waving a weapon around. Somebody could get hurt."

Roger Forbes wasn't interested in what Mitchell Storm had to say on that subject, or on any subject. "I'll do whatever I damned well feel like doing, you pompous ass, and if that includes waving this gun around, I will."

"Let me handle this, Roger," Sylvia intervened, reaching out to take the revolver from him.

He turned cold, ice-cold, blue eyes on her. "Why would I do that, Sylvia?"

"Because I'm your stepmother. Because I'm older and wiser than you are. And because I'm the one in charge.

I always have been and I always will be," she informed him in no uncertain terms.

Roger brayed like a jackass. "Nothing you've done since we arrived on this bloody island has worked out worth a tinker's damn, you silly old bitch."

"Don't use that tone of voice with me, Roger."

"I'll use whatever tone of voice with you that I want to," he threw back in her face.

"You can't talk to me that way," she insisted.

"I can, I have, and I will," he countered, unrepentant.

Her complexion suddenly became blotched with unattractive red spots. "Your father would roll over in his grave if he knew."

"Let him." Roger laughed and it was a repulsive sound. "Who do you think you're kidding? You hated the old goat as much as I did. Why, it wouldn't surprise me to find out that you gave him a helpful push toward those pearly gates yourself," he suggested, raising his eyes heavenward for a moment.

Sylvia Forbes was absolutely livid. "How dare you suggest such a thing?"

"Get off it, Sylvie. Maybe you were a passably decent actress at one time in your life, but that time has long passed. You aren't fooling anyone with the innocent widow act."

"You son of a bitch," she swore at him and would have gone for his eyes with her talons if she hadn't remembered at the last moment who their real enemies were.

To Mitchell's regret.

Sylvia took several minutes to calm herself and collect her wits. "Well, this has turned out to be one fine mess," she announced as if the previous scene had never taken place. "We're stuck with these two and not a penny in treasure."

"Which brings us back to the question: What do we do next?" Roger reiterated.

"I say we shoot *her*," came the answer from the chapel doorway behind them.

Torey had had a *feeling* about Nadine Forbes from the moment she had met the young woman that first evening at Castle Storm, the evening Mitchell had introduced her to his assembled, if uninvited, guests as his fiancée.

Jealousy wasn't a healthy emotion.

In the hands—and in the mind—of an unstable girl it could be more than unhealthy, it could be dangerous.

Nadine Forbes was the perfect example.

"Give me the gun, Roger," his stepdaughter urged him, cajoled him, then demanded of him, holding out her pale, white hand. "I'm not afraid to shoot her."

Roger was obviously more than a little confused by this most recent turn of events. "Shoot who?"

"Miss Storm."

"Miss Storm?" His eyes flew wildly to Torey.

Nadine hadn't bothered with a raincoat or a jacket or even an umbrella. She was wearing a fashionable cotton frock: a lightweight sundress suitable only for the warmest days on the Isle of Storm. She was soaked through right down to her skin. Her white strappy summer sandals were covered with mud. Her hair hung in wet, bedraggled ringlets around her face.

Yet the young woman seemed totally oblivious to her physical appearance.

Nadine was single-minded. "Don't we want *her* out of the way permanently? Doesn't *she* stand between us and the successful completion of our plans?"

"What the hell are you blathering about, Nadine?" Roger asked, his voice laced with incredulity.

She smiled a beguiling smile at her stepfather. "Why, dear grandmama's plans are for me to marry Lord Storm. I am to be the next Lady Storm and a countess in my own right. Surely my elevated position in society will advance both grandmother's and yours."

"I'm afraid those plans have fallen through," he admitted with some chagrin.

"It's not too late," she rebutted.

"It is too late."

"Isn't."

"Is."

"It isn't," she insisted. "Why, I almost succeeded in getting rid of her yesterday, you know."

"You were the one who pushed me out the window," Torey said and she knew it was true.

"Of course I was." The girl seemed proud of her nearly successful and deadly accomplishment. "He—" she raised one hand and pointed a finger at Mitchell "—is supposed to become my lover and husband. Not yours."

"I'm afraid those were my hopes and dreams, dear, and not Lord Storm's intentions," Sylvia admitted, sounding suddenly like the voice of reason.

"That's not true."

"It is true," her step-grandmother assured her.

"It can't be true." A childish pout formed on the sulky mouth. "I'm younger than she is. I'm as pretty as she is. And I'm not the stupid cow Roger said I was."

Roger Forbes had the good graces to blush.

"I know how to please a man," Nadine declared as she stood there, facing them with utter defiance written on her face. "I've watched the two of you," she said, indicating Roger and Sylvia. "I've seen you naked and sweating like a pig and pumping her against the bathroom sink, all the while her pale, old, drooping breasts were swinging back and forth, back and forth, like the pendulum on a clock."

"That is enough, Nadine," Sylvia insisted, taking a very stern tone with the girl.

"You can't stop me from telling the truth, you old biddy," she said, making a face at her step-grandmother. "I know all of your secrets, and I can shout them at the top of my lungs if I wish to. You're the stupid cow. You're the one who is ancient and wrinkled and undesirable. Roger only does it to you because you're blackmailing him. You've been blackmailing him for years. Ever since you deliberately set out to dig up all the dirt on him you could find after you married dear grandpapa. Roger only does it to you to keep you quiet."

"Shut up!"

"I know everything, grandmama, dearest. Why, I even know your real age."

Sylvia grew livid. "Keep your mouth shut, girl, or so help me you'll live to regret it."

"You're sixty-three years old," the girl threw in Sylvia's face. Then Nadine turned to Roger. "How does it feel to know that you've been sticking it to a sixty-three-year-old woman?" She stuck out her tongue at him. "Who's the stupid cow now?"

Every drop of blood drained from Roger Forbes's too-handsome features.

Nadine lunged.

She grabbed the gun from Roger's hand before he knew what had happened.

"I don't like her," the girl announced, pointing the weapon straight at Torey's head. "I think I'll shoot her right between the eyes. I'm going to kill her this time.''

"Goddammit, Storm,'' Roger whined from where he stood, frozen in place, unmoving. "I never meant for it to go this far.''

Suddenly Torey *sensed* what Mitchell was about to do. There was no time or opportunity for him to get to Nadine. He wasn't about to trust either Roger or Sylvia to come to their aid. That left only one course of action. He intended to place himself between Nadine and the gun, and Torey. He was going to use his body to shield her.

She could not allow it.

Torey sniffed, as if she were facing a minor disappointment in her life, and remarked to Nadine in her haughtiest debutante manner. "All right, Nadine, you win.'' She even threw up her hands in defeat. "You can have him.''

That wasn't what Nadine Forbes had expected her to say.

The girl's eyes narrowed suspiciously. Nadine was shrewd in her own way. "You don't mean that.''

"Yes, I do.''

"Why?''

Torey yawned—politely covering her mouth, of course—as if she had, frankly, become a little bored with the whole subject. "It wasn't a real engagement, anyway.''

"It wasn't real?''

She shook her head. "It was a phony engagement. We made it up to put your grandmother off the scent.'' Just for good measure, Torey added, "Do you see an engagement ring?''

The girl shook her head no.

"Have you read any official announcements in any of

the newspapers? Or heard anything about it on the telly?''

Again, Nadine shook her head.

"Of course, I think Lord Storm wanted you all along, but he thought he was too old for you."

"He's not too old for me."

"I agree. In fact, I think he's the perfect age for you."

The girl visibly brightened.

Torey kept talking. "You're young and pretty and you have a lovely figure. Why, I'll bet you know how to please a man in bed, too, if you get my drift."

"Of course I get your drift."

Torey had to be careful and not rush the next leap of logic. "Then the man is all yours, Nadine. Therefore, I don't see any reason for you to have to shoot me," she pointed out gently.

The girl's forehead creased. "You think I'm a stupid cow, too, don't you?"

"Of course, I don't," Torey said sympathetically.

"You feel sorry for me. I can see it in your eyes. I can hear it in your voice. I don't like people who feel sorry for me. I believe I'll have to shoot you, after all."

In the space between heartbeats, Mitchell threw himself across Torey protecting her with his own body.

Nadine cried out. "No!" She never lost her grip on the gun, however. "Why?" she asked Mitchell.

"Because I love her."

"You love me."

He shook his head. "You're a sweet child, Nadine, and you need help. Help that I can't give you. Why don't you put the gun down and we'll see that you get the very best help?"

"I don't want to," she said defiantly.

Without a sound and without any warning, a sturdy

arm reached around Nadine and plucked the revolver right out of her hands.

"I'm afraid what you want and what you're going to get in this particular instance are two entirely different things, young lady," stated Alice Fraser.

Roger and Sylvia Forbes quickly turned tail as if to make a dash for the chapel door. They found the entranceway was blocked by one very large and very angry Iain MacClumpha.

"Nobody moves, nobody so much as breathes unless The MacClumpha gives them permission," he barked out the command. "Is that understood, lasses and laddies?"

Then he glanced down at Mitchell and grinned. "Excepting you, of course, my lord."

"It was all for bloody nothing," Sylvia was still wailing as she was led away some time later by the authorities.

"It looks that way, old thing," Roger commiserated as he trotted along behind her, hands cuffed behind his back.

"I hope they get Nadine professional help," Torey commented as she watched the trio disappear with the police in the lead, and Alice and The MacClumpha bringing up the rear guard.

"I think all three of them could use professional help," Mitchell observed. Then he glanced around the small chapel and sighed. "It's all been for nothing, hasn't it?"

Chapter 24

"I wouldn't say it's all been for nothing," Torey announced optimistically. "The box is very old and very beautiful and no doubt very valuable, as well."

"Ah," Mitchell said, perhaps not with bitterness in his tone, but certainly with a degree of discouragement. "Another family heirloom we can sell in order to fix the leaking roofs of Castle Storm and the bungalows on the island?"

The Storm turned his back, then, and walked out the door of the chapel.

Torey followed and sat down next to him on a large flat rock some small distance away.

The rain had ceased and the sun had come out. There wasn't a cloud to be seen in the sky. By all accounts the rest of the afternoon was going to be lovely.

"I would like to help," Torey said at last, racking her brain to find a way to broach the subject of money without wounding his damnable male pride.

Mitchell gazed out over the deceptively placid waters of the channel. "You've already helped enough."

She cleared her throat. "Do you remember the night of the costume ball at Storm Point?"

The man beside her laughed, but there was a hint of the bittersweet in his laughter. "I remember."

After a pause, she inhaled deeply and said, "I was wearing a set of rubies with my Victorian evening gown."

"As a matter of fact, most of your guests and, in particular, Mrs. Van Allen and Miss Albright were gossiping about your jewelry. The dowagers were speculating whether or not the Storm rubies had been out of the bank vault since your mother died."

Thank you, Mrs. Van Allen, Torey said silently.

Maybe the old woman was going to end up helping the cause, after all.

"As a matter of fact, the dowagers were right. Those rubies had sat in the bank vault for more than ten years, gathering dust and doing no one any good."

"What are you trying to tell me, Torey?"

"I'm trying to tell you that I would like to give the rubies to the people of the Isle of Storm."

"Thanks, anyway, but I don't think the sheep farmers or the fishermen or the townsfolk would have much use for such baubles."

"I don't literally mean give the stones themselves," she hastened to explain.

He waited to hear the rest of her explanation.

"We'd sell the stones. Auction them off at Sotheby's and use the proceeds to fix their roofs and whatever else needs fixing. Starting, I think, with Old Ned's place. I noticed there was a leak in one corner by the fireplace. Or at least I assume that's why he had a pan sitting there to catch the drips."

Mitchell stood and stretched. "Keep your rubies, Torey," he said. There was an undertone of resentment in his voice.

"Why won't you allow me to help?"

He looked down at her. "Clan Storm has never accepted charity and we're not about to start now."

"It wouldn't be charity," she pointed out. "It would simply be getting some of your own back."

"I don't want some of my own back. Not like that. And not from you."

She stood and faced him. "You are a stubborn son-of-a-gun, Mitchell Storm."

There was a rueful smile on the handsome face above her. "It goes with the territory, I'm afraid. All the chiefs of Clan Storm have been stubborn son-of-a-guns."

"Men!" she muttered under her breath.

Meanwhile, he had sauntered back into the chapel and was staring at the mess they'd made of the wall. "At least we solved the age-old mystery and put the legend of a treasure to rest," he said.

"The box is lovely," she remarked. "Is it heavy?"

Mitchell lifted it easily. "Not really."

"May I look at it?" she asked.

"Of course."

"Do you think Lady Victoria would mind if we set it for a moment on the end of her tomb?"

"I don't think she would mind in the least."

Mitchell set the box down on the stone sarcophagus. The sunlight was streaming in the open window and Torey could clearly see the etched vignettes as she leaned over to study them.

"The workmanship is superb," she murmured, absorbed.

"Yes, it is," Mitchell agreed, taking some interest himself in the process of looking.

"There's something for everyone depicted here. Great cities rising up out of the desert. Grand palaces that almost seem to resemble an early Venice. The hills of Scotland. There's even a scene like one of the stained-glass windows.''

''Which one?''

''The one showing Lady Victoria ascending the stairway and the angels waiting to escort her presumably into heaven.''

''The box must have been created some time before Lady Victoria commissioned the windows for the chapel, however.''

Torey was starting to get that *feeling* again. ''But I think we can assume that she studied the box, perhaps even pored over every detail of it before she had it buried in the wall. She may even have been inspired by the heavenly scene etched on the box when she had her own stained-glass window created.''

''Perhaps she was.''

Torey examined the picture on the silver box again. Her heart began inexplicably to pick up speed. Her hands began to tremble slightly and there was a marked change in her breathing.

Mitchell noticed it as well. ''Is something wrong?''

She shook her head.

''You've had a strenuous day. I think it's time we headed back to the house and had a cup of—''

''Mrs. Pyle's special tea.''

''A double dose of her special tea.''

''Not yet.''

''But you're trembling.''

So she was.

''Torey, are you all right?''

''Yes.''

''Then what is it?''

''I'm not certain.''

She closed her eyes for several minutes and tried to clear her mind. Then she opened her eyes and looked anew at the elaborate scene etched on the box. She straightened, walked across the chapel and stood before the stained-glass window that depicted Lady Victoria climbing the stairway to heaven.

"You're on to something," he said softly.

"I am."

Mitchell waited.

"What is it?" he finally asked when it seemed that he could wait no longer.

"There is a discrepancy."

His handsome brow crinkled. "A discrepancy?"

"In the pictures."

"Why wouldn't there be?" She turned and listened to him. "They weren't created at the same time or by the same artisan or even for the same reason."

"But they are almost identical . . ."

"Almost?"

"Except for one or two tiny details."

"What are they?"

"The figure on the box is obviously a man and the figure on the window is a woman."

"What's the second discrepancy?" he inquired.

"The scene on the box is complete. The stained-glass window was never finished." Torey stopped herself. "Or was it finished?" came the whispered speculation. "What if it was left with the appearance of being unfinished for a reason?"

"What reason?"

Torey rubbed her palms together almost in delight. "To keep a secret, of course."

Mitchell stiffened. "What secret?"

"The secret of what Lady Victoria actually did with

285

the treasure Michell brought back from France or from the Holy Lands or from wherever he'd been.''

Mitchell groaned. ''I thought we'd gotten this hidden treasure thing out of our systems. Look, honey, we've found a beautiful old box. What more do you think there is?''

''I think there is a great deal more,'' Torey stated. ''Listen to me one more time, Mitchell. Believe in me just this once.''

He stared down at her. ''I do believe in you.''

She took him to the stained-glass window depicting the young Victoria's ascent into heaven. ''A not uncommon religious theme of that historical era, wouldn't you agree?''

''I would.''

''Is there anything that strikes you as being unusual about this window?''

He examined it closely and then shook his head.

''What about the wise sayings included at the bottom?''

''There are Bible verses quoted, or wise, old sayings included on all of these windows.''

''Do you recall when we decided it was important to view the four windows, not separately, but as a whole?''

''The whole is greater than the sum of its parts.''

''Exactly.

''One inscription explains the vows of the Knights Templar, including their vow of poverty. One states that greed was the reason for the unknown warrior knight's downfall. The clan motto clearly implies that anyone who crosses swords with Clan Storm will pay the price. What was the price?''

''Michell lost his life.''

''Yes, and he may also have lost something more.

Look again at the inscription on the fourth window."
Torey proceeded to read aloud: " 'Do not hold as gold
all that shines as gold,' and 'The richest of heaven's
pavement is trodden gold.' "

Mitchell's mouth twisted into a studied frown. "Go
on."

"The stairway that Victoria is shown climbing is plain
stone."

"I can see that."

Torey grasped his hand and tugged him back to the
ornate box and the similar scene etched on its side.
"What do you see that is different about this illustration?"

Mitchell took a close look. "Well, I'll be."

Torey waited for the realization to hit him.

"Surely you don't think . . ."

"I think. I *sense*. I know. The box didn't hold the
treasure you were seeking, Mitchell. It was a clue left by
Lady Victoria to tell someone, perhaps someone like you
or someone like me, what she had done with the real
treasure."

Torey gazed down at the box again.

There it was clearly delineated: the stairway to heaven
wasn't drawn in silver like the rest of the scene.

It was etched in gold.

"Why is it that the man is always the one with the brute
strength?" Mitchell was asking some time later as he
stood ready with pick, shovel, and crowbar, while Torey
sat nearby and watched.

"A woman's work is never done, either," she reminded him. "We simply do a different kind of work in
a different way."

In other words, she used her brain.

He was supposed to supply the brawn.

Mitchell stood at the bottom of the long flight of stone steps that led from the bottom of the hill, not far from Old Ned's house, all the way up to Saint Victoria's chapel.

Before he started, he double-checked. "You honestly believe this is what Lady Victoria considered her stairway to heaven."

"In a manner of speaking. These were certainly the stairs she ascended every day of her life to pray in the chapel overlooking the place where Michell drowned. This was the stairway that she climbed on her hands and knees in penance every year on the anniversary of his death. She chose to build her church and to be buried in that church at the top of these stairs. Yes, if she decided to conceal Michell's treasure, I believe she hid it under these stone steps."

Mitchell had to admit it made sense in a crazy kind of way.

"You've got a shovel, a pick, and a crowbar," Torey listed, checking over his equipment. "All I want you to do is elevate the stone step enough for me to get quick peek under it."

"Is *that* all?"

"Well, you could always wait until The MacClumpha returns from the mainland if you feel you can't manage it on your own. Of course, once he's dealt with the police, he may decide to take Alice out for dinner and maybe even to a movie. So they might not get home until rather late tonight. Naturally, you could always wait until tomorrow. Assuming you'd get any sleep thinking about 'is it or isn't it?' "

Mitchell swung the pick and brought it down alongside the first stone step. A spray of mud went flying.

"Look at the bright side," Torey said, encouraging him. "The recent rains have made the soil softer to dig in."

He gave her a look that spoke volumes.

This treasure-hunting business seemed to involve a great deal of manual labor, primarily digging, and he seemed to be the one doing all of it, Mitchell grumbled to himself as he worked up another good sweat while Torey sat there sipping from a thermos of lemonade sent along by his housekeeper, Mrs. Pyle.

Torey had become a favorite of Mrs. Pyle's.

Actually Torey had become a favorite of everyone's on the Isle of Storm.

"I think that should do it," she finally said, setting the thermos to one side.

"I can get the crowbar under the edge of the stone step and lift, but it won't be for long. You'll have to be ready. A quick look is all you're going to get," he reminded her.

"I know. I'll look as quickly as I can," she promised him. "On the count of three, then?"

What else would it be?

Torey counted out loud for both their benefit. "One. Two. Three."

Mitchell leaned on the end of the steel crowbar with all of his might and all of his considerable weight.

"It's moving. It's lifting. You've got it!" Torey exclaimed.

She quickly leaned over and peered under the stone.

Sweat had broken out over every inch of Mitchell's skin. He could feel the strain in every bone and muscle of his body.

"Well—?" he grunted.

Torey was speechless.

"What do you see?" he gritted through his teeth.

"Gold."

"Real gold?"

"Real honest-to-God gold."

He wanted to take a quick look for himself so bad he could taste it, but he knew he'd only be able to hold the step for another several seconds. "How much—gold?"

"Bright, shiny coins spilling out of an old leather pouch. Hundreds of bright, shiny coins."

Mitchell exhaled and was forced to let the stone step drop back into place. "Are you sure you saw what was there and not what you wanted to see?"

Torey's face was flush with excitement. "Of course it was there. Of course I saw it."

Then she looked up.

Mitchell found his eyes following hers.

"What is going on inside that lovely and intelligent head of yours, Miss Storm?"

Her gaze went from the second step to the third, from the third to the fourth, and all the way up the hill.

"You don't really think—?"

She nodded her head. "I do."

Mitchell felt like he'd been punched in the gut. "Under every step?"

"Under each and every one," she proclaimed.

Chapter 25

He no longer needed her help.

He no longer needed her money.

He had more than enough gold and money now to fix every leaky roof in Scotland.

He no longer needed her.

It was time for Victoria Storm to say her good-byes. After all, she had known from the beginning that this was merely a visit, a temporary stay in Scotland. It had never been intended as a permanent move. And she never wanted to be counted among those who didn't know when it was time to take their leave.

Torey took the pathway down to the water just as she had that afternoon with Mitchell. There was the *Barbara Allen* moored alongside the dock. Today she intended to row the skiff to the small island by herself. Her final trip to the island and to her tree. There were some good-byes best said in private.

Torey untied the mooring line, stepped down into the small boat, grabbed the oars, and began the relatively short row across the sound to the islet.

She had never named the island, Torey suddenly realized. Now she never would.

Perhaps one day another young woman would make this journey and it would become her island and her tree. She could—indeed, she should—have the honor of choosing its name. After all, naming an island was not a responsibility to be taken lightly.

Torey's shoulders were aching and she noticed tiny blisters were already forming on her palms when she finally reached the shore. She dragged the skiff up onto the sandy beach in the protected cove and started off toward the grove of trees.

She remembered the path well.

It was almost as though she had walked it a hundred times before, instead of only once.

Then, there in front of her, with its great sprawling and protecting branches, was the tree.

She went through the same ritual she had always performed back home.

Did Rhode Island still seem like home to her?

She walked up to the tree, touched her hand to its trunk, leaned her cheek against its bark, and whispered, "Hello. It's me. It's Victoria. I've come to say goodbye."

She would not only be leaving her tree behind, her island, the friends she had made on the Isle of Storm, dearest Alice, and Scotland—her beloved Scotland—she would be leaving herself.

For she was leaving without her heart.

Torey climbed up into the great tree, made herself comfortable and leaned back against a particularly lovely branch. Then she reached for the gold chain and locket around her neck. She held it in the palm of her hand and felt its familiar warmth and comfort.

Mitchell had insisted, of course, that she keep the locket of Lady Victoria and she had accepted. It—*she*—

had been a part of Torey's life for so long. She couldn't imagine giving her up now.

But when he had offered to have an experienced gold-smith pry off the back to see what, if anything, was in-scribed there, Torey had declined. She didn't want to know. She didn't need to know.

She already knew in her heart.

She remembered the first time she'd caught sight of Mitchell Storm. It had been the night of her costume ball and he had been following her, watching her, never tak-ing his eyes off her.

Alice had claimed he was a waiter.

Torey had known better.

She had said it from the first, and it was still true, he was no ordinary man.

She just hadn't wanted to lose her heart to him, hadn't expected to fall so deeply in love with him. She wasn't certain she could survive now without him.

She had discovered that being with Mitchell trans-formed her in some way that she loved, that she cher-ished, that she wanted to hold on to forever.

The Robert Burns poem that Mitchell had recited a portion of to her that afternoon seemed to be particularly fitting.

> *But to see her was to love her,*
> *Love but her, and love forever.*
> *Had we never loved sae kindly,*
> *Had we never loved sae blindly,*
> *Never met—or never parted—*
> *We had ne'er been brokenhearted.*

Torey supposed Burns had simply created a different way of saying it was best to have loved and lost, than never to have loved at all. She wished she could believe the Scottish poet, but at the moment it was of little comfort to her.

She would miss his birthday celebration.

Robert Burns's, that was.

The Burns birth-night had once been a literary festival observed the world over. Homer is a myth, they used to say. Dante a cloud. Shakespeare a power. But Burns is a brother man.

Now his birthday was primarily commemorated in his native land. Every January 25 was a huge celebration of Rabbie Burns and all things Scottish.

She was leaving a part of herself in Scotland, and she was taking part of Scotland away with her.

It was time to live her own life, but what did Victoria Storm, part American, part Scot, want her life to be?

She'd been twenty years old when her mother and father had died within a few short months of each other. Torey realized that with the traumatic loss of her parents she had stayed a child and yet very quickly become an adult.

It was time—past time—she grew up completely.

What didn't she want? She did not want to return to the States and marry Peter Nicholson. She and Peter had never gotten beyond friendship in all the years they'd known each other; surely a sign that they had no future together. They had drifted along because it was comfortable, because it was expected of them, because no one better had come along.

Until now.

What did she want her life to be?

Victoria Storm wanted to be with the man she loved, here, now, in Scotland.

Then why didn't she stay?

"Because you're afraid he no longer has any reason to marry you," she said aloud.

The truth was spoken frequently while sitting in a good tree.

Because she was afraid that Sylvia Forbes may have been right when she had claimed that Mitchell would only want to marry her for one of three reasons: for her money, for revenge, for sex.

He no longer needed her money. Even before he had found the huge horde of gold under Lady Victoria's stairs, he had refused the Storm rubies to help himself and his people.

Surely the factor of revenge must have faded after a century and more. And to make some amends she was leaving all the Victorias with him.

Well, nearly all of them.

She was leaving, of course, and she was taking the locket of Lady Victoria with her.

Sexual attraction: it was strong between them, but she wasn't fool enough to believe it would ever be enough. She wanted a man to love and a man to love her while she was young and someday, one day, when she was no longer young.

Mitchell wanted her. Mitchell had never said one word about loving her, his words to Nadine had been a ruse, of course—about needing her, about making their engagement a real one, about making her visit permanent.

It was time to go.

Torey slipped down from the tree, ran her hand along its branches, and left without another word.

She was nearly back to the main island, and glad of it—her hands were rubbed raw from rowing—when she glanced up and saw The Storm standing on the dock waiting for her.

Chapter 26

He'd panicked when he couldn't find her.

Mitchell had assured himself that she wouldn't just up and leave without giving him a chance to say what needed to be said, but he had still panicked when he couldn't find her.

He had run to the hill and looked down at the dock and seen that the skiff was missing. Then he had known, of course, where she had gone. He'd heaved a huge sigh of relief.

He should have known she would head for the island— her island—and the tree.

She was saying good-bye to everything and everyone. It had taken him several days to realize that. She was quietly and unobtrusively going from place to place, person to person, and giving a little of her time, a little of herself.

How could he make her stay?

The small rowboat came up alongside the dock and he grabbed the line for her and secured it to the mooring.

"It's a lovely afternoon," came out of his mouth.

"Yes, it is," she responded.

"Have you named it yet?"

She held her hand up to shade her eyes and looked at him. "Named what?"

"The island." He swallowed. He offered his hand to her and Torey took it. He swung her up onto the dock. "Your island," he said once they were facing each other.

She rubbed her hands on the sides of her slacks and avoided meeting his eyes. "I'm still working on a name."

He didn't believe her.

"It's your island. It will always be yours," he said sincerely.

They walked along the dock and back up the hill. From there Old Ned's cottage was visible.

Mitchell needed the words. But he couldn't seem to think of them, much less say them.

Instead, he heard himself blurt out, "I hear you've been to visit Old Ned."

"I visit Old Ned quite often," she said, staring down at her damp sneakers.

"He seems confused."

That brought her head up. "He's always been mentally as sharp as a tack."

"Oh, he still is. He just doesn't understand why the bride-to-be of The Storm is leaving the island."

"Oh," was all she could say.

"He blames me."

Torey reached out to touch his arm and apparently thought better of it. She dropped her hand to her side. "I hope you told him it wasn't your fault."

Mitchell heaved a huge sigh. "He doesn't believe me." They walked on for some distance. "No one does."

Her thoughts had been somewhere else. "No one does what?"

"Everybody on the Isle of Storm assumes it's my fault that you're leaving," he said, shuffling his feet as they took the pathway through the informal gardens.

"Who said I was leaving?"

He arched an eyebrow. "We Scots are not an unobservant people, Torey. You've been quietly but systematically going from place to place, person to person for the past few days."

"I guess I wasn't fooling anyone."

"I guess not."

"My leaving isn't a matter of being your fault, Mitchell. You must make that clear to them. There isn't any reason for me to stay, that's all. When it's time to go, it's time to go."

Her words echoed in his brain: *There isn't any reason for me to stay.*

Could he be that wrong? About her? About them? He'd thought there were any number of reasons—and one reason in particular—why she might consider staying.

Who was he kidding?

He shrugged his shoulders. "I was too embarrassed to come right out and admit that we'd—that I'd—created a phony engagement to put Sylvia Forbes and her stepgranddaughter off the scent."

"No one but the two of us ever need to know about that."

"I tried to explain that you have your own life in the States."

"I do."

"I said that you're a city girl—" he stopped and cleared his throat. "—A city woman and that living on

299

a remote island most of the year wasn't your cup of tea.''

"My cup of tea, yes," she repeated, murmuring.

Shit.

He wasn't handling this well at all. He was getting nowhere fast. He had to *say* something, *do* something.

Mitchell tried again. "I've never said the words to you, but I want to say them now."

They paused beneath a trellis of sweet-smelling blooms that arched over the walkway in the informal gardens.

"What words?" Torey prompted.

"Thank you."

"Thank you?"

"Thank you for everything you've done to help me and the people on the Isle of Storm. We will prosper. This will become a good place to live, to raise a family, to work, to spend one's life."

"I think most of the people who live here already feel that way," she commented.

They strolled on under a whole series of arches, past the late-blooming summer roses and a gardener clipping merrily away.

He doffed his hat. "Lady Victoria. My lord."

"Your flowers are lovely," Torey said to him as they passed by the man. "I'm not *Lady* Victoria; I'm just plain Victoria," she said once they were out of the worker's earshot.

"You're a true lady to him, and, believe me, you're anything but plain Victoria."

Keep talking, Storm, he encouraged himself.

"I didn't get any sleep last night," he admitted to her.

"Insomnia?"

"I don't think so."

That made her laugh. "If you didn't sleep, Mitchell, that means you had insomnia."

He could be as stubborn as the next man. Maybe even more than most. "That wasn't it."

"Why couldn't you sleep last night?" she inquired, finally asking the question he'd been fishing for all along.

"I don't like sleeping alone."

He felt her stiffen beside him. "Haven't you spent most of your life sleeping alone?" She reconsidered. "Don't answer that question. It's none of my business."

He went on as if he hadn't even heard, let alone acknowledged, the last part of her conversation. "If it's not the right person beside you, then you're better off sleeping alone," he announced as if that were a news-breaking announcement.

"I agree," she said.

"See," he quickly pointed out.

"See what?"

"We don't always disagree. In fact, we often agree with each other."

She gave him a sidelong glance. "I suppose we do."

Mitchell took in a deep, sustaining breath and blew it out all at once. He was trying to clear his lungs, he told himself. In truth, he was trying to keep himself from grabbing the woman beside him and kissing her into submission, into agreeing with whatever he said or did.

This took finesse and finesse was not a strong suit for the man called The Storm.

He licked his lips and found himself gesturing with both hands. He finally stuffed one of them in the pocket of his jacket. "What if the right person—"

She stopped him. "The right person?"

"The one who if they're not beside you, then you're better off sleeping alone—that right person."

"Ah, that right person."

He picked up his train of thought and continued. "What if the right person for you doesn't think that you're the right person for them?"

Her brow was still wrinkled.

Damn, he hadn't expressed it clearly.

"Then I guess whoever 'you' is has a problem."

"The *you* is me. And I've got a problem," he said, relieved that it was finally out in the open.

"You have a problem?" Torey repeated.

He nodded his head. "I'm in love with a woman who seems determined to leave me."

She went pale. She came to a standstill.

"Perhaps," Torey said looking up at him, "you had better explain that."

When Mitchell had announced earlier that he hadn't said the words to her that he should have, Torey had been waiting for those three little words, the 'I love you' words.

Instead, the big lug had come out and thanked her for everything she'd done to help him and the people on his island.

Then she had convinced herself as they walked through the informal gardens—some of the loveliest gardens anywhere on earth, surely—that even if Mitchell loved her, it didn't mean that he intended or even wanted to marry her.

The two did not always go hand in hand: love and marriage.

Now he wanted to discuss a woman he was in love with who seemed determined to leave him.

This time she wasn't getting her hopes up.

This time she wasn't going to assume he meant her

until he had said every single word she wanted and she needed to hear him say.

It was the least she deserved.

Mitchell opened his mouth. "Do you think I'm funny?"

"Funny?"

"As in amusing?"

"You're hilarious," she said dryly.

"No. Seriously. Do you think I'm amusing and witty?"

"I suppose so."

"Do I make you laugh?"

Torey laughed out loud. "Yes. You definitely make me laugh."

"Well, you see, that's one point in my favor, and yours because I think you're pretty funny as well."

"Thank you. I think."

"Do you like the sound of my voice?"

"Yes." That was a nice, simple question to which she was able to give a nice, simple answer.

He smiled. "I love the sound of your voice. I love the sound of your laughter coming down the hallway when you don't realize that I can hear you. Your laughter rings true and clear like a bell."

Torey slipped her hand into his. God knew, the man was trying and, perhaps sometime this same afternoon, he would get around to telling her that he loved her.

Mitchell looked down at their two hands intertwined and said, "I like holding your hand in mine. I like touching you and having you touch me." He got a certain expression on his face. "I love your touch. I love touching you."

"It makes me happy when you say that," she admitted to him.

"We have a great deal in common, you know," he suddenly announced out of the blue.

"We do?"

He gave it several seconds of thought. "We both hate phonies."

Torey nodded her head.

"We both love dogs and walking in the rain and fireworks."

She wasn't one-hundred-percent certain on the walking in the rain part. She supposed she would have to qualify walking in the rain: How hard was it raining? How cold was the temperature out? Was she walking alone or beside the man she loved?

"I love walking in the rain with you," she finally said.

"We're both named Storm."

"True."

"If we were to marry you wouldn't even have to change your name. Think of the convenience."

"I don't think people consider convenience very high on the list when they're considering marriage."

Mitchell pulled her down on a stone bench. He towered over her for a moment, then went down on one knee and stared straight into her eyes. "Are we considering marriage?"

Her head was spinning. "Is *who* considering marriage?"

"You and me."

Her heart was stuck somewhere in the region of her throat. "I—ah . . . don't know. Are we?"

"We've become very good friends," he pointed out.

"Yes, we have become very good friends," and Torey realized that it was true.

"I understand you," he declared. "Most of the time," he qualified.

"And I understand you," she replied. Some of the time.

"We're great in bed together."

"Are you speaking of sex now, Lord Storm?"

"Yes and no. I like to think of what happens between the two of us as making love."

"I love making love with you and to you." She decided it was time to come out and declare herself.

He was definitely down on bent knee now. He was holding her hand in his. "Somehow, in some way that I still don't understand, Victoria Storm, you have become more necessary to me than breathing . . . than living."

She couldn't breathe.

Mitchell went on. "Without you beside me, all the gold in the world would still make me a poor man."

She was afraid she was going to cry. The words were beautiful. The words were the ones she'd always wished to hear, wanted to hear, needed to hear.

"Without you here to love me, there is no way for me to be happy, there is no place on earth that I can call home."

Her eyes were brimming with tears.

"Darling, why are you crying?"

"Because we're going to be so happy together," she said.

Mitchell brought his face right up next to hers and stared long into her eyes. "I love you, Victoria Storm. I adore you. I worship you. I want to spend every day of my life with you. Will you come with me and be my love? Will you marry me and become my wife?"

"I will," she whispered as his lips touched hers.

He felt like he could conquer the world single-handedly . . . hell, with his bare hands, for that matter.

That's the way Mitchell Storm, Earl of Storm, Chief of Clan Storm, *The* Storm, felt as he strolled back toward Castle Storm with his arm around the woman he loved, the woman he would soon make his wife.

He had promised to make her happy.

He would.

He had promised to love her.

He would.

He had promised to care for her, to cherish her, to respect her, to honor her.

He would every day of his life.

And for whatever came after . . .

His grandfather had been right, in the end. He had told Mitchell to go to America and find Victoria and bring her back to Scotland because she was the key to finding the treasure.

He realized now that his grandfather very likely hadn't meant the treasure of gold.

The sun was beginning to set as they reached the farthest tip of the Isle of Storm that overlooked the sea. The sky was turning into molten gold. The water reflected that same golden hue. Even the green island was taking on the appearance of gold.

They stood there together in silence and looked out on a golden sea, and from somewhere, high on the ramparts of Castle Storm, came the skirl of the bagpipes—perhaps it was even The MacClumpha himself.

It was a single expert piper playing ''Scotland the home, Scotland the brave.''

This was his home, Mitchell Storm realized with a sense of contentment that few men, only a lucky few men, ever feel in their lifetimes.

Scotland was his home and his love was standing beside him.

What more could any man desire?

Epilogue

Beatrice Van Allen knew something peculiar was afoot when her maid knocked on the door of her boudoir and informed her that Miss Albright was waiting downstairs and insisted upon seeing the mistress of the household immediately.

It was the crack of dawn.

Well, it was nearly ten o'clock in the morning, but, as was her custom in the autumn in New York, Beatrice was still abed, a pile of pillows propped up at her back. A covered silver server of hot biscuits lathered with rich, creamy butter and drizzled with her favorite sweet honey lay on her lap, and a pot of steaming tea, replenished every ten minutes on the dot, sat on the bedside table.

Beatrice was nibbling on just such a biscuit when Lola Albright came rushing into her bedroom.

A dainty linen napkin, edged with antique Belgian lace, was touched briefly to Beatrice Van Allen's extensive chins in order to catch a stray drip of honey.

Lola was waving a newspaper in her right hand, and exclaimed in a voice quivering with excitement, "News, Beatrice. Wait until you hear the news."

"Do sit down, Lola, and catch your breath," Beatrice instructed, pretending to a calm she wasn't feeling, to a calm that she hadn't been feeling since her maid had apprised her of Lola Albright's unexpected arrival.

Lola sat.

"Would you care for a cup of tea, my dear?" came the offer. It was not followed up, however, by an invitation for Lola to help herself to a biscuit.

The pale creature with the bright red cheeks shook her head and said vehemently, "I couldn't eat a bite. I'm too excited. I had to be the first to tell you."

Apparently, timing was everything.

"What is this news, then, that has brought you bursting into my bedroom scarcely before the sun is up?"

Lola licked her lips in anticipation. "It's all here in this morning's *Times*."

Beatrice's brow creased in half a dozen places. "I didn't realize you read the *Times*." They all subscribed, of course, but she had assumed that no one ever actually read it.

"I don't usually. It was Henry who told me about the notice in this morning's edition."

"Henry?"

"The doorman at my building," came the brief explanation. "He mentioned it to me as I was taking Spike out for his eight-thirty constitutional."

"I see." Beatrice put the plate of biscuits aside. She had quite lost her appetite by now. "Do go on, Lola."

"Spike was quite miffed at me for making him miss his outing, I'll tell you."

Beatrice could not abide dogs. "I believe Spike will survive one day without his morning walk."

"I've promised him two outings tomorrow in recompense," her friend said with hope of redemption.

"Lola, the news," commanded Beatrice.

"You'll never guess who it's about."

"I don't intend to guess. You are going to tell me."

Lola sat straight in her chair, pushed at the bifocals perpetually slipping down the bridge of her nose and cleared her throat before beginning. At the last moment she glanced up and asked, "Should I read it word for word, or simply tell you what it says?"

"Lola—"

Lola Albright opened her mouth and out it came. "Victoria Storm has married."

That brought Beatrice to attention. "You don't say."

"I do say. Or I should say that the *Times* says. Apparently it was a small, intimate ceremony performed by a bishop—" She studied the small print on the page. "—The Bishop of Canterbury, in Saint Victoria's Chapel on the Isle of Storm." Lola looked up for a moment and uttered a wistful sigh. "How perfectly lovely that Victoria should be married in a chapel that bears her name."

"Go on," urged Beatrice, greedy for every detail.

Lola read on. " 'Attendants for the bride and groom were Mr. Iain MacClumpha and his fiancée, Miss Alice Fraser, and Mr. and Mrs. John Spencer Hollister III.' Then in parentheses the *Times* has added an addendum stating that the latter is the well-known philanthropist, Jake Hollister, and that she is the former Cordelia Jane Bennett of the Buffalo, New York, Bennetts."

"Prominent family, the Bennetts," Beatrice explained. "There's a bit of money there, too. Of course, not quite in the same class as our dear Victoria, but, then, few are."

"The article concludes with a paragraph describing the large celebration given by the earl and his new countess—" Lola suddenly paused, frowned in thought, and then sought confirmation from her companion. "He would be that handsome, dark-haired man that Victoria danced with the night of the summer ball, wouldn't he?"

"Yes, he would be, Lola."

"Anyway, it ends by saying all eight hundred inhabitants of the Isle of Storm were invited to the wedding reception."

"Well, well, well," Beatrice said, talking more to herself than to Lola. "This is news, indeed."

"I told you it was," Lola claimed. "And coming on the heels of the other gossip this week, quite amazing."

"I presume you are referring to the reports that Peter Nicholson has been secretly married to some cowgirl since early summer."

"Not a cowgirl, Beatrice. A rodeo queen."

Beatrice shuddered. "His parents must still be in shock, poor creatures."

Lola waved the newspaper again. "But isn't it wonderful news about dear Victoria and her Scottish peer?"

Beatrice Van Allen puffed herself up and proclaimed to her friend, "Wonderful news, indeed. And it's just as I'd predicted from the start, Lola. They were made for each other."

Then she sighed and considered having another biscuit with honey, after all.

Author's Note

There has been the refrain of an old folk song running through my head for as long as I can remember, certainly since I was a very little girl.

> *Oh ye tak the high road*
> *And I'll tak the low road*
> *And I'll be in Scotland afore ye*
> *For me and my true love*
> *Will never meet again*
> *On the bonnie bonnie banks*
> *Of Loch Lomond*

It wasn't until my first trip to Scotland in 1995, however, that I discovered my Scottish ancestry, in addition to the English, Irish, and German I knew to be in my family background. I gave the genealogist the name of my great-great-great-grandmother, Jane McFarland, and we found that she had descended from Clan MacFarlane, whose lineage was out of the ancient Celtic Earls of Lennox.

Clan MacFarlane took its name from the fourth chief

311

of their kindred, Pharlain—Bartholomew—who lived in the reign of Robert The Bruce. The last native MacFarlane chief emigrated to America in the eighteenth century and his direct line expired in 1886 with the death of the twenty-fifth and last chief, William.

"There are no more MacFarlane chiefs," the genealogist informed me that day in Edinburgh as I heard the sound of bagpipes playing in the distance. "Your lands are forfeit, the great houses have vanished, and the castles are now ruins."

"Where are the castles?" I asked her, knowing I had to see them even if they were no more than a pile of ancient stone and rubble.

The refrain of the old Scottish song ran through my mind and I knew the answer even before she said, "Loch Lomond."